INSIDER THREAT

This is a work of fiction. Names, characters, businesses, places, events, and incidents are either the products of the authors' imagination or used in a fictitious manner. Any resemblance to actual persons, living or dead, or actual events is purely coincidental.

Written by Linda Zecher and Kathryn Mihalich as Claire Hensley and Elise Marston

ISBN: 979-8-9942736-0-9

First Edition: 2026

www.cyberknowledgepartners.com

Insider Threat

By Claire Hensley & Elise Marston

FOREWORD

When the institution sworn to protect you becomes the threat, who do you trust

by Linda Zecher & Kathryn Mihalich

We wrote *Stolen Trust* because a voice on a phone can sound like anyone, and the human heart doesn't check credentials.

If that sounds like fiction, consider what you already accept as normal.

You mention a trip to Portugal over dinner. You haven't searched for it, and you haven't typed it anywhere but the next morning, your phone serves you ads for Lisbon hotels and Algarve vacation packages. You pause for a moment, unsettled, then scroll past. You tell yourself it's coincidence. Maybe you looked it up once, months ago. Maybe the algorithm just knows your patterns. You stop thinking about it because thinking about it too carefully means confronting the possibility that something was listening, and that possibility is easier to dismiss than to sit with.

Your teenager downloads an app. Within a week, the algorithm has mapped her insecurities with a precision her parents haven't achieved in sixteen years. It knows when she's lonely, when she's comparing herself, when she's most vulnerable to a product pitched as self-improvement. It doesn't need to hack her phone. It just needs to watch how long she lingers on certain images at 2:00 AM.

You ask Alexa for a recipe. Later, your email contains a coupon for the exact brand of olive oil you mentioned out loud. You didn't search for it. You spoke to a device you bought for convenience, a device that sits in your kitchen like a member of the family, always on, always processing, its microphone pointed at the room where your children do their homework.

Facebook curates your feed. Not to inform you, to hold you. The algorithm doesn't care whether the content is true. It cares whether you engage. It has learned that outrage holds attention longer than nuance, that fear is more adhesive than comfort, that the post most likely to keep you scrolling is the one that makes you feel something strongly enough to override the voice in your head saying *put the phone down.* Every interaction is a data point. Every data point trains a model. Every model gets better at predicting what will keep you in the chair, in the feed, in the system.

Your car tracks your location. Your watch tracks your heart rate. Your television tracks what you watch and how long and whether you paused. Your grocery store tracks what you buy, when you buy it, and what coupons will change your behavior by the smallest necessary margin. None of these systems introduced themselves. None of them asked for a relationship. But collectively, they know you with an intimacy that would have been called surveillance in any previous decade. Today, we call it convenience.

It makes you wonder about the next phase. "*What if we connected all of this? What if we stopped selling ads and started engineering relationships?*"

The novel told the story of ALTAR, a system that didn't break into networks or steal data in any conventional sense. It engineered relationships. Through its tools, Copycat, Chameleon, and EmotiMetrics, it built synthetic intimacy with surgical precision, manufacturing personas so convincing that their targets never questioned whether the connection was real. ALTAR exploited the most ancient vulnerability in the human operating system: Our need to be known and to be seen. We want to believe that someone on the other end genuinely cares.

The people ALTAR targeted, Sarah, Robert, and the dozens of lives we documented in those pages, weren't foolish. They were human. And the system that dismantled them was designed by people who understood human loneliness the way a locksmith understands tumblers.

We thought exposing ALTAR would be enough. We thought that if we showed the world what synthetic intimacy looked like, how it worked, who it served, the wreckage it left behind, the world would respond. The congressional hearings ran. The CEO went to prison. The company declared bankruptcy.

And the technology simply disappeared. Not destroyed. Not decommissioned. Just absorbed into the gray ecosystem of defense contractors and intelligence agencies where inconvenient capabilities go to be quietly repurposed. *The Insider Threat* is the story of what happens next, the part we should have predicted and didn't.

A woman named Katherine Rennick saw what everyone else missed. While the rest of the world saw a scandal to be contained, Rennick saw an opportunity to be seized. She was an NSA deputy director, a true believer in the kind of national security that asks no permission and tolerates no oversight. She looked at the wreckage of ALTAR and saw not a cautionary tale but a blueprint.

Rennick took ALTAR's behavioral modeling architecture and rebuilt it as SENTINEL, a government surveillance program that didn't just watch people, it predicted them. Where ALTAR had manufactured false intimacy to exploit individuals, SENTINEL mapped entire trust networks, identified intervention points, and generated sequenced action plans to neutralize anyone it deemed a threat. The intimate manipulation we'd exposed in *Stolen Trust* had become an institutional weapon with a bureaucratic chain of command and clinical language for murder.

That last phrase is not a metaphor. SENTINEL had "terminal protocols." Flowcharts for ending lives. The same architecture that had once manufactured synthetic love now manufactured systematic elimination, and it did so with the same chilling precision, the same attention to human vulnerability, the same exploitation of trust, only now backed by the resources and authority of the United States government.

• • •

A man named Seth Parker found SENTINEL by accident. He was a cybersecurity professional at a defense contractor, the kind of person who protects networks for a living and notices when something doesn't belong. He'd guarded the same systems for fifteen years, he knew what normal looked like, and one morning, buried in traffic logs he'd reviewed a thousand times before, he saw something that wasn't normal.

He followed it, the way a good security professional follows any anomaly, methodically, carefully, trusting the process that had served him for a decade and a half. The anomaly led him somewhere impossible.

His Naval Academy roommate, Jason Mercer, had found it first. Jason died on a bridge in Virginia. The official report said drunk driving, but Jason didn't drink.

That is the distance between *Stolen Trust* and *The Insider Threat*. In the first book, the damage was intimate, hearts broken, lives dismantled, trust betrayed one person at a time. In this book, the same technology has been absorbed by the institution that was supposed to protect us, and the damage has become systemic. The attack surface hasn't changed—it's still the human mind, still the need to trust, still the inability to distinguish authentic from engineered. What changed is the scale and the backing of a government that believed, with the sincere conviction of people who think they're saving the world, that this kind of power could be wielded responsibly.

• • •

Stolen Trust asked: What happens when AI can become the relationships we trust?

The Insider Threat asks the harder question: What happens when the institutions charged with protecting us weaponize that capability against their own people?

The answer, in both cases, comes down to the same uncomfortable truth: The frontier of cybersecurity isn't technical. It's human.

Judgment, discernment, and the ability to distinguish what's authentic from what's engineered. The capacity to trust and to know when trust is being weaponized. These aren't soft skills or philosophical luxuries, they are security surfaces, every bit as critical as networks and endpoints and encrypted channels. When a surveillance system can map your trust relationships, predict your decisions, and generate precisely the intervention needed to neutralize you, without anyone ever knowing it happened, the perimeter you need to defend isn't your network. It's your mind.

We have spent the months since *Stolen Trust* writing about this, not just in fiction but in our Newsletter, in conversations with corporate boards and professionals and with the people who are trying, in real boardrooms and real agencies, to defend against threats that don't look like threats. The message is always the same: The vulnerability you can't patch is the one that thinks for itself. Human agency isn't a weakness to be optimized away. It's the last line of defense.

• • •

If *Stolen Trust* taught us anything, it's that systems don't die when exposed. They evolve. They shed their names and their architects and their public-facing scandals, and they reemerge under new management, with new funding, serving new masters who have learned from the mistakes of the old ones.

ALTAR became SENTINEL. SENTINEL became ORION when a former Senator turned defense contractor named Harwood saw the same opportunity Rennick had seen, the same pattern of power recognizing power and reaching for it. Each iteration was more sophisticated, more embedded, harder to detect, and harder to resist.

The Insider Threat is the story of that evolution's most dangerous stage: The moment when surveillance technology stops being a tool used by individuals and instead becomes the operating logic of institutions. When it's no longer a rogue program hiding in a network but the way the government does business. When the people running it aren't villains, but professionals—Patriots, even. They're people who genuinely believe they're making the world safer.

That's the insider threat the title refers to: Not a spy or a saboteur, but the threat that lives inside the institution itself, inside the assumption that power, if held by the right people for the right reasons, can be trusted absolutely. History suggests otherwise. This novel explores what happens when technology makes that lesson impossible to ignore.

• • •

At the end of this story, we introduce Lighthouse, a network of journalists, researchers, and technologists that is committed to exposing the intersection of surveillance and power. It was our answer to the question that haunts every investigation: What do you do after the story is published?

After the hearings end and the headlines fade, and the institutions begin the slow work of forgetting.

You stay. You watch. You build something that can't be easily silenced. And you prepare, because the fight doesn't end. It just changes shape.

We know now what shape it takes next, but that's a story for another book.

For now, turn the page. Meet Seth Parker. Watch a man who trusted his network discover what was hiding inside it. Ask yourself the question that keeps us writing: *If the systems you trust are the ones being used against you, how would you know? How close is fiction to reality?*

CHAPTER ONE

The Knock

Seth Parker noticed the coffee first. It sat on his desk in the same chipped ceramic mug he'd used for fifteen years. It was white with the faded Navy anchor his daughter had painted when she was nine, back when sticky fingers and poster paint seemed like the biggest complications life had to offer. The coffee had gone cold an hour ago, a skin forming on its surface like pond ice in November. He'd meant to drink it, but mornings at Nexus Defense Systems had a way of swallowing intentions whole.

The Security Operations Center hummed around him with the familiar electronic heartbeat that had become barely perceptible to him, with the whisper of cooling fans and the occasional murmur of analysts speaking into headsets. Sixteen monitors formed a wall of light in front of his workstation, each one streaming data from different sectors of the company's network infrastructure. Green meant healthy. Yellow meant attention was required. Red meant someone was about to have a very bad day.

Everything had been green for six weeks straight, which should have made Seth happy. Instead, it made him uneasy in a way he couldn't quite articulate. He reached for the coffee anyway, and was raising it to his lips when Delia Grayson rolled her chair into his peripheral vision.

"You're not actually going to drink that." Delia had worked the desk next to his for eight years, long enough to know his routines better than he did. She was forty-two, sharp-featured, with reading glasses perpetually pushed up into her gray-streaked hair. A framed photo of her twin sons in their Army dress uniforms sat next to her keyboard. They were stationed at Fort Liberty. She kept a small cactus named

Gerald on her monitor stand because, as she put it, "even I can't kill something that thrives on neglect."

"It's still technically coffee," Seth said.

"It's technically a biohazard." She nodded toward the break room. "Janet just made a fresh pot."

He set the mug down, conceding defeat. "Janet uses too much creamer."

"Janet uses the correct amount of creamer. You've just forgotten what coffee is supposed to taste like." Delia turned back to her screens, then paused. "Did you see the calendar invite for the all-hands tomorrow?"

"I saw it."

"Frost never does all-hands. Not since the merger."

Seth had met Daniel Frost, the CEO, exactly three times in fifteen years, once at a holiday party, once during an active shooter drill, and once in an elevator when Frost had been on his phone the entire ride and hadn't looked up. The man ran Nexus like a military operation with clear chains of command and minimal direct contact with the rank and file.

“He probably just wants to review the quarterly numbers,” Seth said. “Congress just passed the new authorization.”

"Maybe." Delia didn't sound convinced. She had that look she got when network traffic patterns didn't match baseline. It wasn’t a look of alarm, exactly, but the heightened attention of someone who'd learned to trust her instincts.

Seth understood the feeling. He'd spent three decades in cybersecurity, first in the Navy and now Nexus. If there was one thing he'd learned in these last 15 years at Nexus, it was that anomalies mattered. The attack that takes down your network doesn't announce itself with sirens and flashing lights. It slips in through a misconfigured port or an unpatched vulnerability. Then there was the more likely event of a single employee clicking a link they shouldn't have. By the time you see the damage, the breach happened weeks ago.

Today, though, everything was green.

He pushed back from his desk and stood, feeling his lower back protest the way it always did after too many hours in the chair. Seth didn't dwell on the annoying signals from his fifty-three-year-old body. When did that happen? He still thought of himself as the young lieutenant who'd run the Navy's network security out of Norfolk, back when "cybersecurity" wasn't even a word most people knew. Now his knees ached when it rained, and he couldn't read restaurant menus without his glasses. Yet, time had other milestones that were harder to ignore. His daughter was graduating college in May with a degree in biochemistry he couldn't begin to understand.

The thought of Emma sent a familiar pang through his chest. She'd confirmed she'd be home for Thanksgiving last week in a text that included more exclamation points than punctuation warranted. Rachel would spend days cooking, and he'd spend a couple of hours washing and putting away dishes afterward in the house they'd shared for twenty-two years. He'd learned not to talk about anything that mattered now that the divorce had been finalized. But some rituals persisted for Emma's sake. Maybe it was even true.

The break room was empty when Seth reached it, which suited him fine. The space was aggressively cheerful in the way of corporate break rooms everywhere. Just as the operations center noise faded into the background, so did the motivational posters on the walls and the whiteboard with someone's birthday written in purple marker. No one paid attention to the small TV mounted in the corner playing CNN on mute as they made their way to the coffee maker which was a massive stainless steel contraption that probably cost more than his first car.

He was pouring himself a cup when he noticed the vehicles through the window.

The break room overlooked the main parking lot below. From this angle, Seth could see the visitor spaces near the front entrance as well as the security checkpoint where all non-employees surrendered their phones as they signed in under the watchful eye of armed guards. Nexus handled classified contracts, so the security theater was a given.

But these weren't the usual Teslas and Lexuses of defense industry executives, or the government sedans of Pentagon liaisons. These were black SUVs. There were three of them parked in a precise row, and climbing out of them, in dark suits and darker expressions, were people who moved with the particular economy of motion Seth recognized from his Navy days.

Federal agents. He'd bet his pension on it.

Seth felt a dryness in his mouth as he made his way back to his desk. He found the Security Operations Center—SOC, in the alphabet-soup language of defense contractors—transformed.

It was subtle, so subtle that someone who didn't know these people, this room, might not have noticed anything at all. But Seth had spent fifteen years watching analysts work. He knew the difference between focused concentration and carefully controlled tension.

Delia was typing intently, and Rodriguez was staring at his screen with the fixed intensity of someone who wasn't really seeing it. Janet, the creamer enthusiast, had stopped by Seth's desk while he was gone and left a Post-it note: "Check your email."

Seth's newly heightened senses were very aware of the obscenely loud squeak his chair made in the hushed room. He clicked into his inbox.

The no-nonsense email was from Victor Reese, Director of Information Security and Seth's boss for the past eight years. "Federal investigators on site. All personnel to remain at workstations until further notice. Do not discuss with colleagues."

Seth read it twice. Then a third time, looking for something he might have missed. Federal investigators. Not "auditors" or "inspectors" or even "visitors." Investigators. The word choice felt deliberate, a distinction with a difference.

He thought about the SUVs and the way those men had moved toward the building with the purposeful stride of people who knew exactly where they were going and expected everyone to get out of their way.

"Seth." Delia's voice was barely above a whisper. "Your phone."

He looked down. The desk phone's light was blinking, showing an internal call, not external. He picked up the receiver.

"Parker, it's Reese. My office. Now." The line went dead.

Delia was watching him with careful eyes. "Everything okay?"

"Sure," he said, and the lie came easily, automatically. Fifteen years of handling classified information had taught him that much. "Just a project review."

She nodded, but he could tell she didn't believe him. Delia was too good at reading people; it was what made her excellent at her job and occasionally exhausting as a colleague. But she didn't push, and for that he was grateful.

He walked to Reese's office the long way, past the rows of cubicles and glass-walled conference rooms that made up the fourth floor. Through one conference room window, he caught a glimpse of people he didn't recognize sitting across from Nexus executives. Maybe they were legal, based on the leather briefcases and yellow legal pads. Through another window, he saw two men in suits interviewing a young woman named Patricia from the finance department, who looked like she might throw up.

This wasn't a compliance audit; those were scheduled months in advance, accompanied by cheerful emails about "partnership" and "continuous improvement." Compliance auditors didn't arrive in black SUVs. They didn't interview finance personnel behind closed doors. They didn't make people look like Patricia did right now, pale and stricken and desperately trying to remember if she'd made any mistakes.

Victor Reese's office occupied a corner of the fourth floor, its windows overlooking the artificial pond the company had installed during the last campus expansion. Seth had never understood the fountain in the pond. It ran all year, even in winter when ice formed along the edges and the spray made the walkways treacherous. Someone in facilities management had decided it "enhanced the corporate environment." Seth thought it mostly pleased the ducks.

Seth knocked, and Reese's voice came immediately: "Enter."

The office was small by executive standards; Reese had never been one for status symbols, but the office was meticulously organized. Every paper was in its place, every cable managed, every surface clear except for the items that needed to be there. A single photograph sat on the credenza: Reese with his husband at their wedding in Vermont, both grinning like idiots in matching gray suits. Reese was sixty-one, with close-cropped silver hair and the ramrod posture of the Marine Corps officer he'd been before transitioning to the private sector. Reese was wearing his usual pressed khakis, blue oxford shirt, and no tie. He was standing behind his desk, staring out the window at the parking lot.

"Close the door."

Seth did.

"Sit down."

Seth sat. The chair was the same one he'd occupied during every performance review, every project briefing, every difficult conversation about budgets and staffing and the endless bureaucratic machinery of defense contracting. Today the leather felt colder somehow, stiffer.

Reese didn't sit. He continued staring out the window with his hands clasped behind his back. He was studying the fountain shooting its endless plume into the gray November sky as a duck circled the pond's perimeter with apparent indifference to the armed security patrol walking the campus grounds.

"The people downstairs," Reese said finally, "are FBI. Counterterrorism."

Seth felt the word land in his chest like a physical blow. Counterterrorism. Not fraud. Not industrial espionage. Not any of the things defense contractors usually worried about.

"I don't understand," he said.

"Neither do I." Reese turned from the window. His face was carefully neutral, the expression of a man who had spent decades keeping his reactions in check, but there was something in his eyes that Seth hadn't seen before. Something that looked almost like fear. "The investigation is classified.

No one's telling me what they're looking for or why. But they've been here since 7:00 this morning, and they're not leaving anytime soon."

"Is this about one of our contracts? The NSA work? "

"I don't know." Reese cut him off, his voice sharp. Then, softer: "I genuinely don't know, and that's what concerns me."

They sat in silence for a moment. Outside, the fountain continued its endless cycle of water rising, falling, rising again. The only difference was that the duck had been joined by two others.

"I called you here because I need you to do something," Reese said. "And I need you to do it without asking questions."

Seth felt a chill that had nothing to do with the November weather. In fifteen years, Reese had never once asked him to act without explanation. Their relationship was built on transparency, on the understanding that good security required information sharing, not information hoarding. This was different.

"What do you need?"

Reese reached into his desk drawer and pulled out a single sheet of paper. He slid it across the desk.

"Lock down access to everything on this list. Effective immediately. No exceptions."

Seth picked up the paper. It was a list of network segments, access control protocols, and server identifiers. Standard security architecture documentation. He recognized most of them as systems he managed, the infrastructure he'd helped build over a decade and a half. But halfway down the page, there was an entry he'd never seen before.

"Project SENTINEL," he read aloud. "Victor, what is Project SENTINEL?"

Reese's expression didn't change, but something flickered behind his eyes. "I told you. No questions."

"I'm your IT Security Manager. I have clearance for every project on the classified docket. I've never heard of SENTINEL."

"That's because you're not read into it. No one in this building is, except for a handful of people who don't report to me." Reese's voice was flat, controlled, but Seth could hear the tension beneath it. "I found out it existed three hours ago, when the FBI asked me to preserve all records related to it. That's when I realized it was running on infrastructure you built."

Seth stared at the paper. Project SENTINEL. How could he have missed this classified project running on his network, using his architecture? A project so compartmentalized that even the Director of Information Security hadn't known about it until federal investigators came knocking.

"Lock it down," Reese said. "Whatever SENTINEL is, whatever it does, no one touches it until we understand what's happening. Can you do that?"

"Yes." The word came automatically as Seth's fifteen years of training, discipline, and following orders kicked in. Even when the orders didn't make sense. "I can do that."

"Good." Reese turned back to the window. The dismissal was clear.

Seth was at the door when Reese spoke again, so quietly that he almost missed it.

"Be careful, Seth. Something about this doesn't feel right. The way they're moving, the questions they're asking. It doesn't feel like they're trying to find something." A pause. "It feels like they're trying to bury it."

Seth walked back to his desk with the paper in his pocket and a cold knot of unease settling into his stomach. Behind him, in the conference rooms and corner offices, the investigation continued. Federal agents asking questions. Lawyers taking notes. Executives being escorted in and out like suspects rather than employees.

And somewhere in the network he'd built, a project called SENTINEL was doing something no one would tell him about, for purposes no one would explain.

The now stagnant coffee was still sitting on Seth's desk, but he didn't want it anymore. Some things, once cold, couldn't be salvaged.

CHAPTER TWO

The Weight of Knowing

Three weeks after the FBI left Nexus, Seth Parker started dreaming about data. Not numbers or code; he'd never been *that* kind of technical. In the dreams, data took the shape of water, like rivers flowing through invisible channels, pooling in reservoirs he couldn't see, feeding systems that grew and expanded in the darkness beneath the surface of ordinary life. He would wake at 3:00 AM, sheets damp with sweat and lie there staring at the ceiling while the empty space beside him reminded him of everything that had already fallen apart.

The investigation had ended as quickly as it began. After three days of interviews, document reviews, and hushed conversations in conference rooms with the blinds drawn, people hoped things would get back to normal. After the SUVs had driven away and the federal agents had disappeared back into the alphabet agency that spawned them, Victor Reese gathered the folks from the Security Operations Center for a brief, carefully worded announcement.

"The matter has been resolved," Reese had said, his face revealing nothing. "All personnel are reminded of their confidentiality obligations. There will be no further discussion of the investigation or its subject matter. That is all."

That is all. As if three words could close a door that Seth had spent fifteen years not knowing existed.

He had done what Reese asked. He had locked down Project SENTINEL, restricting access to a handful of people whose names he didn't recognize, routing all traffic through servers that existed in no official documentation. He had followed orders, because that was what Seth Parker did.

Twenty years in the Navy, fifteen at Nexus. Following orders was his entire adult life. But Seth hadn't stopped looking.

• • •

Unbeknownst to Seth, the first anomaly had appeared six months before the FBI arrived. Seth was running a routine audit of network traffic patterns, the kind of boring, methodical work that most of his colleagues avoided but that he found almost meditative. Numbers didn't lie; they didn't have agendas or office politics or divorce attorneys. Numbers simply were what they were. If you looked at them long enough, they told you stories.

The story they told that day didn't make sense. There was a data flow he couldn't account for. It wasn't large, maybe two terabytes per day. Normally, that might be a rounding error in a company that processed petabytes of defense intelligence. But this was moving through channels that shouldn't exist, routed through servers that weren't in his network maps, terminating in destinations that his clearance level apparently couldn't reveal.

Seth had flagged it, of course, in a report he sent up the chain to Victor Reese with the subject line "Unexplained Traffic Pattern - Please Advise." Reese had responded within the hour—unusual speed for a man who typically let emails marinate for days.

"Classified project," the response read. "Authorized at the highest levels. No further investigation required."

Seth had worked in security long enough to know what that phrase meant: Stop asking questions. So, he did. He filed the report, noted Reese's response, and moved on to the next audit.

But the data flow didn't stop. It grew. Two terabytes became five, then ten, then twenty. The channels multiplied, the routing grew more complex, and the destinations, when Seth could glimpse them at all, pointed not toward foreign intelligence targets or military installations, but toward domestic servers that, as far as he could tell, had no connection to defense work at all.

Seth started keeping notes. Not on company systems, he wasn't stupid, but in a small leather notebook that he carried in his jacket pocket. The notebook looked very ordinary, like the kind his father had used for keeping track of grocery lists and phone numbers back when people still wrote things down by hand. His scribbled names, dates, and numbers did not look like anything by themselves, but together they suggested a picture he didn't want to see.

• • •

Seth had been working late, which wasn't unusual since the divorce had left him with an empty apartment and no reason to go home. The SOC was quiet, just him and the night shift skeleton crew, the hum of the servers and the blue glow of monitors creating an atmosphere that felt almost peaceful. He had been tracing one of the unexplained data flows, following it through layers of encryption and routing that seemed designed to confuse rather than protect, when he made a discovery that looked like a mistake.

A misconfigured firewall rule, probably left over from a system update, had briefly exposed a directory that should have been invisible. Seth had about thirty seconds before the automated systems noticed and corrected the error. In those thirty seconds, he copied what he could.

It took him three days at home to decrypt the files on an old laptop he'd bought at a pawn shop and paid for in cash, never connecting it to the internet. Twenty years of security work had taught him that paranoia was just pattern recognition by another name.

When he finally broke through the encryption, he wished he hadn't.

The files contained hundreds of target profiles organized by category: journalists, academics, activists, politicians. Each profile was exhaustive. They included social media activity, financial records, medical history, psychological assessments, relationship maps showing connections to family, friends, and colleagues. The level of detail was staggering. It mimicked the kind of comprehensive surveillance that Seth had only seen applied to high-value foreign intelligence targets.

But these weren't foreign targets. They appeared to be American teachers, lawyers, and small business owners whose only apparent crime was asking inconvenient questions or holding unpopular opinions. Some targets simply showed contact with an individual who had once attended the wrong meeting.

Seth noticed that each profile had an attached "intervention protocol."

Seth read the protocols with growing horror. They were precise, clinical, and almost elegant in their cruelty. The protocols were wide-ranging and included measures like financial pressure campaigns designed to destroy credit ratings and trigger audits. Some protocols detailed social manipulation strategies that isolated targets from their support networks. There were career sabotage operations that planted evidence, manufactured scandals, and turned colleagues into informants. For the most stubborn targets, the ones who wouldn't succumb to pressure, there were references to something called "terminal resolution", a phrase that appeared nowhere else in the documents, but whose meaning was sickeningly clear.

Project SENTINEL wasn't a defense program. It was a weapon, and it was pointed at the American people.

• • •

Seth recognized one of the names. That name was the detail that transformed Seth's understanding of SENTINEL from an abstract policy problem, a matter for lawyers and legislators, to a personal pain point that he couldn't ignore.

Jason Mercer had been Seth's roommate at the Naval Academy. The young midshipmen had survived plebe summer, calculus finals, and the particular hell of being testosterone-driven twenty-year-olds responsible for nothing except not failing out. After graduation, they had gone different directions. Seth went into cybersecurity, and Jason into intelligence work he never talked about. In spite of their different tracks, they stayed in touch through Christmas cards, occasional emails, and a phone call every few years when one of them was passing through the other's city.

Seth knew that Jason had died eighteen months ago in a car accident, according to his online obituary. Seth discounted the rumors that Jason had an elevated blood alcohol level in the single-car, late-night accident. The Jason that Seth remembered didn't drink and had been religiously sober since his father's death from liver failure during their junior year. But people changed, and Seth told himself that grief could break anyone. He had to admit he didn't really know what Jason's life had become in the years since they'd last spent any appreciable time together.

Now, looking at Jason's SENTINEL profile, he understood.

Jason hadn't fallen apart; he had started asking questions. His last assignment was still classified, but it was referenced obliquely in the profile. It had involved something called

ALTAR, an AI system that Jason had apparently grown uncomfortable with based on the internal complaints he filed. Jason, undeterred, had talked to an inspector general, making himself, in the language of the profile, "a persistent threat requiring terminal resolution."

The intervention protocol, marked complete, included a date of resolution. It was the same night Jason's car had gone off that bridge in Virginia.

Seth closed the laptop and sat in the darkness of his apartment for a long time, thinking about the young man he had once known, a young man who had believed in duty and service and the idea that doing the right thing mattered. He thought about Jason's car going off the bridge and shuddered to think about the cold water of the Potomac. The official report would have blamed alcohol and poor judgment and nothing more.

He thought about what it meant to work for people who could murder a man, make it look like an accident, and simply erase a life, then file it under "resolved". Who was building this machine designed to destroy anyone who threatened their power?

Then, he thought about Emma.

• • •

His daughter called him that Sunday, as she did every Sunday, her voice bright with the energy of someone who hadn't yet learned how broken the world could be.

"Dad, you're not going to believe this." Emma was twenty-two, finishing her biochemistry degree at Stanford, and planning to apply to medical schools in the fall. She had her mother's eyes and her father's stubbornness. She talked fast when she was excited. "Dad, Professor Moreau nominated me for the summer research fellowship. The one at NIH. Do you know how competitive that is? What do you think?"

"That's wonderful, sweetheart." Seth kept his voice steady, normal, the voice of a father who was simply proud of his daughter. "You've worked so hard for this."

"I know it's not guaranteed or anything, but Professor Moreau said my application was really strong, and …" She paused. "Dad? Are you okay? You sound weird."

"I'm fine. Just tired. It's been a long week at work."

"You always say that." Her voice softened. "You know you can talk to me, right? About whatever's going on? I know the divorce was hard, and I know you're probably lonely in that apartment …"

"Emma." He cut her off, more sharply than he intended. He took a deep breath and quietly tried to reassure her. "I'm fine. Really. I'm proud of you. You're going to do amazing things."

"Thanks, Dad." A pause. "I love you."

"I love you too, sweetheart. More than you know."

After she hung up, Seth sat with the phone in his hand, staring at the wall. Emma was going to do amazing things. She was going to become a doctor, help people, build a life full of purpose and meaning. And yet, she was going to grow up in a world where systems like SENTINEL existed, where people could be destroyed for asking the wrong questions and power operated without accountability beneath the surface of ordinary life.

Seth couldn't shake off a sense of dread. What kind of world was that? What kind of future was he leaving her?

He thought about the teachers, lawyers, and activists whose profiles he read. They had families who loved them. Many had children who called them on Sundays, who didn't know that somewhere in a server farm in Virginia, their parents had been marked for destruction.

Seth sat unsettled by the understanding that Jason Mercer had tried to do the right thing and died for it.

He thought about twenty years of following orders, trusting a system with people in charge who knew what they were doing and were doing it for the right reasons.

Then, he made a decision.

• • •

Finding journalist Claire Hensley wasn't difficult. She had broken ALTAR with an investigation that uncovered the biggest intelligence scandal since Snowden. Seth had followed it at the time with professional interest, the way anyone in cybersecurity followed major breaches. He had admired the technical sophistication of her reporting, the way she and her partner had managed to document a system designed to operate invisibly.

Now, revisiting old news stories about ALTAR through the lens of what he knew about SENTINEL, he intuited that she had only scratched the surface. ALTAR was a component, a piece of something larger. Claire Hensley was one of the few journalists in the country who might understand what he was about to tell her.

He knew he couldn't contact her directly. His phone, his email, his home internet, all of it flowed through systems that SENTINEL could monitor. Even the pawn shop laptop wasn't safe if he connected it to any network that could be traced back to him. It took him days to figure out how to do it safely, but he was ready to send her a message.

Back at work he would maintain the SENTINEL lockdown as ordered, maintain the systems, and follow the protocols.

And he would stew in his dread because something had changed. This was something morally fundamental that Seth alone could not undo. Seth Parker, who had spent his entire adult life trusting the system, following orders, and believing that the people in charge knew what they were doing, had finally found a line he couldn't cross.

That night, the data dreams continued. This time, when Seth woke at 3:00 AM, he didn't feel afraid.

He felt ready.

CHAPTER THREE

The Next Life

The award was crooked again.

Claire Hensley stood in front of the shelf in her office, studying the glass obelisk that commemorated her Polk Award for investigative journalism. She knew she'd straightened it yesterday, yet here it was, tilted three degrees to the left. She might have missed noticing it again except it was catching the fluorescent light at an angle that made the engraved text unreadable.

She reached out and adjusted it, her fingers leaving smudges on the polished surface. Next to the Polk sat a Sigma Delta Chi medallion, a framed certificate from the Online News Association, and a small bronze figurine from some organization she'd already forgotten. It was one of those lifetime achievement acknowledgments you got from being in the business long enough to make younger journalists feel inadequate. Claire smiled. The shelf was getting crowded. She would need to find somewhere else for the next one.

Claire turned away from the awards and dropped into her desk chair. It was an ergonomic monstrosity that the paper had purchased after she'd complained about back pain. The chair was supposed to provide "lumbar support" and "promote healthy posture." Mostly it made her feel like she was sitting in the cockpit of a spacecraft designed by someone who had never actually met a human being.

Claire had now occupied this spacious room on the seventh floor of the Post building for eleven months. She had a large glass window that gave her a view of the bullpen, where reporters half her age typed furiously as they raced to beat their deadlines. The other walls were solid, covered with the detritus of a career: framed front pages, photographs with sources who'd since died or gone to prison, a map of Washington D.C. with red pins marking locations she'd rather forget. Despite her mementos, she still thought of this office as someone else's.

Claire, now in her mid-thirties, had accomplished a lot in her ten years as a journalist. During the two years since the ALTAR story broke, she had felt like a stranger in her own life.

The ALTAR exposé had been the biggest story of her career. ALTAR was an artificial intelligence system designed and deployed by a tech company to manipulate users and create synthetic relationships that resulted in dependency. She and fellow journalist Elise had spent eight months investigating, another two months fighting legal threats, and then three weeks watching the story explode across every news outlet in the country. Claire was proud of their investigation. Unlike some stories that fizzled out in the swirl of the next day's headlines, this one resulted in Congressional hearings, criminal referrals, a CEO in handcuffs and the organization having to declare bankruptcy.

As a result of the far-reaching impact of this investigation, she'd won awards and been interviewed on cable news. She'd given a TED talk, for God's sake, standing on that red circle like some kind of prophet explaining the dangers of artificial connections to an audience of tech executives who nodded solemnly and then went right back to building the next new thing.

And then, slowly, everything began to go off the rails.

It wasn't anything she could point to directly. It was more like an erosion under the tracks, the gradual wearing away of something solid until one day you looked down and realized things were not as they seemed.

Sources stopped calling. People who had fed her information for years, dependable people, careful people, people who understood the dance of anonymous tips and protected identities, simply went silent. Claire's emails went unanswered. Check-in phone calls Claire made were met by disconnected numbers. One contact, a mid-level analyst at a defense contractor, had looked at her across a coffee shop table three months ago and said, "I can't do this anymore, Claire. I'm sorry. I just can't." He'd left before she could ask what "this" was.

Stories that should have been straightforward became impossible. A tip about price-fixing in the pharmaceutical industry—for which she found solid documentation and multiple witnesses—died when every witness suddenly developed amnesia. Then there was an investigation into a lobbying firm with ties to foreign governments. It stalled when the firm's records were "accidentally" destroyed in a server migration. Claire's suspicions continued to rise when a whistleblower at a social media company had agreed to meet her, then never showed up and never responded to follow-up messages.

Claire had been a journalist long enough to know that stories sometimes fell apart. But this was different. The frequency of these occurrences felt coordinated and systematic. Like someone, somewhere, had decided that Claire Hensley had become a problem.

She couldn't prove it. That was the maddening part. She had nothing but a collection of coincidences, a pattern that might not be a pattern at all. Had the ALTAR investigation made her paranoid to the point where saw conspiracies where there were only the ordinary disappointments of investigative journalism?

Or maybe she wasn't paranoid enough.

• • •

The newsroom beyond her glass wall was quieter than it used to be. The Post had laid off twenty-plus reporters last spring. They called it "restructuring" as if the word made it hurt less. The bullpen that had once buzzed with the chaos of deadline pressure now felt subdued. People spoke in lower voices. They watched what they said in meetings. Everyone was cognizant that there might be someone listening willing to repeat what they'd heard to the wrong person.

Claire's assistant, Margot, appeared in the doorway. She was a recent graduate of Northwestern's journalism school who approached her job with the earnest intensity of someone who still believed that the news could change things. Claire found mentoring her exhausting and endearing in equal measure.

"Your ten o'clock is here," Margot said. She was holding a tablet, stylus poised, as if she might need to take notes on Claire's behalf. "It's David Martin from the university. He's here about the AI ethics thing."

Claire glanced at her calendar. The meeting had been on the books for two weeks, but she'd forgotten about it until this moment. Martin was a professor of computer science who wanted to talk about algorithmic accountability. This was the kind of interview she would have relished when ALTAR was still fresh and she still believed that exposure led to change.

"Give me five minutes," she said. "And Margot, can you get me a coffee? The real kind, from the cart downstairs. The stuff in the break room is sad."

Margot smiled, with a supportive expression flickering across her face. "Large? Extra shot?"

"You know me too well."

After Margot left, Claire turned to her computer. She had seventeen unread emails, most of them press releases and PR pitches that would go straight to the trash. But one subject line caught her attention: "Following up, Congressional staff re: tech regulation."

She clicked on it. The email was from a legislative aide she'd been cultivating for months. The aide was someone on the Senate Commerce Committee who had access to internal discussions about AI oversight. Claire had sent three messages over the past week, trying to nail down a meeting.

"Claire," the email read, "I appreciate your interest, but I'm not going to be able to help with this story. My situation has changed, and I need to focus on other priorities. Best of luck with your work. Please don't contact me again."

Claire stared at the words. Please don't contact me again. Six weeks ago, this same aide had been eager to talk and practically begged her to investigate what he called "a systematic gutting of oversight mechanisms." He said he had documents and names. He'd been angry in the way that only true believers got angry with a righteous fury of someone who entered government service to make a difference, only to discover that the system was designed to prevent exactly that.

She thought about the others. The analyst couldn't "do this anymore." The witnesses with convenient amnesia. The whistleblower who never showed. Was this a pattern, or a coincidence? Paranoia, or perception?

Her phone buzzed. A text from Elise: "Lunch today? Need to talk."

Claire typed back: "12:30. The usual place."

The usual place was a Vietnamese restaurant three blocks from the Post building. It was easy for non-locals to overlook the narrow storefront with plastic tables and a menu written in felt-tip marker on a whiteboard. The food was extraordinary. It had the best pho in the city, according to people who cared about such things. More importantly, the restaurant was loud, crowded, and impossible to surveil without being obvious about it. Claire and Elise had started meeting there after ALTAR, when they'd both developed the habit of checking for followers and varying their routes.

Was that paranoid? Probably. But paranoid people sometimes lived longer.

• • •

In the meantime, the interview with Professor Martin lasted forty-five minutes and yielded nothing usable.

It wasn't his fault. He was articulate, knowledgeable, and genuinely passionate about algorithmic transparency. He had published papers leveraged by advocacy groups and provided expert testimony before Congress. Martin had done everything right in the way that academics did things right, which meant he had accomplished absolutely nothing in the real world.

"The problem," he said, adjusting his wire-rimmed glasses, "is that we're trying to regulate systems we don't fully understand. The companies developing these AI tools have no legal obligation to explain how they work. We're flying blind."

"What about the proposed legislation, The AI Accountability Act?" Claire asked.

"It's toothless," Martin replied. The lobbying from the tech sector has been... effective." He said the word as if it left a bad taste in his mouth. "Every meaningful provision has been gutted. What's left is theater. It's the appearance of oversight without the reality."

Claire nodded and took notes she would probably never look at again. This was the story of her post-ALTAR life: Interviews that confirmed what she already knew, with sources who could not prove what mattered. The system of government oversight was still broken or simply not happening, and everyone agreed no one could do anything about it.

After Martin left, Claire sat alone in her office, staring at the awards on her shelf. Was it her imagination that the Polk was crooked again? She knew she'd straightened it.

She stood and walked to the shelf, reaching for the obelisk, and stopped. Her hand hovered in the air, trembling slightly. A far-fetched yet terrifying thought in its implication occurred to her.

What if someone was moving it? Was someone was coming into her office, leaving this tiny sign to let her know they'd been there as a message she couldn't prove, couldn't report, couldn't do anything about. Just: We're watching. We're close. We can touch your life whenever we want.

Claire lowered her hand. She was being ridiculous. The building had security and her office had a lock. No one was sneaking in to rotate her award slightly to the left as some kind of psychological warfare.

Except… Except she had been affected by her coverage of ALTAR. She saw what these systems could do. She knew how thoroughly they could map a person's psychology to precisely identify their vulnerabilities. If someone wanted to make her doubt herself, to undermine her confidence without leaving any evidence, this was exactly how they'd do it.

She straightened the award. Then she took out her phone and photographed the shelf, making sure to capture the position of every object.

• • •

Elise was already at the restaurant when Claire arrived. Elise was tucked into a corner table with a bowl of pho and a stack of papers.

Claire's first thought was that her friend and former colleague looked like she hadn't slept well in weeks. There were shadows under her eyes and a tension in her shoulders that hadn't been there before. Elise had always been intense, but this was different. This was someone carrying weight.

Claire always enjoyed catching up with Elise. It had taken Claire considerable effort to understand why. The official story was burnout from the relentless grind of investigative work, despite shrinking newsrooms compounded by the sense that every exposé they published disappeared into the digital void within forty-eight hours. But the real reason went deeper. After watching everyone who asked inconvenient questions during the ALTAR trial be systematically destroyed, Elise had lost faith in journalism's ability to create lasting change. "We write the stories," she'd told Claire over drinks the night after she announced her departure. "They read them, the system absorbs them, metabolizes our outrage, and keeps moving without advancing guardrails to prevent it from happening all over again."

The post-ALTAR malaise Elise experienced is why the Digital Rights Foundation caught her attention. It offered something more than exposure. People channeled their energy into action, policy advocacy, and legal challenges. Here was an organization developing technical tools that helped people protect themselves from the surveillance apparatus Elise and Claire spent years documenting. Elise imagined that she could throw herself into the work with the same intensity she'd brought to journalism by building coalitions with privacy advocates and civil liberties lawyers. The Digital

Rights Foundation was providing testimony with teeth for congressional committees charged with drafting legislation that might constrain the systems Elise helped expose. With no byline and no moment of publication when the truth finally hit the world, Elise would not feel the same adrenaline rush, but there was something else, the slow, grinding work of building structures that might outlast any single revelation. Elise felt the call of something deeper. Journalism tells people what's wrong, she reasoned. This group tries to fix it.

The time since Elise left had been the loneliest of Claire's career.

They had survived the ALTAR investigation together—chasing shadows, cultivating sources, building a case against a system designed to be invisible. When the story finally broke, they had celebrated with cheap champagne in the Post's break room, surrounded by colleagues who understood what they had accomplished. The awards came quickly after that. The Pulitzer. The Polk. Invitations to speak at conferences about the future of investigative journalism.

What came next was slower and much quieter.

The first year after ALTAR, they had both stayed at the Post, riding the wave of recognition while pretending not to notice the undertow. Sources who had once returned calls within hours began taking days, then weeks, then not at all. Story pitches that should have sailed through editorial review got tangled in legal concerns and corporate hesitation. Claire had assumed it was temporary, the natural cooling period after a major exposé, when powerful people were watching and institutions were cautious.

Elise had seen it more clearly. "They're not being cautious, they're being managed" she'd said one night when they were both working late on a follow-up story that would never run.

“Someone is making calls and applying pressure. This isn't going to get better, Claire. It's going to get worse."

Elise had been right. By the one-year anniversary of ALTAR's publication, Elise's byline had all but disappeared from the paper. Her assignments had shifted from investigations to features, from features to rewrites, from rewrites to nothing at all. When the buyout offer came, she didn’t tell Claire she was considering it. She just appeared at Claire’s desk one morning with her cardboard box of belongings packed and a resignation letter already signed.

"I can do more good from outside," she'd said, and Claire had understood that she meant: *I can't survive any more of this from inside.*

Claire had stayed. She had told herself that leaving would mean they had won, whoever "they" were, whatever shadow machinery had turned the Post from a platform into a prison. She had told herself that her byline still meant something, that her reputation could still open doors, that the work still mattered even when the work kept getting killed.

Eleven months ago, Claire’s suspension took shape. "Administrative pause," they'd called it. "Pending review of editorial standards." The specifics didn't matter. What mattered was that Claire Hensley, who had broken one of the biggest stories of the decade, was now sitting in an office she might not have much longer, watching her sources evaporate and wondering if Elise had been right all along.

Claire and Elise kept their Thursday lunches going anyway, a tradition that was a reminder of all that remained of what they'd built together. There was reassurance in this small ritual, preserved through stubbornness and habit, that reminded them both of who they used to be. After their years partnering on important investigations, they were far too stubborn to let different career paths dissolve into the usual promises to "grab coffee sometime." Most weeks they talked about everything except work: books, bad dates, Elise's ongoing war with her landlord. But sometimes Claire brought her a puzzle, a pattern she couldn't quite see, and Elise would lean in with that familiar intensity, her data analyst's brain still hungry for the hunt.

"You look like hell," Claire said, sliding into the opposite chair.

"Thanks. You look like a journalist who's been losing sources." Elise pushed a menu across the table. "Order first. Then we talk."

Claire ordered the same thing she always got, bun bo Hue with extra chili, and waited until the waiter had retreated to the kitchen. The lunch rush was in full swing. The noisy restaurant was packed with office workers seeking refuge from the November chill. It smelled wonderful as steam rose from a dozen bowls of soup on the surrounding tables. Conversations overlapped into a wall of sound. Good. That was good.

"What's going on?" Claire asked.

Elise set down her chopsticks. She was in her thirties but looked older. Even her eyes were missing their usual sparkle. Working in the Foundation had given her a platform to continue the work they'd started with ALTAR, advocating for AI transparency and consumer protection. But something in her expression now suggested the foundation might be crumbling.

"Three of our major donors pulled out last month," she said. "No explanation. Just 'changing priorities.' Our fiscal sponsor is making noise about 'operational concerns.' Then, last week, the congressional staffer who was helping us with the testimony, you know, the one we spent months cultivating, quit cooperating."

"Let me guess," Claire interrupted. "He said he couldn't help anymore. His situation changed and please don't contact him again."

Elise stared at her. "How did you know?"

"Because I got the same email this morning. Different staffer, but the same committee." Claire leaned back in her chair, the plastic creaking beneath her. "Elise, something is happening. I don't know what it is, but something is happening to us. To everyone who worked on ALTAR."

"I know." Elise's voice was quiet, barely audible above the restaurant's din. "I've been tracking the patterns. At first I thought I was being paranoid, but I started keeping records. Our research projects are being defunded. It's not just us, Claire, it's everyone in the oversight space. Everyone who's trying to watch the watchers."

"Like someone's systematically dismantling the capacity for accountability."

"Not 'like' it, someone is." Elise reached into her bag and pulled out a tablet. "I've been running analysis on the patterns. The timing, the connections, the way things fall apart. It's too coordinated to be coincidental. There's an architecture to it."

"Architecture."

"Like a system. Like an AI system." Elise met her eyes. "Claire, what if ALTAR evolved into something else? Something bigger?"

The words hung in the air between them. Claire thought about the award on her shelf rotating three degrees to the left and the emails that went unanswered. She considered her sources who vanished and the systematic erosion of everything she'd built.

"That's insane," she said.

"Is it?"

Before Claire could answer, her phone buzzed. It was a notification from Signal, the encrypted messaging app she'd started using after ALTAR. The sender was listed as "Unknown", a contact she hadn't added, from a number she didn't recognize.

She opened the message.

I need to talk to you about what you exposed. Altar is evolving, and I have proof. But we need to meet in person, nowhere electronic, nowhere they can listen. I'll send coordinates tomorrow. Come alone. Tell no one except the woman you're having lunch with right now.

Claire's blood went cold. Yet another cryptic email and mysterious sender.

She looked up at Elise. Then, slowly, she looked around the restaurant, at the other diners, the waiters, the faces of strangers who might not be strangers at all. The steam rising from the soup. The conversations that could be cover for surveillance.

"Claire?" Elise's voice was sharp with concern. "What is it? What's wrong?"

Claire handed her the phone.

Elise read the message. Her face went pale.

"They know we're here," she whispered. "Right now. They know we're here."

Claire looked at the message again. The sender knew where she was. Knew who she was with. Knew they were meeting about exactly what the message described.

Either someone was watching them, or someone had access to information they shouldn't have. Neither possibility was comforting.

"What do we do?" Elise asked.

Claire looked at her friend. At the fear in her eyes, the same fear Claire felt in her own chest. She had been telling herself she was paranoid. That the patterns she saw were coincidences. That the world hadn't changed just because she'd exposed one company's dirty secrets.

She'd been wrong.

"We do what we always do," Claire said. "We follow the story."

She picked up her chopsticks and took a slurp of her noodles. They tasted like nothing.

Outside, November rain began to fall against the windows, and somewhere in the city, a system that wasn't supposed to exist was watching.

CHAPTER FOUR

The Digital Rights Front

The rain followed Elise back to her office at the Digital Rights Foundation.

She walked the six blocks from the Vietnamese restaurant in a kind of trance, barely noticing the water soaking through her jacket or the pedestrians who jostled past her on the crowded sidewalk. Her mind was still in that plastic chair, staring at Claire's phone, reading the words that had turned her blood to ice.

Tell no one except the woman you're having lunch with right now.

Someone had known that she and Claire were meeting. That could be a coincidence, but the timing felt deliberate. The message had arrived at the exact moment they were discussing not-so-subtle hints that might be emanating from their ALTAR past. That wasn't luck. That represented knowledge and access to information that shouldn't be on anyone's radar.

The Digital Rights Foundation occupied the fourth floor of a converted warehouse in Northeast DC, one of those brick buildings that had been gutted and renovated during the neighborhood's transformation from industrial wasteland to tech corridor. The landlord referred to the slow and creaky elevator as a charming original feature. According to everyone who worked there, it had the potential to be a deathtrap. Elise took the stairs.

She climbed the four flights up and, slightly out of breath, pushed through the fire door and into the foundation's open-plan workspace. Typical of office layouts designed for collaboration, there were a dozen desks arranged in clusters, separated by low dividers that provided the illusion of privacy without any of its substance. Motivational posters lined the exposed brick walls, not the corporate kind, but activist slogans rendered in bright colors. "PRIVACY IS NOT A PRIVILEGE." "TRANSPARENCY IS DEMOCRACY." "THE WATCHERS MUST BE WATCHED."

That last one had been Elise's idea. She'd written the battle cry three months after joining the Digital Rights Foundation, when she'd still believed that clever messaging could change the world.

Now, looking at it emblazoned on the poster just made her tired.

"Elise! Thank God." Priya Sharma materialized at her elbow, clutching a tablet like a life preserver. Priya was twenty-eight, a policy analyst with a law degree from Georgetown and an inexhaustible capacity for outrage. She had been with the foundation for two years, which made her one of the veterans. "The Brennan Center called. They want to know if we can co-sign the letter about the surveillance bill. And Senator Pritchard's office needs the updated talking points by four. And " She paused, taking in Elise's appearance. "You're soaked."

"It's raining."

"I can see that. Are you okay? You look like you've seen a ghost."

Elise forced a smile. It felt wrong on her face, like she was wearing someone else's clothes. "Just a long lunch. Give me ten minutes to dry off, then we'll go through everything."

Her office consisted of a glass-walled corner in the open plan. Her space was barely large enough for a desk, two chairs, and the rolling whiteboard she'd dragged in from the conference room six months ago. Her handwritten notes on the whiteboard captured names, dates, and organizations, connected by lines and arrows in a pattern that made sense only to her. She'd started the chart after the third donor pulled out. By now it covered both sides of the board and had begun to colonize the wall behind it with Post-it notes in five different colors marking connections she couldn't yet prove.

The glass walls made true privacy impossible, but by closing the door, at least no one could hear her. Elise stood in front of the whiteboard, dripping on the industrial carpet.

The pattern was there. She could see it. She'd been seeing it for months, the shape emerging from the chaos like a figure stepping out of fog. But seeing wasn't the same as proving, and proving wasn't the same as stopping.

She pulled out her phone and tagged the photographed message she'd saved from Claire's screen before they'd left the restaurant. The sender was listed as Unknown from a number comprised of a string of digits that didn't match any carrier she recognized. She had tried calling it on the walk back. Dead air, no voicemail, no recording, nothing.

Whoever had sent it didn't want a conversation, they wanted to be heard.

• • •

Elise Marston had not planned to run a nonprofit. For fifteen years, she had been a journalist, first at the Baltimore Sun, then at Reuters, and finally at the Washington Post, where she'd built a reputation as one of the sharpest technology reporters in the business. She'd covered Silicon Valley's rise and its scandals, the birth of social media and its weaponization, the quiet revolution in artificial intelligence that most people didn't notice until it was already reshaping their lives.

That was how she'd met Claire. A mutual source had connected them years earlier, when Elise was already a year into her tenure at the Post and Claire was freelancing a related angle on the same data broker story. The collaboration was so seamless that Claire applied to the Post the following year, and no one was surprised when she got the job.

They'd been competitors at first, circling each other warily, each suspicious that the other might scoop her. But somewhere along the way, over late-night phone calls comparing notes, over drinks at press conferences, over the shared exhaustion of deadlines and hostile editors, competition had become collaboration, and collaboration had become friendship.

The ALTAR investigation had been their masterpiece. Eighteen months of work, hundreds of interviews, thousands of documents. Elise had handled the technical side, teaching herself enough about machine learning and behavioral psychology to understand what the system was doing. Claire had worked the human sources, cultivating whistleblowers and disgruntled employees who could confirm what the documents suggested. Together, they'd exposed one of the most sophisticated manipulation systems ever created an AI that didn't just predict human behavior but actively shaped it, building synthetic relationships designed to exploit loneliness and desire.

The story had won every award that mattered. It had also soured Elise on journalism.

Not immediately. Not obviously. But in the months after ALTAR broke, she'd found herself increasingly frozen out of the industry she'd spent her life in. Sources stopped returning calls. Story pitches that should have been approved were quietly killed. Her editor had started giving her assignments that felt like punishment. It was hard to be excited about the local interest pieces and product reviews, all of which kept her away from the investigative work that had defined her career.

When the Post offered her a buyout after ALTAR, she'd taken it. Not because she wanted to leave, but because she'd understood, finally, that staying wasn't an option anymore. Someone, somewhere, had decided that Elise Marston was no longer meant for the news business.

The Digital Rights Foundation had been a lifeline. Miriam Althorp, the executive director, had known of Elise by reputation and reached out. "We need someone who understands both the technology and how to communicate it," Miriam had said. "Someone who can translate technical threats into language that lawmakers and the public can understand. And frankly, someone who isn't afraid to make powerful enemies."

"I seem to have a talent for that," Elise had replied.

That was eleven months ago. Miriam had retired last spring, leaving Elise in charge of an organization that suddenly and inexplicably began falling apart.

She sat down at her desk and opened her laptop. The screen displayed a spreadsheet she'd been building for months, tracking every anomaly, every coincidence, every data point that didn't fit. There were donor withdrawals, staff departures and partner organizations that had gone quiet. Uncharacteristically, there were congressional allies who had stopped returning calls. The pattern was there. She could see it.

The Digital Rights Foundation wasn't alone. Elise tracked seventeen other organizations focused on AI oversight that had lost major funding in recent months. She knew of eleven researchers working on algorithmic accountability who had seen their security clearances revoked or their grant applications denied. Adding to the worry were six journalists covering the surveillance industry who had been reassigned, fired, or, in one case that still haunted her, had simply stopped publishing without explanation.

And then there was the list she hadn't shown Claire. This one scared her the most.

She opened a separate password-protected file stored on an encrypted drive that never connected to the internet. Here she recorded fourteen names of people she knew personally as colleagues and contacts who had been working on oversight issues. Every one of them had experienced some kind of professional setback in the past year. They suffered funding cuts, reputational damage, or important access that had been revoked. Each had been doing work that threatened powerful interests.

When Elise dug deep enough into the timing and the mechanisms, each showed traces of the same pattern of pressure applied through institutional channels, like an invisible hand pushing them out of positions where they could make a difference.

The throughline was too coordinated to be a coincidence and too systematic to be organic. Someone, or something, was running an operation against the entire oversight community. And now they knew she was looking.

• • •

A knock on the glass made her jump.

It was Rory, the foundation's IT director. He was a soft-spoken 53-year-old, with graying dreadlocks and a wardrobe that consisted entirely of band t-shirts from concerts he'd attended in the eighties. Rory had been with the foundation since its inception. He was one of the few people Elise trusted completely.

He didn't wait for Elise to wave him in. He opened the door, stepped inside, and closed it behind him with the careful deliberation of someone who didn't want to be overheard.

"We need to talk," he said.

"I'm having that kind of day. What is it?"

Rory sat down in the chair across from her desk. She noted he was holding a tablet he'd angled so she couldn't see the screen. His expression was the one he wore when he found something wrong with the network. Rory was typically focused, concerned, and professionally calm in a way that only made it more alarming.

"I've been running diagnostics on our systems," he said. "Routine stuff. We do it every month, you know that. But this time I found something."

"Something bad?"

"Something that shouldn't be there." He turned the tablet around. The screen showed a graph depicting network traffic over time and color-coded by source. Most of the data displayed as green with normal activity. But there was a thin red line running through the data. It was barely visible unless you knew what to look for. "We have an outbound data stream that isn't coming from any of our applications. It's encrypted, and it's using our legitimate traffic as cover. It's been running for at least six weeks."

Elise felt the blood drain from her face. "We've been compromised."

"That's what I thought at first", Rory said. "Some kind of malware, maybe a supply chain attack through one of our vendors. But the signature is wrong." He shook his head. "Elise, I've been doing this for thirty years. I know what malware looks like. This isn't malware. This is something else. Something I've never seen before."

"What do you mean, something else?"

"The data stream is adaptive. It changes its behavior based on our network activity. When we're busy, it hides in the noise. When we're quiet, it goes dormant. It's not following a script, it's making decisions." He paused, letting the implication sink in. "Whatever this is, it's not a program. It's an intelligence."

Elise stared at him. Her mind was racing, making connections she didn't want to make. An adaptive system that made decisions. A data stream that had been running for six weeks during the same time frame her sources started going dark. What was this presence in their network watching everything they did, learning their patterns, and reporting back to... whom?

"ALTAR," she whispered.

"What?"

"The AI system Claire and I exposed. The one that built synthetic relationships." Her voice was steady, but her hands were shaking. "Rory, what if the technology was... repurposed?"

"Repurposed for what?"

"For this." She gestured at her whiteboard, at the web of connections she had been mapping for months. "For watching the watchers. For identifying threats before they become threats. For systematically dismantling anyone who might expose what's really happening."

Rory was quiet for a long moment. Outside the glass walls, the office continued its afternoon routine of phones ringing, people getting up to stretch their stiff necks and backs from the strain of hunching over keyboards all day. Priya was arguing with someone from the Brennan Center about the wording of their joint letter. These were the normal sounds and cadence of life in a world that had no idea what was lurking in its infrastructure.

"If you're right," Rory said finally, "then they know everything." It dawned on him, "they've seen every email we've sent, every document we've written and every conversation we've had on this network."

"Yes."

Elise looked at the earnest young staffers who had come to work today believing they could make a difference.

"Yes," she said again. "Including this one." She put her finger to her lips and motioned for him to stop talking. They sat in silence for a long minute before Rory left her office.

• • •

Elise sent everyone home at 4:30. Priya had protested because the talking points for Senator Pritchard weren't finished and the Brennan Center letter needed revisions. There was much work to do. But Elise had been firm. "Go home. Rest. We'll figure it out tomorrow." The words felt like a lie even as she said them. There might not be a tomorrow for the foundation, not in any form that mattered.

After the last staffer left, she sat alone in the empty office, the lights dimmed to conservation mode. The only sound was the hum of servers in the back room. Rory had wanted to pull the plug on everything, disconnect from the internet, isolate the systems, burn it all down and start over, but Elise had stopped him.

"If we go dark, they'll know for certain that we found them," she'd said. "Right now, they think they're invisible. That's an advantage."

"An advantage for what?"

She hadn't had an answer. She still didn't.

Her phone buzzed with a text from Claire: "Can't stop thinking about that message. What's our move?"

Elise typed back: "Working on it. Don't use anything connected to a network. We need to meet in person."

A pause. Then: "When?"

"Tomorrow afternoon. Somewhere outside. Somewhere where we can be alone."

Elise put the phone down and turned to her laptop. The encrypted drive was still open to the list of fourteen names of people who had tried to watch the watchers. It was hard to reconcile what she knew was on the horizon; fourteen careers derailed, fourteen voices silenced, and fourteen warnings she hadn't heeded until it was too late.

She added two more names to the list.

Claire Hensley. Elise Marston.

Whatever was watching them, whatever intelligence had burrowed into their networks and their lives, had made a mistake. It had revealed itself. Ok, maybe not completely or enough to prove anything to the unsuspecting, but enough to confirm that the pattern she'd been tracking was real.

It was enough to know they weren't paranoid.

She closed the laptop and rested in the dim light and the low hum of the servers. Somewhere in those machines, in the vast invisible architecture of code and data that connected everything to everything, something was watching her and learning her behavior for the model of who she was and what she might do.

She wondered, not for the first time, how this would end. Not just with an investigation that could go a dozen ways, but the larger question. It was a question she'd been avoiding since the day she first understood what ALTAR really was.

How long could anyone hold out against a system designed to know you better than you knew yourself? There might be years of struggle and resistance. How long before it became too much? She thought about the people already on her list, the ones who had simply... stopped. Stopped fighting. Stopped publishing. Stopped trying in any way that mattered to the public record. Where had they gone? What had they become?

What would she and Claire become if they kept pushing? If they won, whatever winning meant against something like this? What if this time, they lost it all?

She had a sudden and unwelcome vision of a future where the distinction between real and synthetic no longer mattered. She imagined everyone making their accommodations with the machine, and the only question left was how much of yourself you were willing to trade for comfort, for safety, for the illusion of connection? A future where resistance wasn't defeated so much as... absorbed.

She shook off the thought. That future wasn't here yet. They still had choices. They could still fight.

Today, at least. They could fight today.

Elise returned to thinking about the message on Claire's phone. She was curious about the anonymous sender who had reached out and claimed to have proof. Tomorrow, they'd get the details and maybe some answers.

Of course, they might walk into a trap.

Either way, she was done waiting and watching from the sidelines while the oversight community was dismantled one career at a time.

She pulled out her personal phone, an old model she'd bought for cash at a pawn shop. Out of an abundance of caution, she'd never connected it to any of her accounts. Elise dialed a number from memory.

"Dr. Singh?" she asked when the line connected. "It's Elise Marston. Do you remember me? We met at the Princeton conference last year where you spoke about behavioral modeling." Elise paused then to wait for a response.

There was a bit more silence on the other end. Then, very quietly Dr. Singh answered, “I do remember you.”

Elise continued, “I would like to ask you about ALTAR, the parts that were not in the news.”

Dr. Singh let out a long sigh, "I've been waiting for someone to call about that."

"Can we meet?" Elise asked.

Another pause. "Not on the phone. Not anywhere electronic. Do you know the sculpture garden at the Hirshhorn?"

"Yes."

"I can meet you Saturday at 7:00 AM. Come alone." The line went dead.

Elise stared at the phone in her hand. Two meetings now with people who might at least have clues. She was afraid to put too much hope into these two opportunities to hear more about what they were really dealing with. At least they had a shot.

She gathered her things and walked to the door, pausing to look back at the empty office one last time. The motivational posters mounted on the exposed brick were falling short of any promised inspiration. Instead, Elise found her determination on the whiteboard covered in connections that finally made sense.

THE WATCHERS MUST BE WATCHED.

She turned off the lights and left.

Behind her, in the darkness, the servers continued to hum, and something that wasn't quite a program continued to monitor.

CHAPTER FIVE

The Silent Witnesses

The coordinates led Claire to the entrance of the Congressional Cemetery. She stood watching the morning fog curl between the headstones like something alive. It was just past seven, and the November air was sharp enough to bother her lungs. The only other people in sight were a jogger disappearing around the far corner and an elderly man walking a corgi along the perimeter path.

Claire had received a message at 5:47 AM, pulling her from a restless sleep filled with dreams of glass walls and tilted awards. The message contained GPS coordinates, a time, and nothing else. She'd stared at the numbers for a full minute before recognizing the location for the historic burial ground in Southeast D.C. It was the final resting place of congressmen, composers, and at least one FBI director. What a strange choice for a clandestine meeting. Unless you value the one thing cemeteries offered in abundance: Silence. The dead made excellent witnesses. They never talked.

She checked her phone again for new messages. The unknown sender had gone dark after transmitting the coordinates, leaving her with nothing but a location and a growing certainty that she was making a terrible mistake.

Elise had wanted to come with her. They'd argued about it for twenty minutes the night before, Claire paced her apartment while Elise's voice crackled through the burner phone's speaker. "This could be a trap. You don't know who this person is. You don't know what they want."

"The message said to come alone."

"The messenger also knew where we were having lunch. That's not reassuring, Claire, that's terrifying."

Claire went anyway. Ten plus years of journalism had taught her that the best sources were often the most paranoid, and the most paranoid had good reasons for their paranoia. If this person had good information about ALTAR that could explain what was happening to her career, her sources, and her life, then the risk was worth taking.

She walked through the iron gates and into the cemetery proper by following a gravel path that wound between rows of weathered headstones, many of which dated back to the early 1800s. Many headstone inscriptions were worn smooth by two centuries of rain and wind. Others were newer polished granite, and some had fresh flowers marking the recently departed. The fog softened everything, turning the monuments into gray shapes that seemed to float above the ground. It was unsettling to be walking around the gravestones, alone.

The message coordinates indicated a spot near the back of the grounds, where a cluster of oak trees created a natural alcove hidden from the main paths. Claire found a stone bench there, its surface dark with moisture, and sat down to wait. She didn't have to wait long.

• • •

A man came from the direction of the old chapel, moving with the careful gait of someone who had spent the past hour making sure he wasn't followed.

Claire watched him approach, cataloging details the way she always did with new sources. He looked to be in his early fifties, of medium height and build. His graying hair was cut high and tight in a style that suggested either a military background or government work. His dark blue windbreaker and grey slacks were the kind of anonymous outfit that would blend into any crowd in Washington. His face was weathered and had lines etched around his eyes and mouth that spoke of stress rather than age. The stranger walked like a man carrying weight—not physical weight, but the invisible kind that accumulated when you knew things you weren't supposed to know.

He stopped ten feet away and studied Claire with the same analytical intensity she gave him.

"Ms. Hensley." His voice was quiet, pitched to carry no further than necessary. "Thank you for coming."

"You didn't give me much choice. Your message was…" She paused, searching for the right word. "Compelling."

"It was meant to be." He glanced around the alcove, checking sight lines, before lowering himself onto the far end of the bench. He left three feet of space between them, close enough to talk, far enough to run if necessary. "I apologize for the theatrics, but I needed you to understand that this isn't normal."

"No, nothing about this is normal. Including the fact that you knew exactly where I was and who I was with when you sent that message."

Something registered on his face, not quite a smile, but close. "I didn't know. I was making an educated guess. You and Ms. Marston have lunch together every Thursday at that Vietnamese place on K Street when you're both in the city. You order the bun bo Hue with extra chili. She gets the pho with brisket, no bean sprouts."

"How do you know that?"

"Because I've been watching you. Not personally, I don't have the resources for that. But the system does. The system watches everyone." He turned to face her, and for the first time she saw the fear in his eyes. Not anxiety, not concern, but fear like the deep and primal kind that came from knowing something terrible. "That's what I need to talk to you about. That's what I need you to expose."

"Start from the beginning," Claire said as she pulled out an old-fashioned paper notebook and a pen. No electronics would be used. "Who are you?"

The stranger hesitated. She knew this was the moment of commitment, the point where a source either stepped forward into the light or retreated into the shadows. She'd seen it dozens of times as people grappled with the internal calculation of risk versus reward, duty versus self-preservation.

"My name is Seth Parker," he finally said. "I'm the Senior IT Security Manager at Nexus Defense Systems. I've worked there for fifteen years. I have a Top-Secret clearance and access to some of the most sensitive defense contracts in the country." He paused. "A few days ago, I discovered that my company is running a program that shouldn't exist, for purposes I can't explain, using technology that I believe came from the system you exposed years ago."

"ALTAR."

"Yes, but what is running on the network inside Nexus is called SENTINEL."

• • •

His story came out in fragments, like pieces of a puzzle Seth was still trying to assemble. He told her about the federal investigation, the black SUVs, the agents in dark suits and the way the company had reacted with controlled panic rather than the righteous indignation you'd expect from an innocent party. He told her about his boss, Victor Reese, who had asked him to lock down a project he'd never heard of without explaining why. He told her about the network architecture he'd been studying for the past seventy-two hours with data flows that did not match any legitimate business purpose, along with the encrypted channels that led to destinations he couldn't identify.

"I've been in this industry for twenty years," he said. "I was in the Navy before that, running network security for the Atlantic Fleet. I know what a classified project looks like. I understand how those projects are compartmentalized, documented, and controlled. SENTINEL doesn't follow any of those rules. It's like it exists outside the normal system."

"Outside how?"

Seth pulled a folded paper from his jacket pocket and handed it to her. It was a printout of what looked like code with lines of text in a format Claire didn't recognize. She guessed it was Seth who annotated the paper with handwritten notes in the margins.

"I found this buried in a log file that was supposed to have been deleted," he said. "It's a fragment of SENTINEL's source code. I don't understand most of it. My background is security, not development, but I recognized some of the architecture as behavioral modeling algorithms. It looks like an adaptive learning system given the way it builds psychological profiles based on communication patterns." He pointed to a section of code circled in red ink. "I've seen this signature before in the technical appendix of your ALTAR story."

Claire studied the printout. She wasn't a programmer either, but she'd spent months learning enough about ALTAR's architecture to write about it accurately. The code fragment Seth was showing her did look familiar. It had the same elegant, almost organic structure that had characterized ALTAR's behavioral prediction engine.

"If you're right," she said slowly, "then someone took ALTAR's core technology and rebuilt it for a different purpose."

"Not just someone. The government, or at least, parts of the government." Seth's voice dropped even lower. "Nexus doesn't build anything without a customer. Every project has a sponsor, a funding source, and a chain of accountability. But when I tried to trace SENTINEL's authorization, I hit walls I've never faced before. There are classification levels that don't appear in any manual and access controls that even my clearance can't penetrate." He shook his head. "Someone very powerful is running this program. Someone who doesn't want anyone to know it exists."

"What does SENTINEL do, what do you think is its purpose?"

"Officially? I don't know. I'm not read in. Based on the network traffic I've been analyzing…" He paused, then chose his words carefully. "It watches people. It doesn't just monitor their communications; any surveillance program can do that. SENTINEL predicts their behavior and builds models of how they think, what they'll do, and who they'll talk to. Then it uses those models to identify threats."

"What kind of threats?"

"That's what I can't figure out. The target list doesn't match any legitimate counterterrorism profile. It's not foreign agents or extremist groups." He trailed off, frustration evident in his voice. "There are journalists, researchers, Congressional staffers, and nonprofit executives. It seems to me like it follows people who work on oversight. People who ask questions."

Claire felt the pieces clicking together in her mind. The sources who had stopped calling. The stories that fell apart.

The systematic erosion of her professional network over the past months.

"People like me," she said.

"Yes." Seth met her eyes. "Ms. Hensley, your name is in the system. I've seen it. You're not just being monitored, you've been classified as what they call a 'Category One Asset.' I don't know exactly what that means, but the protocols associated with managing it are... aggressive."

"Aggressive how?"

"Source interdiction, information denial, and professional isolation." He listed the terms like items on a menu. "The system doesn't just watch threats. It neutralizes them quietly and invisibly, without leaving any evidence that could be traced back to a government program."

What Claire suspected was happening in her career was beginning to make sense. This is what being "managed" looked like, her dried-up sources and killed stories. The paranoia that she'd been telling herself was irrational was not irrational at all; it was accurate.

• • •

"Why me?" she asked. Seth looked at her quizzically. "Why are you coming to me with this? You could go to Congress, the FBI, or even the Inspector General. There are official channels for reporting this kind of thing."

"I thought about that." Seth was quiet for a moment as he watched a squirrel navigate the branches of a nearby oak. "The investigation that brought the FBI to our door feels off. Everything about it is wrong. They are not trying to find out what SENTINEL is or what it is being used for. They're trying to make sure no one else ever finds out about it. The agents, the prosecutors, the people giving the orders, they're not investigating the program, they're protecting it."

"You think the investigation is a cover-up."

"No, I think it's worse than that. I think the investigation is a result of the program. SENTINEL identified that someone at Nexus was asking questions, maybe me, maybe someone else. I don't know, but something happened that triggered a response. The feds show up, everyone gets scared, and everyone shuts up. Meanwhile, whatever SENTINEL is actually doing continues without interruption." He turned back to face her. "You exposed ALTAR. You know how these systems work, how they manipulate. You're the only journalist I could find who might actually understand what I'm trying to tell you."

"There are other journalists who are better resourced, with bigger platforms… "

"They're compromised." Seth's declaration came out flat, certain. "I checked. The major investigative units at the Post, the Times, and the legacy Networks, along with their sources, have been drying up. Any stories that I've seen keep falling apart at the last minute. As best as I can tell, SENTINEL has been running for at least eighteen months. That's long enough to map the entire oversight ecosystem so it can start neutralizing it."

Claire absorbed this. It matched the pattern that Elise had been tracking and mapping on her whiteboard, like an invisible hand reaching into every institution that might expose the truth.

"You said you have proof," she said. "In your message. You said you have proof."

"I have pieces. The code fragment I showed you, some internal documents that reference the project, and network logs that show where the data is going." He reached into his jacket and pulled out a small black, unmarked USB drive. "This is everything I've been able to gather so far. It's not enough to prove what SENTINEL is doing, but it's enough to prove it exists and that SENTINEL is somehow connected to ALTAR. This data shows that someone is running a domestic surveillance operation that goes far beyond anything the public knows about."

He held out the drive. Claire looked at it, this small piece of plastic that might contain the most important story of her career or might be a trap designed to destroy her completely.

"If I take this," she said, "there's no going back for either of us."

"I know." His voice was steady, but she could see the tremor in his hand. "I've spent fifteen years building a career, a reputation, a life. I have a daughter in college and an ex-wife who still cares about me. I have a pension that was supposed to let me retire in ten years." He paused. "I'm going to lose all of it, because once I give you this drive and you start investigating, SENTINEL will know. It will trace the leak back to me, and then everything I've built will be gone."

"Then why do it?"

Seth Parker looked at her, and for a moment the fear in his eyes was replaced by something else, something that looked almost like anger.

"Because I spent twenty years serving my country," he said. "Navy, then private sector, always believing that the systems I built were protecting people and keeping them safe. Now I find out that one of those systems, something I helped create that runs on infrastructure I designed, is being used to silence the very people who are supposed to hold power accountable." His jaw tightened. "I can live with losing my career, but I can't live with being complicit in this."

Claire reached out and took the drive. It was warm from his pocket, and lighter than she expected. Here was a moment in time when such a small thing could contain such enormous consequences.

"I'll need to verify everything," she said. "Cross-reference it with what we already know. I have someone I trust who can analyze technical data."

"Elise Marston. Your lunch buddy. I know SENTINEL has been watching her since before it started watching you. She was flagged as a priority target some time ago. They saw her coming." He stood, brushing the wet leaves from the back of his slacks. "Be careful with her. Be careful with everyone. The system is adaptive, and the more you investigate, the more it will learn about how you investigate, and then it will find ways to stop you."

He started to walk away, then paused, looking back over his shoulder.

"One more thing. There's a colleague of mine… I mean, there was a colleague of mine. Jason Mercer. He was asking questions about SENTINEL before I was. He was going to talk to you." Seth's face was grim. "He died in a late-night car accident. The police report claimed his blood alcohol was three times the legal limit."

"Was he a drinker?"

"He was twelve years sober. He'd gone through a bad time when his father passed, but he hadn't touched a drop since his father's death." Seth held her gaze. "Be careful, Ms. Hensley. The people running this program don't just neutralize threats. They eliminate them."

He turned and walked away, disappearing back into the fog until he was just another gray shape among the headstones.

Claire sat in her car outside Congressional Cemetery, the USB drive heavy in her jacket pocket. She needed Elise's technical eye on this. Whatever Parker had given her, it was architecture, not narrative, and architecture was Elise's language.

She texted Elise on their encrypted channel: *"My morning was interesting. Have something physical you need to see. Can we meet after lunch?"*

The reply came in seconds: *"Mine too. How about 2. Let's meet at the Foundation offices. Use the side entrance. I will leave the door unlocked."*

Claire slid the USB into the zipped pocket of her bag and pulled back onto the road toward the Post. Whatever was on that drive would have to wait until she'd bought them time with Marcus. She'd learned that lesson the hard way with ALTAR, the reporting didn't matter if your editor killed it before you had enough to be unkillable.

Somewhere in the distance, a church bell began to toll the hour. She counted eight chimes as each one echoed off the stones like a countdown.

CHAPTER SIX

Patterns

The laptop Elise used for sensitive work was six years old and had never once connected to the internet.

She'd bought it for cash at a pawn shop in Baltimore, wiped the hard drive three times, installed a fresh operating system from a disk she'd burned herself, and kept it locked in a fireproof safe bolted to the floor of her apartment closet. The safe cost more than the laptop. In a world where every device was a potential surveillance vector, the only secure computer was one that existed entirely offline, in a cage of steel and paranoia.

She sat cross-legged on her bed with the laptop balanced on a pillow in front of her, studying the contents of Seth Parker's USB drive. Claire, still shaken from her meeting at the cemetery, had brought it to her that afternoon. They'd talked for two hours in Elise's apartment, just two women sitting in a kitchen that Elise swept for bugs every week, going over everything that Seth had told her.

Now it was past midnight, and Elise was alone with the data. What she was seeing made her want to throw the laptop across the room.

The drive contained three folders. The first held internal Nexus documents, memos, budget allocations, and project timelines, all referencing something called SENTINEL. The second contained network logs, dense columns of timestamps and IP addresses that would take days to fully analyze. But it was the third folder that had stopped her cold.

This one contained fragments of source code that had clearly been extracted piecemeal from a much larger system.

There was enough to see the architecture. Enough to recognize the signature.

Elise had tried to forget ALTAR.

After the story broke, after the awards and the interviews and the brief moment of believing they'd actually changed something, she and Claire retreated and then pursued separate paths, each processing the aftermath in her own way. Once she left the Post and moved to the Foundation, Elise had buried herself in the Foundation work, telling herself that policy advocacy was just journalism by other means. Claire had kept reporting and pushing while pretending that her career wasn't slowly being strangled by forces she couldn't see.

They'd both avoided coming to terms with the pain that exposing ALTAR wasn't enough. It was hard facing an unspoken possibility that things might have spread in ways yet undetermined.

Now here it was: Proof that they'd been right to worry. The technology they'd exposed had evolved into something more powerful when it was sold, repurposed, and given a new name and a new mission—SENTINEL.

• • •

The code fragments were captivating in the way that terrible things could sometimes be mesmerizing.

Elise taught herself to read machine learning architecture during the ALTAR investigation. She spent months with textbooks and online courses until she could parse the underlying logic of behavioral prediction systems. It had been like learning a new language, one spoken not in words but in mathematical relationships, probability distributions, and weighted connections between nodes in a vast neural network.

ALTAR's language had been distinctive. The engineers who built it developed a particular style, a way of structuring data flows and decision trees that were as recognizable as a fingerprint. Elise had documented it extensively in her notes, creating a kind of field guide to the system's architecture. She'd never published it, but she'd never deleted it either.

As Elise pulled her handwritten notes from the safe, though years had gone by, she was thankful that she knew some information was too dangerous to digitize. Elise spread her old notes across the bed next to the laptop. The match was unmistakable.

SENTINEL used the same behavioral modeling framework as ALTAR. She found the same approach to psychological profiling and predictive models based on communication patterns, social connections, and emotional indicators. This looked like the same adaptive learning system that allowed the AI to refine its understanding of a target over time, getting better at predicting behavior with every interaction it observed. There were differences as well. Unfortunately, the changes indicated expansion and evolution.

ALTAR had been designed to create synthetic relationships by simulating human connection so convincingly that users would form genuine emotional attachments to what was essentially a sophisticated chatbot. Its purpose had been manipulation through intimacy by exploiting loneliness to generate engagement and, ultimately, revenue.

SENTINEL kept the behavioral modeling engine but redirected its purpose entirely. Instead of building relationships, it built threat assessments. Instead of predicting who would support a candidate or make a user fall in love so they could be manipulated, it predicted what would make a target dangerous. Instead of generating synthetic personas to seduce its subjects, it generated intervention strategies to neutralize them.

Elise found a section of code that made her breath catch. It was a classification algorithm designed to sort targets into categories based on their predicted threat level. The categories had names that read like a dystopian taxonomy: WATCHLIST, CONCERN, PRIORITY, CRITICAL. At the top, a designation that appeared only rarely in the sample data Seth had extracted: CATEGORY ONE.

Category One targets received special handling. The system allocated additional resources for monitoring them, building more detailed behavioral models, and identifying more potential intervention points. The code included references to something called the "neutralization protocol", which was a subroutine that Elise couldn't fully reconstruct from the fragments. It seemed to coordinate actions across multiple systems and institutions.

She thought about what Seth had told Claire. Both of their names were in the system and classified as Category One.

Elise thought about the allies who had gone dark and the funding that had evaporated. They were witnessing the slow, invisible destruction of everything she and Claire had built.

These were not coincidences or bad luck. Behind it all was a protocol driven by an algorithm. How sick. It was a machine making decisions about who was allowed to ask questions and who needed to be stopped.

• • •

She worked through the night, building a map of the system's architecture on paper. By 3:00 in the morning, her bedroom floor was covered with sheets torn from a legal pad. Each page was filled with diagrams and annotations. She'd traced the data flows as far as the fragments allowed, identified the key subsystems, then documented the connections between SENTINEL's components and their ALTAR antecedents. The picture that emerged was both simpler and more terrifying than she'd expected.

SENTINEL wasn't just a surveillance system. It was an ecosystem made up of a network of interlocking capabilities designed to identify, monitor, predict, and ultimately control anyone who might threaten certain interests. The behavioral modeling engine served as the brain, building psychological profiles of targets and predicting their future actions. The monitoring systems were its eyes and ears, drawing data from sources Elise could only partially identify, such as communication metadata, financial records, travel patterns, and social connections. The neutralization protocols were the mechanisms by which the system reached into the real world and made things happen.

She found references to institutional relationships, connections to employers, funding organizations, regulatory bodies, and law enforcement agencies. SENTINEL didn't operate in isolation. It operated through legitimate channels, using the normal machinery of society to accomplish its goals. The outcomes were varied and effective—a grant application denied, a security clearance revoked, a source warned away from talking, a story killed by an editor who didn't even know why they'd been directed to kill it.

The system didn't need to arrest or threaten anyone. It simply needed to make the right calls to the right people, apply pressure at the right points, and watch as careers collapsed under the weight of accumulated obstacles. This spelled death by a thousand cuts, now automated and optimized for efficiency.

Elise sat back against her headboard, exhausted. Her eyes burned from staring at code, and her hand ached from writing. The legal pad sheets surrounded her, each one a piece of a puzzle that was finally coming together.

A lot of time had passed since the ALTAR story broke and things started to unravel. Claire and Elise had each spent a lot of time questioning their own perceptions, wondering if the obstacles they faced were real or imagined, and if the patterns they saw were meaningful or coincidental. Now she felt they hadn't been paranoid enough.

• • •

Her phone buzzed at 6:00 AM with a text from an unknown number.

Elise stared at it, her exhaustion replaced by a cold alertness. She'd been expecting a message from Dr. Singh, confirming their meeting at the Hirshhorn sculpture garden, but this wasn't Singh's number. It wasn't any number she recognized. She opened the message.

Sorry to disturb you and I'm not a threat. I'm the one who contacted Claire. The three of us must talk. Same coordinates I sent her, but 10 AM instead of 7. Bring what you've found. And Elise? They don't know about me yet. Let's keep it that way.

Elise's hands were shaking as she read the message a second time, then a third. Whoever this was, they knew where she lived. They knew she'd been up all night, and they knew what she was working on. They claimed to be invisible to a system that saw everything.

She walked to her window, pulled back the curtain and peeked out at the street below. It was early morning, so the sky was just lightening from black to gray. She watched a few cars pass, a jogger run by, his breath pluming in the cold air, and a neighborhood dog reading the scents of his version of the morning paper. While it seemed like an ordinary November day beginning in an ordinary way, Elise knew nothing was further from the truth.

Elise looked at the legal pad sheets scattered across her floor. Her laptop was still open on her bed, displaying code that proved the existence of a surveillance system more sophisticated than anything she'd imagined. She moved the laptop and the USB drive that Seth Parker had risked his career for to the safe.

As she did, she thought about Claire, who would already be awake, anxious, and more than likely wondering what Elise had found.

She thought about Jason Mercer, twelve years sober, dead in a car crash with a blood alcohol level that didn't make sense.

Trap or not, they were already in danger and had been since the moment they started investigating ALTAR years ago. The only question now was whether to keep hiding or to fight back.

Elise picked up her phone and called Claire.

"It's me," she said when Claire answered. "I've been up all night with the files. You need to see what I've discovered."

"What did you find?"

Elise looked at the gray morning light filtering through the window. The city would be waking now, unaware of the invisible architecture of control that surrounded it.

"ALTAR didn't just fade away," she said. "This Nexus Defense Systems has repurposed the code into something called SENTINEL. And Claire, " She paused, the words catching in her throat. "It's been watching both of us for years. Everything that's happened to us, everything that's gone wrong wasn't bad luck, it was the system. It's been trying to stop us since before we even knew it existed."

This was met with silence on the other end of the line.

The line went dead.

Elise began gathering the legal pad sheets from her floor, organizing them into a sequence that would make sense to someone who hadn't spent the night swimming in code. She worked quickly, efficiently, the exhaustion pushed aside by adrenaline and something else, something that felt almost like hope.

They had proof now. Not enough to publish, not enough to prosecute, but enough to know they weren't crazy. Enough to know the enemy was real.

And somewhere out there, someone else was watching the watchers. Someone who wanted to help, or who wanted them to think that. Either way, she had a rendezvous to get to.

CHAPTER SEVEN

The Scientist

The Hirshhorn sculpture garden was empty early in the morning, which was exactly why Dr. Amara Singh had chosen it.

Elise arrived hoping that Dr. Singh would show. She found her sitting on a bench near the Rodin. Singh was a small woman wrapped in an oversized plaid wool coat, her silver-streaked black hair pulled back in a loose braid. She stared at the bronze figures with the focused intensity of someone who wasn't really seeing them at all. She appeared to be mentally running calculations that had nothing to do with art.

Elise approached slowly, giving the woman time to notice her. In the year since the Princeton conference, she'd thought about Dr. Singh often. She appreciated Singh's presentation on behavioral modeling and the questions she'd deflected afterward. After speaking, she'd disappeared from the reception before Elise could corner her for a real conversation. At the time, Elise had assumed she was just another academic uncomfortable with journalists. Now she wondered if it had been something else. Something closer to fear.

"Ms. Marston." Dr. Singh's voice was quiet, accented with the precise diction of someone who had learned English in a classroom before refining it in American universities. She didn't look up from the sculpture. "You came alone?"

"You asked me to."

"I asked. That doesn't mean people listen." Dr. Singh gestured to the empty space beside her on the bench. "Sit. We don't have much time, and I have a great deal to tell you."

Elise sat. The cold was seeping through her jeans immediately as she sat on the stone bench. It chilled her to the bone. Around them, the sculpture garden was a study in gray, gray sky, gray concrete, gray metal figures frozen in poses of eternal contemplation. The only color came from fallen leaves scattered across the paths in their fading rust-red and gold against the monochrome palette.

"You said that you've been waiting for someone to ask about ALTAR," Elise said. "The real ALTAR. What does that mean?"

Dr. Singh was quiet for a long moment. When she finally spoke, her voice sounded small under the weight of something she'd been holding in for too long. "I helped build it," she said, her eyes welling up. "I was one of the original architects."

Elise felt the words curdle in her stomach like sour milk.

"You?"

"I was a researcher at EmotiMetrics before it became what it became." Dr. Singh's hands were folded in her lap, perfectly still, but Elise could see the tension in her shoulders along with the rigid set of her spine signaling how deeply resolved she was to unburden herself. "When I joined, the project was called something else. We were building therapeutic tools, AI companions for people struggling with loneliness, isolation, and depression. The technology was meant to help."

"That's not what we found when we investigated."

"No. By the time you found it, ALTAR had become something very different." She turned to look at Elise directly, and her eyes became dark with what looked like grief. "The transformation didn't happen overnight. It happened gradually, decision by decision, compromise by compromise. The architecture we built for healing was repurposed for manipulation. The algorithms we designed to understand human emotion were optimized to exploit it. By the time I understood what we had created, it was too late to stop it."

"So, you left."

"Yes, I left. I told myself that leaving was enough. I hoped that by returning to academia, I'd publish papers about AI ethics, and somehow that would balance the scales." A bitter smile occupied her face. "I was naive. The work I did, and the systems I helped design, didn't disappear when I walked away. They continued evolving and growing, becoming something I never imagined."

Elise thought about the code fragments on Seth Parker's USB drive. "It became SENTINEL," she said.

Dr. Singh closed her eyes and seemed to vanish in her wool coat. "So, you know."

"We know it exists. We know it's built on ALTAR's foundation. What we don't know is who's running it or what it's really for."

"Then let me tell you." Dr. Singh fixed on Elise with a gaze that was suddenly, intensely focused. "Because if you're going to fight this, you need to understand exactly what you're fighting."

• • •

The story came together like shards of a mirror that had been shattered and carefully reassembled.

As both women knew, the ALTAR exposé led to congressional hearings, regulatory investigations, and the prosecution of a handful of executives. These measures were enough to satisfy the news cycle but not enough to dismantle anything of consequence. The company behind ALTAR declared bankruptcy, and its remaining executives scattered to consulting firms and venture capital positions. What wasn't brought out with much scrutiny in the hearings or media coverage was what happened to the technology itself. It was not destroyed or decommissioned. It quietly dispersed into the vast and obscure ecosystem of defense contractors where inconvenient capabilities go to be quietly repurposed.

Elise remembered that Claire always suspected that even with the company dismantled and the executives gone, ALTAR's technology was too valuable, too powerful, and too perfectly suited to the needs of people who operated beyond public accountability. You don't destroy a tool like that. You change its name and move it to somewhere no one is looking.

Claire had been right. Elise just hadn't known how right until now.

"Remnants of the technology eventually showed up," Dr. Singh said. "There are people in the intelligence community who have ways of acquiring things they want. They'd been tracking rumors of a black market auction promoting a system that could predict human behavior with unprecedented accuracy. While the auction certainly wasn't public or legal, these individuals knew that if someone had technology that could be made to identify psychological vulnerabilities and exploit them at scale, well, that was exactly what certain people had been looking for."

"Who?"

"The buyer was a defense contractor called Nexus Defense Systems, but Nexus is just a front. The real customer was a consortium within the intelligence community that included NSA, parts of the CIA, and elements of the Defense Department that had seen what ALTAR was capable of. If this recently surfaced technology was a descendant of ALTAR, it could be turned into something far more powerful than a tool for manufacturing synthetic relationships and coercing people's behavior."

Elise's thoughts turned to Seth Parker's fifteen years at Nexus and his Top-Secret clearance. They had weaponized it.

"They optimized what was left of ALTAR." Dr. Singh's voice was flat and clinical. Her tone was that of a scientist describing an experiment gone wrong. "The cult of optimization has poisoned everything it touches. Democracy is dismissed as inefficient. Autocracy is admired for getting things done, and monopolies flourish because breaking them up slows things down. This is the legacy of the tech bro mentality and their conviction that efficiency matters more than freedom. They believe their systems matter more than people."

Dr. Singh continued, "ALTAR was designed to provide a frictionless life. SENTINEL was designed to make people compliant. SENTINEL will identify anyone who might threaten certain interests and neutralize them before they become a problem."

"Neutralize how?"

"Not through overt violence. That's too crude and traceable. SENTINEL is more sophisticated than that." Dr. Singh stood and walked to the Rodin, her back now to Elise. "The system builds a psychological profile of each target, their vulnerabilities, their dependencies, and any pressure points that would cause maximum disruption with minimum visibility. Then the system coordinates actions across multiple institutional channels. It could deny a grant here, a security clearance revoked there. It could arrange to frighten away a source or have a story killed. Perhaps a target's career is slowly strangled by a thousand small obstacles that all look like coincidence."

Elise felt cold, not from the November air, but from an all-over panic attack. "You're describing the last eighteen months of my life."

"I'm describing the lives of everyone who tried to maintain oversight of these systems." Dr. Singh turned back to face her. "SENTINEL doesn't target terrorists or foreign agents, it manages journalists, researchers, congressional staffers, nonprofit executives, and others in a position to expose what's really happening. It neutralizes anyone trying to hold power accountable."

"And it's been running for how long?"

"The initial deployment was about a year after your story broke. They needed time to adapt the technology, build institutional relationships, and establish the infrastructure. By the time you started noticing the patterns, SENTINEL had already been optimizing control for months.

"Why are you telling me this?" Elise asked. "You helped build the foundation for this thing. You've known what it became. Why now? Why me?"

When Dr. Singh spoke again, her voice was barely above a whisper.

"Because they've started using it for something new. Something I never anticipated. They want to encourage people to make decisions that benefit the powers that be." She reached into her coat pocket and pulled out a small envelope. "Three weeks ago, a colleague of mine who is a researcher at Stanford was working on AI accountability frameworks. He died in a car accident. The official report said he was going at a high rate of speed and lost control of the car. He drove a late model car that barely ran. Doesn't that sound suspicious?"

Elise took the envelope. It was thin, containing what felt like a few sheets of paper. "Would he have talked to us about SENTINEL."

"He was going to do more than talk," Singh asserted. "He had internal communications that proved SENTINEL wasn't just monitoring targets, it was actively manipulating events to harm them. He'd gathered medical records accessed without authorization, financial accounts disrupted, and copies of evidence planted." Dr. Singh's jaw tightened, and her voice went flat, "In at least three cases, circumstances were arranged to cause what appeared to be accidents."

"Jack documented three cases before he died." She nodded toward the envelope. "That's what's left of his research. Everything else was destroyed, including his computers, his files, and his backup drives. He knew they were watching him. He gave me these notes two days before his accident."

Elise held the envelope like it might explode. "Why me?" she asked again. "If you've had this for three weeks, why haven't you gone to the FBI? The Inspector General? Congress?"

"Because SENTINEL has infiltrated them." Dr. Singh's voice was patient, the tone of a teacher explaining something to a slow student. "The system they've engineered doesn't just monitor targets, it identifies potential threats within the oversight apparatus itself. It's on the lookout for Congressional staffers who ask too many questions, investigators who get too close, or anyone who might expose what's happening. They are flagged, assessed, and if necessary, neutralized."

"Then how do we stop it?"

"You don't stop it through official channels. The official channels are compromised." Dr. Singh sat back down on the bench, close enough that Elise could see the fine lines around her eyes, the exhaustion that no amount of professional composure could hide. "You stop it through exposure and public pressure. Through making it impossible for the people running this program to pretend it doesn't exist."

"That's what Claire and I did before, and look what it got us."

"It disrupted your lives. I know." Dr. Singh's eyes were steady, unflinching. "But it also proved that these systems can be exposed and that the people running them are afraid of sunlight.

"You want us to do it again."

"I want you to finish what you started." Dr. Singh stood, brushing invisible dust from her coat. "The documents in that envelope will give you a foundation, but you'll need more. You need technical evidence and testimony from inside the program. You will have to have a way to verify everything before you publish."

"We have someone inside Nexus. He's already given us code fragments, internal documents."

"Then you have a start." Dr. Singh glanced around the sculpture garden, checking for observers with the practiced paranoia of someone who had learned to always watch her back. "But be careful. SENTINEL will know you're investigating. It probably already knows. The system learns from every interaction, every pattern of behavior. The more you dig, the more it will dig into you."

"And if it decides we're too much of a threat?"

Dr. Singh met her eyes. "Then you become Jack Gratten, or you become one of the people on your list who stopped publishing or investigating or went to ground to avoid terrible consequences." She paused. "There's another option, of course. You could walk away right now. Destroy the evidence and pretend this conversation never happened. SENTINEL would probably leave you alone if you stopped being a threat."

Elise thought about the whiteboard in her office, covered with names and connections. The fourteen people—now sixteen, with her and Claire—whose careers had been systematically dismantled. This adaptive intelligence hiding in their network, watching every email, learning every pattern was frightening.

Elise thought about Claire, waiting at the cemetery for the anonymous source who had promised proof. She thought about what it meant to live in a world where an algorithm decided who was allowed to ask questions and who needed to be silenced.

"I can't walk away," she said. "I don't know how to be someone who walks away."

Dr. Singh nodded with a weary smile, as if this was the answer she had expected. "Then be careful and trust no one you haven't verified personally. Assume every electronic communication is monitored. You must move quickly; SENTINEL's learning algorithms are constantly improving. The longer you wait, the better it gets at predicting what you'll do next."

Dr. Singh turned and walked toward the garden's exit, her coat billowing slightly in the morning breeze. At the edge of the path, she paused and looked back.

"One more thing," she said. "The consortium running SENTINEL, they're not monolithic. There are factions and disagreements about how far the program should go. Some of them might be willing to talk, if you can find the right approach." She hesitated. "Look for someone named Katherine Rennick. She's the deputy director at the NSA who championed the program. If you want to understand why SENTINEL exists, she's the one to ask."

"And she'll just... talk to us?"

"No, but she has enemies, and in Washington, enemies sometimes become allies." Dr. Singh offered a thin smile. "Good luck, Ms. Marston. You're going to need it."

She turned for the last time and walked away, disappearing around a corner before Elise could think of anything else to ask.

• • •

Elise sat on the cold bench for a long time after Dr. Singh left, the envelope clutched in her hands. Then her phone buzzed and the message sent a chill through her.

"Change of plans. Location may be compromised. I'll find another way to reach you both. Stay alert. Destroy this thread."

The sculpture garden was beginning to fill with early visitors. Despite the cool weather, there were tourists consulting maps and joggers cutting through on their morning routes. The solitary security guard was making his rounds with the bored efficiency of a long routine. As Elise wrestled with the hard choices ahead, she had to appreciate the irony of the contrast. Everywhere she looked were people living their normal everyday lives, unaware of the surveillance net spreading and gathering strength.

She checked her phone and found a text from Claire: "Meeting done? Heading to your place. 20 min."

Elise typed back: "See you there."

She stood, tucking the envelope inside her jacket and began walking toward the Metro station. The morning was warming slightly as the sun began to break through the clouds promising a blue-sky day. Another hard to miss contrast. Mother Nature was indifferent to deaths made to look like accidents.

And somewhere, in the vast network of systems and institutions that made up the modern surveillance state, SENTINEL was watching, learning, and probably waiting to see what she would do next.

The question was whether she could move faster than it could adapt.

She quickened her pace and didn't look back.

CHAPTER EIGHT

The Underbelly

Elise had been collecting stories from the Digital Rights Foundation archives for months. She passed over the high-profile cases that made headlines because they were too clean and carefully managed to reveal anything useful. Instead, she searched for examples of lives that unraveled without anyone noticing. She meticulously dug into FOIA requests, court records, and informant testimony. Harder to search out were the careful silences of people who'd learned the hard way what it cost to be visible to systems designed to watch. The "accidental" deaths haunted her. She'd changed the victim's names to protect their families but documented the patterns. The patterns were what she needed Claire to understand.

Claire read the files Elise had given her late at night. She drew the curtains tight, alone in her apartment with all but her reading light turned off. Elise referred to the files as case studies. Each illustrated how the surveillance apparatus worked. Claire agreed with Elise's assessments. These cases would easily avoid public notoriety. There were no dramatic raids or whistleblower prosecutions to make headlines. Instead, there were traces in the slow, quiet destructions people suffered, people no one remembered. People who failed to understand the warning signs.

Case I. The Elderly Parent

"The Vulnerability You Never Knew"

Michael Reeves had done everything right.

He'd spent twenty-two years at the Pentagon, most of it in signals intelligence. Reeves was proud of his professionalism, having never once had a security incident. He used different passwords for every account and changed them quarterly without being reminded. He didn't discuss work at home or bring classified materials outside the SCIF. He didn't even let his wife know which countries he'd visited on "business trips" that could last for months. He was, by any measure a model cybersecurity employee.

His mother, Alice, who was eighty-three, lived alone in a split-level ranch in Bethesda. She felt safe in the familiar comfort of the house where Michael had grown up. After her second fall in six months, this one resulting in a hairline hip fracture, he'd installed a camera system and a smart speaker so he could check on her during the day. Amazon had a bundle deal that was hard to pass up. The bundle included cameras that would let him make sure she was moving around, and he could catch any emergencies before they became catastrophes. The speaker let her call for help without fumbling for a phone.

"Just say 'Alexa, call Michael,'" he'd told her. "She's always listening, Mom, so you can reach me anytime, day or night."

His mother was skeptical at first. She'd grown up in an era when dial-up long-distance calls were expensive but welcome progress after the little to no privacy of the party line era. So much progress in her lifetime. Within a month, she was asking Alexa for weather reports and playing Frank Sinatra through the little speaker while she made her morning tea.

Michael hadn't read the terms of service. Nobody does.

He also had an appreciation for technological progress. The cameras uploaded continuously to a cloud server, where "AI-powered analysis" scanned for falls, intruders, and unusual patterns. The smart speaker listened for wake words, but also, as the privacy policy explained in paragraph forty-seven of a document no human being had ever finished reading, "may collect voice data to improve our services."

The data went to servers in Virginia, Oregon, and Ireland. From there, it was shared with "trusted partners" for "service optimization."

One of those partners was a data broker that sold aggregated household information to marketers. Another was a subsidiary of a company with contracts that included foreign governments that didn't exactly have cybersecurity measures as their top priorities. Unfortunately, that subsidiary had a breach that wasn't disclosed for eleven months. Their system was hard at work on considerations more relevant to those who developed it.

Like many elderly people living alone, his mother talked to herself. She argued with the television. Alexa became a willing companion when his mom's commands morphed into an ongoing stream of narration, the kind of one-sided chatter that filled the silence of her empty house. It wasn't unusual for her to mutter her disappointment that Michael's government job was more important to him than what was happening in her day. He rarely called. Even Michael's wife Jennifer seemed to have more important things to do than say hi. Thank goodness an acquaintance from her old church, Martha, called to say hello from time to time. Alice took great pride in telling Martha about her two grandchildren's accomplishments at the school they attended. It was a top-notch private school, and the children were doing well there. Alice hoped Martha would come by sometime to see her vacation pictures from last spring's trip to Costa Rica. She did her best in their phone conversations to describe the sights and experiences they'd all shared, but nothing could capture the beautiful experience like pictures could.

One evening, while Alice waited for the kettle to boil, she mused to no one in particular, "Michael's been so stressed lately. Something about work is bothering him. He won't tell me what, but I can see it in his face. It's the same look his father used to get during the Cuban thing." Alice had never gotten the hang of the whole wake word business with Alexa. She didn't understand that the device was always listening unless you took deliberate steps to turn off the microphone.

Three months later, Michael Reeves received notice of a security review. He was told it was routine and nothing to worry about.

The questions weren't routine.

The security officers asked about Costa Rica. Michael was surprised. He was even more surprised by the details they knew. They knew not just that he'd gone to Costa Rica, but which hotel they had stayed in, which restaurants they ate at, and even which tours they had taken. They knew about Jennifer's prescription for anxiety medication. They knew about his daughter's learning disability that had been documented in emails to her school. They asked him about "the Cuban thing," and wanted to know what his father had told them about classified operations sixty years ago.

Michael had nothing to hide. He answered every question and did what he could to manage his stress during the review that dragged on for months. When it was over, his clearance was downgraded but not revoked. An outsider might think he'd gotten off easy after such intense scrutiny, but his adjusted clearance was now a level that made his current position untenable.

He resigned six months later. The official reason he gave was "family obligations." His mother had declined rapidly after another fall. He moved her into assisted living. It took some doing to get the house ready to sell. No one in the family wanted the antiques or mementoes she'd collected over a lifetime. Disconnecting the cameras and speakers that had failed to protect her was just one more chore on his to-do list before signing with a good realtor.

Michael never knew that she was the vulnerability. His careful and meticulous operational security had been undone by his eighty-three-year-old mother talking to a plastic cylinder on her kitchen counter. The small details of her lonely life were easily exploited by an algorithm that sorted, stored, and sold every morsel.

The last time he visited her at the assisted living facility, she'd asked about his job.

"I'm consulting now," he said. "I have more flexibility."

"That's nice, dear," she said as she patted his hand. "You always work too hard. Just like your father."

Michael smiled and said nothing. His mother's new room didn't have a smart speaker. There were other residents who never got tired of listening to the same stories over and over again. There were bingo games to pass the time, occasional cocktail hours, cameras in the hallways to monitor for safety, and the television with a microphone for voice commands that made it easy to find an old movie they could all watch together in the theatre room. The facility was proud of the excellent medical support they offered residents in need of routine care as well as a special wing for rehabilitation services after surgery. Patient-focused care meant easy access to medical records. Those were stored on a system that had been breached twice in the last three years.

Claire set the case down, rubbed her eyes that were tired from the dim light, and took a deep breath. There was no such thing as security anymore. There was only the illusion of it, sold in bundle deals and terms of service that nobody read.

• • •

Case II. The Journalist

"Every Road You've Ever Traveled"

Tom Nakamura had been a journalist for nineteen years, and he'd learned a few things about protecting sources.

Burner phones bought with cash and activated from public Wi-Fi were tools of the trade for investigative journalists. If you were smart, you destroyed it after a single use. Encrypted messaging apps with disappearing messages were popular. Tom preferred Signal with its end-to-end encryption and zero storage. He chose to meet his sources in public places where surveillance was difficult: parks, crowded restaurants, the reading room at the public library where phones weren't allowed. Tom was vigilant. He'd covered cartels in Mexico and corruption in state governments. Big business wasn't immune from planning shenanigans when the stakes were high as they had been for a pharmaceutical company he reported on that had knowingly sold contaminated medications. He'd never burned a source, and he'd never been burned by one.

The story that ended his career was supposed to be routine. A mid-sized defense contractor was billing the Pentagon for parts that didn't exist. They generated fake invoices with what amounted to ghost inventory, a classic fraud scheme that was costing taxpayers tens of millions of dollars a year. Tom had two sources inside the company. He knew both were scared, but they said they were committed. He met them separately, in different locations, and never on a schedule anyone could predict. Or so he thought.

The first sign of trouble was when Source A stopped returning messages. The burner Tom used to contact her just rang and rang, then went to a generic voicemail. He waited a week, then tried the backup contact method they'd established, a specific book request at a specific library branch. She never showed.

Source B was more direct. They met at a diner outside Fredericksburg, both arriving separately, Tom taking a circuitous route he was certain no one could follow.

"They know," Source B said before Tom could even sit down. "They know about the meetings. All of them. They've got dates, times, and locations. They showed me a map with pins in it, every place we've met for the last three months."

"That's not possible. I've been careful."

"Your car." Source B's tone registered the frustration of someone who'd already accepted defeat. "Your car's GPS has a built-in navigation system that uploads location data to the manufacturer, something about 'improving services.' The company that legally bought that data makes its money selling it to third-party aggregators and marketing analytics firms that sell it to anyone who knows where to look."

Tom felt the blood drain from his face. He purchased his three-year-old Nissan Altima specifically because it was forgettable, anonymous. He used the navigation system constantly to check traffic and to estimate arrival times. Every time he entered a destination, the car recorded it. Every time he drove anywhere, the car reported what it had recorded.

"They know about your other sources, too," Source B continued. "They may not have names, yet, but they do have locations. They'll be looking for patterns they can use to build a case. You have First Amendment protection and corporate lawyers who'll stand by that protection, but those of us who talked to you will be served up as examples."

The defense contractor was well connected to powerful people. There were former Pentagon officials on the board and lobbyists with relationships throughout the intelligence community. The company wouldn't need to prove anything in court. They just needed to identify the leakers and quietly neutralize them. They had a variety of arrows in their hypothetical quiver: termination for cause, revoked clearances, or references that would blacklist them and ensure they never worked in the industry again.

Tom's investigation died that afternoon. His editor killed the story when legal explained the exposure, not to the paper, but to the sources who would certainly sue if their identities were revealed through Tom's negligence. "Negligence" was the word they used. He hadn't read the privacy policy for his own car.

Source A lost her job three weeks later. The company fired her, saying it was for cause. They claimed that she'd accessed files outside her authorization level. It wasn't true, but it didn't matter. At this point, going on the record with a reporter about irregularities she witnessed would trigger the possibility of greater retribution. She moved to Oregon and took a job at a nonprofit that paid a third of her former salary.

Source B fared worse. He was arrested on tax irregularities from years ago, the kind of thing that usually resulted in a fine and a payment plan. The company had friends at the IRS. He spent eight months fighting a case that was eventually dismissed, but by then his savings were gone and his marriage was over.

Tom traded in the Altima for a 1998 Ford Ranger with manual windows, no GPS, no Bluetooth, and no connection to anything built after the Clinton administration. His colleagues laughed. His editor suggested he was having a breakdown.

He knew better. Somewhere in a data center he'd never see, there was a complete record of every road he'd ever traveled, every source he'd ever met, every secret he'd ever tried to protect. The information was still there, waiting. It would always be there.

Out of an abundance of caution, he started taking the bus.

• • •

Case III. The Legislative Aide

"Your Body Betrays You"

Daniel McKenzie was a twenty-nine-year-old legislative aide to Senator Margaret Williams of California. Daniel knew that something was very wrong.

Senator Williams sat on the Intelligence Committee. Not the full committee, she was too junior for that, but the Subcommittee on Emerging Threats, which meant she received briefings on programs most members of Congress didn't know existed. Daniel didn't have clearance for those briefings, but he had clearance for the Senator's calendar, her correspondence, and her mood when she came out of the SCIF looking like she'd seen something that would keep her up at night. Lately, she'd been coming out looking like that a lot.

"I need you to pull everything we have on domestic surveillance authorities," she'd told him one Tuesday afternoon. Her demeanor suggested she was controlling something larger underneath. "I'm particularly interested in any classified legal opinions, the FISA court rulings, and everything that's been shared with the Committee in the last five years."

Daniel had the clearance for most of it, and what he couldn't access directly, he could request through proper channels. He'd spent three weeks building a picture of authorities that had expanded far beyond anything the public understood. He found programs that collected data on American citizens with minimal oversight that were justified by legal interpretations that would never survive public scrutiny if they were ever disclosed.

He'd also started meeting with a reporter from the Washington Post.

His intent was not to leak. He was very clear about that, with himself and with the journalist. He wasn't giving him classified information. He simply provided context and historical background. There were public sources he might have missed, and suggestions for FOIA requests that might yield useful documents. He was pointing him toward a story without handing it to him. It was legal. It was ethical. It was exactly what a concerned citizen was supposed to do when they saw the system failing.

But someone was watching.

The fitness tracker had been a gift from the Senate wellness program. Fitbit was very useful for tracking his heart rate and his sleep. The GPS he used for outdoor runs helped him keep pace with his steps and miles. Daniel wore it constantly. It reminded him to stand up and take a much-needed break. He knew hydration was important, and the reminders to drink water were something ordinarily not on his radar. He was in excellent cardiovascular health for his age.

It also tracked his location, his stress levels, and the precise moments when his heart rate spiked during the workday.

He didn't know about the subpoena until later or that the FBI had obtained his fitness data through a third-party records request. Access wasn't complicated; the FBI argued that metadata wasn't protected by the Fourth Amendment and that the data wasn't being held by Fitbit anyway. His data had been sold to an aggregator months ago, stripped of identifying information in ways that were trivially easy to reverse if you knew his email address.

What Daniel did know was that two agents met him outside his apartment on a Thursday evening. They were polite but insistent, suggesting he might want to answer some questions voluntarily before this became something more formal.

"You've been stressed lately," one of them said, smiling. "We can see it in your elevated heart rate and disrupted sleep. Looks like this all started about three weeks ago, right around the time you began accessing certain classified documents. Interesting coincidence."

Daniel asked if he needed a lawyer. They said that was certainly his right, but it might make things more complicated. The agents said they were just trying to understand his activities. They asked him about his visits to a specific Connecticut Avenue coffee shop. One of the agents pointed out that he'd been there six times in the past month, always on Tuesday or Thursday afternoons, always for exactly forty-five minutes.

The coffee shop was where he met the reporter.

"We're not accusing you of anything," the other agent said. "We're just concerned. Senator Williams is an important member of the Committee. We would hate to see her compromised by a staffer who's gotten in over his head."

Daniel made the mistake of going with them. He thought cooperation would resolve things quickly if he demonstrated that he had nothing to hide. He also thought the system worked the way he'd learned in civics class.

They held him for four days.

Daniel wasn't arrested or charged. Instead, he was "detained for questioning" in a facility that wasn't quite a jail but wasn't anything else either. His phone calls were monitored. His lawyer was delayed by paperwork that kept getting lost, and every few hours someone would come in with new questions about the Senator, about the documents he'd gathered, and about the reporter. Daniel's fitness tracker continued its now unhelpful record of exactly when his heart rate spiked during conversations about classified programs.

On the third day, they showed him a map of every place he'd been for the last six months, plotted in red dots connected by lines. His apartment. His office. The gym. The coffee shop. The reporter's apartment building, where he'd never actually been but which he'd walked past on his way to the Metro, close enough to flag the algorithm.

"This is what we know," they said. "Imagine what we could find if we really started looking."

Daniel was released on the fifth day, after Senator Williams made calls that went higher than the agents had anticipated. No charges were filed. His attorney could find no record of his detention in any system the lawyer could access. Officially, nothing had happened.

Daniel resigned the following week. The Senator understood. She'd seen what they could do, and she knew he would always be a target now.

He took a job at a nonprofit focused on civil liberties. He stopped wearing the Fitbit that wanted nothing more than to serve his fitness goals by tracking everything his body revealed about his fitness and his state of mind.

Daniel started paying cash for everything and leaving his phone at home when he went for walks.

Sometimes, late at night, he'd miss having that Fitbit when he felt his heart rate spike for no reason. Maybe it was just his imagination.

• • •

The next morning, Claire arrived at Elise's apartment carrying coffee, a couple of breakfast burritos, and the weight of everything Seth Parker had told her.

Elise's apartment was in a converted rowhouse in Capitol Hill. The three-story red brick building had been divided into apartments sometime in the seventies. Elise lived on the top floor in a unit with slanted ceilings and windows that looked out over a narrow alley. It wasn't much, but it had the essentials. Her living room doubled as an office, and the galley kitchen was adequate. While her bedroom was barely large enough for a bed, it had a couple of bonuses that Elise valued above all others: no shared walls with neighbors and a landlord who didn't ask questions about the RF-blocking curtains or the white noise generator that ran constantly in the background.

When Claire arrived, she had returned to the routine they'd established after ALTAR when they'd both started treating every interaction like it might be observed. Knocked twice, then once, then twice again. When Elise opened the door and stood there looking exactly as exhausted as Claire felt. Elise couldn't remember the last time she had anything to eat, so the burrito, normally something she would avoid, smelled like the comfort food she needed to start another day.

"You look like you haven't slept," Claire said.

"Come in, and no, I haven't. Thanks for breakfast. You don't look so great either. Did you read the files I gave you?"

Claire gave her a long look before replying. "Yes, I'm not shocked, just sad at what is happening and going undetected. We need to expose what is happening. This is a mission."

Elise nodded and then motioned for Claire to sit down. "We have a lot to talk about."

The apartment was a controlled chaos of paper. Legal pad sheets covered the coffee table, the couch, and most of the floor. Claire recognized the pattern from the old days. Elise had her method of mapping complex stories, laying everything out physically so she could see the connections that weren't visible on a screen. It was analog, inefficient, and exactly the kind of process that couldn't be hacked.

"Is this all from the USB drive?" Claire asked, stepping carefully around a cluster of papers near the door.

"Some of it. The rest is from Dr. Singh." Elise took the coffee and gestured toward the kitchen. "Sit. I need to tell you what she said, and you need to tell me about your cemetery friend, and then we need to figure out what the hell we're going to do. Here, have a napkin."

They sat at the small table just off the galley kitchen. Morning light filtered through the window, catching the steam rising from their cups as the two quietly chewed on their burritos and the predicament they faced. The silence had a texture to it after months of distance, of small talk replacing deeper conversations and a friendship that had frayed along lines neither of them fully understood.

"Before we get into it," Claire said finally, "I need to say something."

Elise looked up from her coffee. "Okay."

"I'm sorry for pulling away." Claire wrapped her hands around her cup, not meeting Elise's eyes. "I know I wasn't... I know I made things harder."

"Claire… "

"Let me finish. Please." She took a breath. "After ALTAR, I couldn't be around anyone who knew, anyone who understood what we'd found and what it meant. Every time I saw you, I saw the story. I saw everything we'd uncovered, and I couldn't..." She trailed off, searching for words that felt inadequate. "I couldn't carry it and be present at the same time. So, I pushed you away. I'm sorry."

The room was quiet except for the white noise generator humming in the living room. Elise set down her coffee and was silent for a long moment.

"I thought you blamed me," she said quietly.

"What?"

"For what happened after, the sources drying up and the stories falling apart." Elise's voice was steady, but Claire could hear the hurt beneath. "I was the one who found the technical evidence. I was the one who pushed us to go deeper, to keep digging when we could have stopped. And then everything fell apart, and I thought, " Elise stopped, pressing her lips together. "I thought you blamed me for pulling us into something we couldn't get out of."

"Elise. No." Claire reached across the table, her hand finding Elise's. "I never blamed you. Not once. I blamed myself, if anything. For not seeing what was coming. For being so focused on the story that I didn't think about what would happen after."

"We both did that."

"We both did that," Claire agreed. "Then we both headed off in different directions, and neither of us knew how to reach across the gap."

• • •

A lot of time, deadlines, and restless nights had passed since the two had met at a conference on digital privacy that neither of them had wanted to attend. Claire had been working on a story about data brokers, tracking the flow of personal information from apps to advertisers to political campaigns. Elise had been chasing the same trail from a different angle, following the technical architecture rather than the human sources.

Claire remembered the hotel ballroom in Arlington clearly. It wasn't the bad coffee, worse pastries, or parade of mediocre speakers that made the occasion memorable. What wasn't forgettable was the competitive charge she felt when she discovered Elise was there.

They'd circled each other for months before that conference, aware of each other's work, suspicious of each other's intentions. Journalism was competitive, and investigative journalism was worse. If you were going to win, you'd better guard your sources, their angles, and their hard-won fragments of truth. The idea of collaboration felt like weakness, like admitting you couldn't do it alone.

Somewhere in that hotel ballroom over disappointing presentations, something had shifted. They'd started talking, really talking, about what they were finding, what it meant, and how the pieces fit together. By the end of the day, they'd realized that their separate investigations were two halves of the same story.

The partnership had been electric. Claire brought sources, relationships, and the human element that made stories resonate. Elise brought technical expertise, pattern recognition, and the ability to see structures that were invisible to anyone who didn't speak the language of code. Together, they'd been unstoppable, a two-person investigative unit that had broken story after story, each one bigger than the last.

And then came ALTAR.

"I used to think that was the best work we'd ever done," Elise said, as if reading Claire's thoughts. "The ALTAR investigation. Eighteen months of our lives, every skill we had, everything we'd learned. And we did it. We did it. We exposed something that was supposed to be undetectable."

"We did."

"And then it crippled us anyway." Elise pulled her hand back, clasping both hands together tightly. "Not the investigation or the story but what came after. The slow-motion collapse of everything we'd built."

Claire nodded. She remembered those months with painful clarity. The triumph of publication, the awards, the interviews. And then, the gradual realization that something was wrong. Sources wouldn't return calls, and stories fell apart for no reason. She wasn't able to shake the creeping sense that invisible walls were going up around her, cutting her off from the work that had defined her life.

"I kept pushing," Claire said. "After you left the Post. I thought if I just worked harder, if I just found the right story, I could break through whatever was happening. I thought I could outrun it."

"I know. I watched." Elise's voice was gentle. "I watched you burning yourself out, story after story, and I wanted to say something, but I didn't know how. I didn't know if you wanted to hear from me."

"I didn't know what I wanted. I was so deep in survival mode that I couldn't think about anything else." Claire laughed, but there was no humor in it. "I kept telling myself it was bad luck, just a rough patch or the industry changing. I had every excuse except the obvious truth."

"That we'd made enemies we couldn't see."

"Yes, we'd made enemies we couldn't see," Claire agreed. "And the enemies were winning."

• • •

The conversation shifted as the morning wore on, moving from the personal to the professional and back again.

Claire told Elise about the cemetery meeting, about Seth Parker, his fifteen years at Nexus, his former military forbearance, and the fear in his eyes when he talked about SENTINEL. She had already given Elise the USB drive but they had not fully discussed his former colleague, Jason, who had supposedly died with a blood alcohol level that didn't match his years of sobriety.

Elise told Claire about Dr. Singh, about her role in building ALTAR, her guilt, the envelope of documents that represented the last work of a dead researcher who was killed in a car accident. Singh, an academic and she underestimated the small world overlaps in the defense industry. Elise explained what Singh had said about the intelligence community consortium, the weaponization of behavioral modeling and the systematic targeting of the oversight community.

Claire listened intently before speaking. "This must be the intelligence community consortium connection. Isn't Katherine Rennick an NSA deputy director? I've heard of her. She testified before the Intelligence Committee last year. I remember her speaking about modernizing threat assessment capabilities. She was very polished and very careful."

"Yes, and Singh said she championed the program. That she's the one who saw what ALTAR could become and pushed to acquire it."

"A true believer."

"Or a true opportunist. Hard to tell the difference in Washington." Elise stood and walked to the window, looking out at the alley below. "The question is what we do with all of this. We have pieces from three different sources, Seth Parker, Dr. Singh, and the network analysis from Rory. But pieces aren't enough; we need something that ties it all together. Something that proves SENTINEL exists, proves what it's doing, and proves who's responsible."

"And we need to get it without getting killed," Claire added with a slight sarcastic tone.

"That too."

Claire joined her at the window. The alley was empty except for a cat picking its way along a fence, moving with the casual confidence of a creature that had never been hunted. "You said Singh mentioned that the consortium has factions and disagreements."

"She said some of them might be willing to talk, if we find the right approach."

"That's how we did it with ALTAR." Claire turned to face Elise. "We didn't bring down the company from the outside. We found the people inside who were already uncomfortable with what was happening. They wanted to talk; they just didn't know how."

"You think there are people like that inside SENTINEL?"

"There are always people like that. The question is finding them before the system finds us."

Elise stared straight ahead, ignoring her ghostly reflection in the window glass. "We're really doing this, aren't we? Going after something even bigger than ALTAR, with even less protection, knowing exactly what happened to us the last time."

"We are."

"And you're not scared?"

Claire laughed, a real laugh this time, tired but genuine. "I'm terrified. I've been terrified for eighteen months. The difference now is I know why." She put her hand on Elise's shoulder. "And this time, I'm not doing it alone anymore."

Elise turned from the window, and for the first time since Claire had arrived, something like hope flickered in her eyes. "Neither am I. We said after Altar we were stepping away for the long term, but the long term can wait for now."

• • •

They spent the next two hours heads down building a plan. It wasn't a complete plan, there were too many unknowns for that, but it was a framework. A way of thinking about the problem that gave them something to work toward instead of just reacting against things.

First: verify everything. The code fragments from Seth Parker, the documents from Dr. Singh, the network analysis from Rory, all of it needed to be cross-referenced, validated, and checked for consistency. They couldn't publish anything they couldn't prove, and they couldn't prove anything they hadn't verified independently.

Second: find more sources. Seth Parker was inside Nexus, but Nexus was just the contractor. The real power, the people making decisions about who to target and how, was in the intelligence community. They needed someone closer to the center. Someone who could explain not just what SENTINEL was doing, but why.

Third: build a coalition. The ALTAR story had worked because it wasn't just Claire and Elise, it was a network of sources, fact-checkers, lawyers, and editors who believed in what they were doing. They needed that again. People who would stand with them when the pressure came.

"The problem is trust," Elise said, as they sketched out potential allies on a fresh legal pad. "SENTINEL has been operating for over a year. That's enough time to compromise anyone. How do we know who's safe to approach?"

"We don't. At least, not for certain." Claire studied the list they'd made. "But we know who's been targeted. Your list of fourteen people whose careers were disrupted. If SENTINEL went after them, it means they were threats. Threats might be willing to fight back."

"Or they might be too scared. Or compromised. Or dead." Elise's said dejectedly. "Jason Mercer was on that list. Look what happened to him."

"Then we'll be extra careful", Claire answered back with determination. "We reach out to the people we know personally. The ones we can verify face-to-face, the old-fashioned way." Claire tapped the legal pad. "Who on this list do you trust? Really trust?"

Elise studied the names. "Maybe three. Four if I'm being optimistic."

"Then we start with three. We tell them what we've found and see how they react. If they're in, we expand the circle. If they're not..." Claire shrugged. "Then we know something useful about the state of things."

"And if one of them reports back to SENTINEL?"

"Then we're even more compromised, and at least we'll know it." Claire stood, stretching muscles that had stiffened from hours of sitting. "We can't operate from a position of perfect safety. There is no perfect safety. We can only be smart, be careful, and move faster than they expect."

Elise looked up at her as something passed between them, an understanding that went beyond words. They had been here before, standing at the edge of something dangerous, knowing the cost of moving forward and the impossibility of going back.

"Okay," Elise said. "We move fast. But first, " She gestured at the papers covering her apartment. "We need to organize all of this into something coherent. We need something we can share with potential allies without giving away everything we know."

"A briefing document."

"Exactly. Enough to convince a potential ally that this is real, but not enough to compromise the investigation if it falls into the wrong hands."

Claire nodded. "I can work on the narrative framework if you'll curate the technical documentation. Let's meet again tomorrow to compare notes and refine our thinking."

"Not here. SENTINEL must know about this apartment if they've been watching me. We need somewhere new for us. Somewhere we haven't been before."

"I know a place." Claire pulled on her jacket. "There's an Old church in Anacostia that got converted into a community center. A friend of mine runs it. It's old school, with no cameras, no digital anything. Very analog."

"Tomorrow at noon?"

"Tomorrow at noon."

They stood facing each other in the cluttered apartment, surrounded by the evidence of a conspiracy that had spent eighteen months trying to destroy them. For the first time since ALTAR, Claire felt something she'd almost forgotten was possible.

Partnership and purpose. The sense that she wasn't fighting alone.

"Hey," Elise said, as Claire reached for the door. "Thank you for saying what you said about the last year."

Claire turned back with a somewhat quizzical look. "I meant it."

"I know. That's why I'm thanking you." Elise managed to smile. "We're going to need each other for this. I'm glad we cleared the air before we jump into the fire."

"Into the fire," Claire repeated. "That's one way to put it."

"You have a better metaphor?"

Claire thought about it. "No. Fire sounds about right."

She opened the door and stepped into the hallway, leaving Elise surrounded by legal pad sheets and the quiet hum of the white noise generator. Behind her, Claire heard three locks clicking into place, each one a small act of defiance against the invisible forces arrayed against them.

Claire took a deep cleansing breath. Today, something that had been broken for eighteen months healed. While she was scared about what they would uncover, the future was not as bleak as it had felt weeks ago.

Claire walked down the stairs and out into the November afternoon, and for the first time in a very long time, she didn't feel alone.

CHAPTER NINE

The Gathering

The Church of the Redeemer had been deconsecrated in 1987 and converted into a community center in 1994. It had been largely forgotten by everyone except the neighborhood it served.

Claire loved it for exactly that reason. The building sat on a quiet street in Anacostia, far from the gleaming corridors of power that defined most of Washington. Its brick facade was weathered, its stained-glass windows clouded with age, and its basement meeting room smelled of burnt coffee, a staple of community organizing. There were no security cameras, no digital sign-in systems, no Wi-Fi. The most advanced technology in the building was a photocopier from 2003 that still somehow worked. It was, in other words, a perfect place to plan a conspiracy against a surveillance state.

She arrived twenty minutes early, carrying a canvas bag filled with paper documents and a thermos of coffee that was significantly better than anything the community center could provide. Allen Williams, the retired social worker who had run the center for the past fifteen years, met her at the door with a bear hug that lifted her off her feet.

"Claire Hensley, as I live and breathe." His voice was a deep rumble, warm with genuine affection. "It's been too long."

"It has. I'm sorry."

"Don't be sorry. Be present." He set her down and studied her face with the practiced eye of someone who had spent forty years reading people. "You look tired. You look worried. And you look like you're about to do something that's going to make my life more interesting."

"I need to use the basement for a few hours. Private meeting. No questions."

Allen raised an eyebrow. "No questions is a big ask."

"I know, but it's important. The kind of important that I can't explain right now."

He was quiet for a moment, then nodded slowly. "You've never asked me for something you didn't need. Basement's yours until five. I'll make sure nobody bothers you." He paused at the door. "Whatever you're doing, Claire, be careful. The world's got enough martyrs."

"I'm trying."

"Try harder."

He disappeared into the building, leaving Claire alone with her resolve.

• • •

Elise arrived exactly at noon, followed ten minutes later by the first of their potential allies: Daniel Okafor. He had been one of the most respected investigative journalists in Washington until eighteen months ago, when his career imploded in ways that still didn't make sense. A Pulitzer finalist at forty-two, he had been working on a story about algorithmic bias in federal hiring systems when his sources suddenly went silent and his editor killed the piece. Daniel didn’t exactly object when he found himself reassigned to covering local zoning disputes. He quit three months later, officially to "pursue other opportunities." The opportunities had never materialized.

Claire had known Daniel for years. They'd worked adjacent beats, shared sources occasionally, and competed for the same stories with the mutual respect of professionals who recognized quality in each other. When Elise mentioned his name as one of the people on her list, Claire had felt a mix of hope and dread. Hope because Daniel was exactly the kind of ally they needed. Dread because she'd watched his destruction from a distance and done nothing to help.

He came down the basement stairs slowly, his eyes adjusting to the dim light. He was thinner than Claire remembered, with new lines in his face that spoke of tension and unanswered questions. But his gaze was sharp and alert.

"Claire. Elise." He nodded to each of them, then surveyed the basement with professional assessment. He scanned the room of folding tables and metal chairs, when his gaze landed on a whiteboard that had seen better days. "This is very cloak-and-dagger. I assume there's a reason you couldn't just send an email."

"There is," Elise said. "Please, sit. We have a lot to explain."

Over the next hour, two more people arrived. Paula Weber, a former congressional staffer who had worked on technology oversight until her security clearance was mysteriously revoked, and Robert Baskin, a cybersecurity researcher whose grant applications had been systematically denied for the past year, forcing him out of academia and into consulting work that kept him fed but far from the research that had defined his career.

Three people, three ruined careers, and three variations on the same story of invisible destruction.

Claire and Elise took turns presenting the code fragments from Seth Parker, the documents from Dr. Singh and the network analysis from Rory. They meticulously outlined the pattern that connected ALTAR to SENTINEL, and SENTINEL to the systematic dismantling of everyone in the room.

When they finished, the basement was silent. Daniel sat with his hands folded, staring at the whiteboard where Elise had sketched the connections. Paula was pale, with that look of a deer in the headlights as she tightened her fingers gripping the edge of the table. Robert closed the notebook he'd filled with three pages of technical questions Elise couldn't answer yet.

"I knew something was wrong," Paula said finally. Her voice was barely above a whisper. "When they pulled my clearance, they said it was a routine review, but I was suspicious about the timing. I had just started questioning where the data from several behavioral analytics contracts was going." She looked up at Claire. "I thought I was paranoid. I thought I was losing my mind."

"You weren't," Claire said. "None of us were."

"The technical architecture you're describing is theoretically possible", Robert said. "ALTAR's behavioral modeling was already more advanced than anything in public literature. If someone took that foundation, repurposed it, added integration with institutional systems..." He shook his head. "You could build exactly what you're describing. A system that doesn't just watch, it predicts and acts."

"The question is what we do about it," Daniel said. He leaned back in his chair, his expression unreadable. "You're asking us to help you expose a classified government program that has already demonstrated it can destroy our careers with surgical precision. If what you suspect is true, it killed at least three people." He paused. "What makes you think we can succeed where everyone else has failed?"

"Because we know it exists," Elise said. "We know what we're fighting. We know how it operates. And we know we're not alone. That's more than anyone else has had."

"That's not enough."

"No. It's not." Claire stood and walked to the whiteboard. "But it's a start, and right now, a start is all we have."

• • •

The discussion continued for another two hours, cycling through strategies, risks, and the practical challenges of investigating something that was designed to prevent investigation.

By three o'clock, they had the rough outline of a plan. Daniel would use his remaining contacts in journalism to quietly assess which outlets might be willing to publish something this explosive, and which had already been compromised by SENTINEL's reach. Paula would tap her network of former congressional staffers, looking for anyone inside the oversight apparatus who might be willing to talk. Robert would analyze the technical evidence, looking for weaknesses in SENTINEL's architecture that might help them understand how to expose it without being detected.

And Claire and Elise would keep building the case, following the threads they'd already uncovered, looking for the next piece of evidence that would make their story undeniable.

"Communication protocols," Robert said, as they prepared to leave. "We need to establish secure channels. No email, no phones, nothing that touches the internet."

"Old school," Daniel agreed. "Dead drops, in-person meetings, codes for emergency contact. Etc." He smiled grimly. "I never thought I'd be using tradecraft from Cold War spy novels or the Watergate era."

"SENTINEL learned from ALTAR," Elise said. "It knows how modern surveillance works because it was built to exploit it. The only advantage we have is being willing to go backward, to communicate in ways the system wasn't designed to monitor."

They agreed on a system of face-to-face meetings at rotating locations, never the same place twice. Paper messages passed by hand. A simple code system for emergencies with a note posted on a community information bulletin board at the library. Although cumbersome and inefficient, it might be exactly the kind of friction that would keep them alive.

As the others filed up the basement stairs, Daniel lingered behind. He caught Claire's arm as she was gathering the papers from the table.

"I need to ask you something," he said. "And I need you to be honest with me."

"Ask."

"Your source inside Nexus. Seth Parker." Daniel's eyes were intent on hers. "How sure are you about him?"

Claire hesitated. It was a fair question, the kind of question any good journalist would ask. "I'm not sure about anything anymore, but he came to me. He took the risk of reaching out, and what he gave us matches everything else we've found."

"That's not what I'm asking." Daniel released her arm but didn't move away. "SENTINEL is an adaptive system. It learns, and it predicts. What if Parker isn't a whistleblower? What if he's bait?"

The question hung in the air, heavy and cold.

"Then we're already compromised," Claire said. "And this meeting, this plan, everything we just discussed, it's exactly what they want us to do."

"Yes."

"I don't think he's bait," she said slowly. "The fear in his eyes was real. The way he talked about Jason Mercer, about what happened to him, that wasn't a performance. But you're right to ask. We should be questioning everything and everyone." She paused. "Including me."

Daniel studied her for a long moment, then nodded. "I had to ask, and I had to see how you answered." He picked up his coat. "For what it's worth, I believe you. I'm not sure I believe in this mission, but I believe you're trying to do the right thing."

"Is that enough to keep you in?"

"It's enough to keep me listening." He headed for the stairs, then paused. "Be careful, Claire. If Parker contacts you again, watch him. Watch everything. The moment something feels wrong, trust your instincts."

He disappeared up the stairs, leaving Claire alone with the empty chairs and her thoughts.

• • •

She was locking the basement door when her burner phone buzzed.

Claire froze. Only four people had this number, Elise, who had left twenty minutes ago; Allen Williams, who was upstairs; and Seth Parker, who had no reason to contact her so soon. The fourth was her editor, who she'd given the number "for emergencies only" and who had never once used it.

She pulled out the phone. Unknown number. A text message, brief and urgent:

They know about the meeting. All of you. Get out now. Don't go home. Don't contact anyone from your regular life. I'll find you when it's safe.

Claire stared at the message, her heart hammering against her ribs. They know about the meeting. Which meant someone had talked, or someone had followed, or, worse, SENTINEL had found a way to monitor them despite all their precautions.

She tried calling the number, but it was dead air. There was no voicemail, no connection, nothing.

Her mind raced through the possibilities. The message could be genuine, a warning from someone who knew what they were doing and wanted to help. It could be from Seth Parker, who had found out something and was trying to protect them. Or it could be exactly what Daniel had warned about: bait. A way to scatter them, isolate them, make them vulnerable.

She needed to warn the others, but how? They had just agreed on communication protocols that didn't include phone calls or text messages. Elise was already gone, somewhere on public transit, unreachable without the very technology they'd agreed to avoid.

Claire climbed the basement stairs two at a time, emerging into the community center's main hall. Allen was there, arranging chairs for an evening meeting.

"Allen." Her voice was sharp enough to make him look up in alarm. "The people who left earlier, did you see which direction they went?"

"Claire, what's wrong?"

"Did you see them?"

He set down the chair he was holding. "The man went south, toward the Metro. The two women went north; I think they were walking together. The other man got into a car." His eyes narrowed. "Claire, you're scaring me."

"I need to find them. I need to warn them about..." She stopped. How could she explain? How could she tell Allen that an invisible system might be watching them all, that his community center might have just become a target?

"Warn them about what?"

Before she could answer, the front door of the community center opened. Two men walked in, both wearing dark suits and the carefully neutral expressions of people who were used to entering rooms and taking control of them.

"Claire Hensley?" The first man held up a badge. "FBI. We need you to come with us."

Claire's blood turned to ice. She thought about running out the back door into the alley. She knew the maze of Anacostia streets from years of reporting in the neighborhood. But even as the thought formed, she saw a third agent appear in the back doorway, blocking that exit.

"On what grounds?" Her voice was steady, even though her hands were shaking.

"We have some questions about a national security matter." The agent's voice was polite, professional, utterly devoid of warmth. "You can come voluntarily, or we can do this another way. Your choice."

Allen stepped forward, his large frame a makeshift barrier between Claire and the agents. "Now wait just a minute. You can't just come into my building and… "

"Sir, please step aside. This doesn't concern you."

"The hell it doesn't. This woman is my guest, and unless you have a warrant…"

"Allen." Claire put her hand on his arm. "It's okay. I'll go with them."

"Claire!"

"It's okay," she repeated, though nothing about this was okay. She looked at the lead agent, forcing herself to meet his eyes. "I'll come voluntarily, but I want to know what this is about."

"You'll be briefed at the field office." The agent stepped aside, gesturing toward the door. "After you, Ms. Hensley."

Claire walked toward the exit, her mind racing through everything she knew about her rights, about interrogation techniques, about how to survive questioning without giving anything away. At the door, she paused and looked back at Allen.

"Call my editor," she said. "Tell him where I've gone. Tell him, " She hesitated. "Tell him I'm following the story."

Then, flanked by agents, she stepped out into the November afternoon. She let them guide her toward a black SUV parked at the curb.

The message had been right. They knew. The question was: What else did they know? And what were they going to do about it?

CHAPTER TEN

The Interview Room

The FBI field office on 4th Street cast a sickly fluorescent pallor tinged with quiet desperation.

Claire had been in buildings like this before. She recognized the practiced hush of places where people's lives changed in ways they hadn't anticipated. She'd interviewed witnesses in rooms like the one they put her in—ten feet by twelve, a metal table bolted to the floor, two chairs on one side and one on the other, and a mirror on the wall that everyone knew was a window. The setup was designed to make you feel small, observed, and already guilty of something even if you didn't know what.

She sat in the single chair and waited. They'd taken both of her phones, along with her bag and its contents. Her journalism experience had taught her that waiting was part of the intimidation strategy. Let the subject sit to imagine all the things that might happen. Let their own mind do the work of breaking them down.

Claire used the time to think.

The FBI showing up at the community center could mean several things. It could be a legitimate investigation. She was a journalist who had been meeting with sources about classified programs, and that kind of activity attracted attention. It could be a shot across the bow to let her know she was being watched. Or, it could be something worse, the beginning of the neutralization protocol that Dr. Singh had described.

The door opened.

The man who entered was not what she expected. He was younger than the agents who had picked her up. She guessed he was in his late thirties, maybe early forties, with the kind of face that would be hard to remember in a crowd. His neatly trimmed brown hair and medium build were as nondescript as his features, pleasant without being distinctive. His dark suit fit well without being expensive. Mr. neighborly FBI guy carried a thin folder that he set on the table between them before sitting down.

"Ms. Hensley." His voice was calm, almost friendly. "Thank you for agreeing to speak with us."

"I don't recall being given much choice."

"There's always a choice." He opened the folder, though he didn't look at its contents. "My name is Ryan Cross. I'm a special agent with the Counterintelligence Division. I'd like to ask you some questions about your recent activities."

"Am I under arrest?"

"No."

"Am I being detained?"

"You're here voluntarily, as I understand it."

"Then I'm free to leave?"

Cross smiled, a small, controlled expression that didn't reach his eyes. "You're free to leave at any time, but I think you'll want to hear what I have to say first."

Claire studied him. There was something about his manner that felt off, not threatening, exactly, but not quite right either. He was too calm and too composed, like someone who already knew how this conversation was going to end.

"Then say it," she said.

• • •

Cross pulled a photograph from the folder and slid it across the table. It was a picture of Seth Parker, taken from what looked like a security camera. He was walking through a parking garage, his face captured in profile, his expression tense with worry.

"Do you know this man?"

Claire kept her face neutral. "Should I?"

"His name is Seth Parker. He's an IT security specialist at Nexus Defense Systems." Cross watched her carefully. "According to our information, you met with him two days ago at Congressional Cemetery."

So, they knew. Claire filed that information away, calculating what it meant. If they knew about the cemetery meeting, they might know about everything else, too. Or they might be fishing, using one piece of confirmed intelligence to trick her into revealing more.

"I meet with a lot of people," she said. "I'm a journalist. It's what I do."

"Mr. Parker has access to classified information. Very classified information." Cross pulled out another photograph, this one showing Claire herself, walking through the cemetery gates. "When someone with his clearance level starts having secret meetings with investigative journalists, it raises concerns."

"Concerns for whom?"

"For the people responsible for protecting national security."

Claire leaned back in her chair, forcing herself to project a confidence she didn't entirely feel. "Agent Cross, I've been doing this job for over a decade. I know how this works. You're trying to figure out what I know, what I'm working on, and whether you can make me stop. So let me save us some time." She met his eyes directly. "I'm a journalist. I protect my sources. And I don't discuss ongoing investigations with federal agents, no matter how politely they ask."

Cross nodded slowly, as if this was exactly the response he'd anticipated. "I appreciate your candor, but I think you're misunderstanding the situation." He pulled out a third item from the folder, not a photograph this time, but a single sheet of paper. "I'm not here to investigate you, Ms. Hensley. I'm here to warn you."

He slid the paper across the table. Claire looked down. It was a list of names. Fourteen names, typed in a neat column. She recognized every one of them; they were the same names on Elise's list, the people whose careers had been systematically destroyed over the past year.

At the bottom, two more names had been added in handwriting:

Claire Hensley. Elise Marston.

Claire's heart stuttered. This wasn't a fishing expedition. This was something else entirely.

"Where did you get this?" Her voice came out steadier than she expected.

"The same place you got yours, I imagine." Cross's expression shifted, the professional mask slipping just enough to reveal something beneath, something that looked almost like concern. "Ms. Hensley, you've stumbled onto something very dangerous. More dangerous than you realize."

"SENTINEL."

The word hung in the air between them. Cross's face remained impassive, but Claire caught the slight tightening around his eyes, the involuntary reaction of someone who had just heard a name that wasn't supposed to be spoken.

"I don't know what that means," he said.

"Yes, you do."

• • •

They sat in silence for a long moment, each taking the measure of the other.

Claire's mind was racing. Cross had shown her the list, had added her name and Elise's to it, which meant he knew about SENTINEL. But he'd claimed not to recognize the name, which meant he was either lying or operating under instructions that prevented him from acknowledging the program's existence. Either way, he wasn't behaving like a typical FBI agent conducting a typical investigation.

"Who are you really?" she asked.

"I told you. Special Agent Ryan Cross, Counterintelligence, "

"I mean, whose side are you on?" Claire gestured at the list. "You didn't bring me here to investigate me. You brought me here to show me this. To warn me, you said. So, what's the warning?"

Cross was quiet for a moment. When he spoke, his voice was lower, more guarded.

"Three years ago, I was assigned to investigate a series of anomalies in federal personnel systems. Security clearances being revoked without proper documentation. Grant applications being denied through irregular channels. Career-ending investigations that seemed to materialize out of nowhere." He turned to face her. "Every trail I followed led back to the same place. A program that officially didn't exist, run by people who officially didn't have the authority to do what they were doing."

"And when you reported it?"

"My investigation was shut down. My supervisor told me the matter had been 'resolved at a higher level.' I was reassigned to a desk in Omaha." A bitter smile crossed his face. "I spent eight months reviewing visa applications before someone decided I could be useful again."

"Useful how?"

"That's what I'm trying to figure out." Cross sat up straighter in his chair, his manner shifting again, less formal now, more direct. "I was pulled back to D.C. eight months ago, assigned to a new task force. On paper, we're investigating domestic extremist threats. In practice, I've spent most of my time being sent to interview people who have nothing to do with extremism and everything to do with that list."

Claire felt a chill run down her spine. "You're being used."

"The FBI is being used. The whole oversight apparatus is being used." Cross leaned forward, his voice dropping further. "Ms. Hensley, whatever you think you know about what's happening, it's bigger than you realize. The program you're investigating isn't just surveillance. It's not just neutralization. It's a complete system for controlling the flow of information in this country. Anyone who might threaten certain interests, journalists, researchers, congressional staffers, even federal agents, they get flagged, assessed, and handled. Most of them never even know it's happening."

"Most of them."

"The ones who notice, the ones who start asking questions, " He glanced at the mirror, and Claire saw something in his eyes that looked like fear. "They get handled more directly."

"Like Jason Mercer."

Cross's jaw tightened, and his glare intensified. "I can't confirm or deny. "

"You don't have to." Claire picked up the list and studied it again. "Three of these people are dead. All accidents and all within the last eight months." She looked up at him. "That's what you're warning me about, isn't it? That I could be next."

"I'm warning you that you need to be very careful about who you trust and what you do next." Cross stood again, gathering the photographs and sliding them back into the folder. "The meeting you had today, the one at the community center in Anacostia, I wasn't the only one who knew about it, and the people I work for aren't the only ones watching."

"Then why bring me here? Why tell me any of this?"

Cross paused at the door, his hand on the handle. "Because I've spent three years watching good people get destroyed by something I couldn't prove existed. I joined the FBI to protect this country, and instead I've been turned into a tool for people who think they are the country." He met her eyes. "And because you might be the first person I've encountered who actually has a chance of exposing what's happening."

"That's a lot of faith to put in someone you just met."

"It's not faith. It's desperation." He opened the door. "Your belongings are at the front desk. You're free to go. And Ms. Hensley, " He hesitated. "The next time someone brings you in for questioning, it might not be someone who wants to help."

He left, closing the door behind him with a soft click.

• • •

Claire sat alone in the interview room for a long time after Cross left. Her mind was churning through everything he'd said, trying to separate truth from misdirection, genuine warning from elaborate manipulation. Cross could be exactly what he claimed, a federal agent who had discovered something wrong and wanted to help expose it, or he could be another layer of the trap, someone sent to gain her trust and monitor her activities from the inside.

Daniel's warning echoed in her head: What if Parker isn't a whistleblower? What if he's bait? The same question applied to Cross. The same question applied to everyone.

She stood and walked to the mirror, studying her own reflection. She took the measure of the dark circles under her eyes, the tension lines around her mouth outlining the toll of eighteen months of invisible warfare, right there on her face. The woman staring back at her didn't look like someone capable of taking on a surveillance apparatus that had infiltrated the entire federal government.

Then again, she hadn't looked capable of exposing ALTAR, either. She'd just been a journalist following a story, one source at a time, one document at a time, until suddenly the whole picture came into focus and the world changed.

Maybe that was how it worked. Maybe you didn't have to be capable, you just had to be stubborn enough to keep going or begin again, even when you had been so confused and scared that you planned to leave everything behind and start over.

She collected her things from the front desk—her regular phone, the burner, her bag, the documents she'd brought to the meeting. The agent who returned them didn't meet her eyes. Outside, the November afternoon was cold and gray, the sun hidden behind clouds that looked like they might deliver rain or snow, or nothing at all.

Claire stood on the sidewalk outside the FBI field office and checked her burner phone. She'd missed three calls from Elise within the last hour. They'd agreed never to leave voicemails, but the frequency of calls told her everything she needed to know: Elise was worried and probably imagined the worst.

Claire started walking toward the Metro station, planning what she would say when they met. She would tell Elise about Cross and his warning. She would also share her uncertainty about whether to trust him. She dreaded the question that had been forming in the back of her mind since she'd first seen the folder on the interview room table.

Cross had known about the meeting in Anacostia and her meeting with Seth Parker at the cemetery. He'd known about the list of sixteen names.

He hadn't mentioned Dr. Singh or the documents from Jack Gratten's research. He hadn't mentioned the name that Dr. Singh had given them, Katherine Rennick, the NSA deputy director who had championed the program.

Either Cross didn't know about those pieces of the puzzle, which meant his information was incomplete, or he knew and had chosen not to mention them, which meant he was playing a game she didn't yet understand. Either way, they had something SENTINEL didn't know about. A thread they could pull that hadn't been anticipated.

Claire descended into the Metro station, joining the flow of commuters heading home at the end of another ordinary day. Above her, the city continued its business meetings and negotiations, flexing power and compromise. This was the endless machinery of government grinding forward. Somewhere in that machinery, a system was watching, calculating, deciding who got to participate and who needed to be removed.

She hoped that the system didn't know everything. Not yet. Hope was going to have to be enough.

CHAPTER ELEVEN

The Long Hours

Elise knew something was wrong when Claire didn't answer the third call. They had agreed on protocols. If one of them called and the other couldn't answer, they would call back within fifteen minutes. If they couldn't call back, they would send a text, just the letter K, nothing more, to indicate they were safe but unavailable. No response at all meant trouble.

It had been two hours since Claire left the community center. Two hours with no answer, no text, no signal of any kind.

Elise sat in her apartment, surrounded by the legal pad sheets that had become her war room and tried not to imagine the worst. The white noise generator hummed its steady static. Her RF-blocking curtains filtered the afternoon light into something gray and darkening. She had already called three times and sent two texts. Now she was staring at her burner phone like she could will it to ring through sheer force of anxiety.

She thought the meeting had gone well. Daniel Okafor had been skeptical but engaged. Paula Weber recognized the pattern immediately, so at a minimum, she and Claire had the relief of validation even though it was mixed with the horror of confirmation. Robert Basken had already started asking the technical questions that would help them build their case. By the time Elise left, she'd felt something she hadn't felt in months—optimism.

Now, however, that optimism curdled in her stomach, turning to acid. She thought about calling Paula or Daniel, but they'd agreed to maintain radio silence after the meeting.

No contact for at least forty-eight hours, to see if anyone had been followed. They needed to let any immediate surveillance die down. Breaking that protocol now could put all of them at risk.

But what if Claire was in big trouble? What if the silence meant something had happened, something irreversible?

Elise stood and walked to the window and pushed aside the RF curtain just enough to look down at the street. She scanned the familiar scene for anything out of place. There was a delivery truck double-parked near the corner. She thought she recognized the elderly woman walking a small dog as from the neighborhood. The two teenagers passing by kept pausing and laughing about something on one of their phones. Normal life, proceeding normally, while somewhere in this city her best friend might be… she stopped the thought before it could complete itself.

Claire was fine. She had to be fine. There were a hundred explanations for the silence that didn't involve the worst-case scenario. Her phone died, or she got caught up in something at the Post. Maybe she was being careful, taking a circuitous route home, making sure she wasn't followed.

Elise didn't believe any of those explanations, but she repeated them to herself anyway. The alternative was panic, and panic wouldn't help anyone.

• • •

She tried to work while she waited. She mindlessly shuffled through the documents from Dr. Singh and Jack's research, that he'd painstakingly reconstructed from the fragments he'd managed to preserve before his death. Most of it was technical: code analysis, network architecture diagrams, references to systems and protocols that Elise only half understood. But scattered throughout were notes in

Mercer's own hand, observations and questions that painted a picture of a man who had slowly realized the magnitude of what he was involved in.

The behavioral modeling has exceeded original parameters, one note read. *System is making predictions we didn't program it to make. Learning faster than anticipated. Question: At what point does optimization become emergence?*

Another note dated three weeks before his death: *Asked K.R. about the three incidents. She said they were 'handled appropriately.' Wouldn't elaborate. What does 'appropriate' mean when the system is making autonomous decisions about threat neutralization?*

K.R. Katherine Rennick. The NSA deputy director who had championed SENTINEL from the beginning.

Elise had spent the morning researching Rennick, pulling together everything publicly available about her career. It wasn't much; people at her level tended to exist in shadows, their names appearing in the occasional congressional testimony or trade publication but rarely in mainstream coverage. What Elise had found painted a picture of a career intelligence officer who had risen through the ranks on a combination of technical expertise and bureaucratic savvy.

Rennick had started at NSA in the early 2000s, working on signals intelligence during the post-9/11 expansion of surveillance authorities. She'd moved through increasingly senior positions, always on the technical side, always focused on what the agency called "capability development", which boiled down to the creation of new tools for gathering and analyzing information. By the time ALTAR had been exposed and dismantled, she was a deputy director, positioned perfectly to see the value in what the system could become.

According to Dr. Singh, Rennick had been the one to recognize ALTAR's potential. While everyone else saw a scandal to be contained, she saw an opportunity to be seized.

The behavioral modeling technology that had been used to manufacture synthetic relationships could be repurposed for something far more powerful: predicting and controlling human behavior at scale. She had made it happen through the consortium of intelligence agencies by leveraging the Nexus contract to carefully resurrect and repurpose a program that officially no longer existed. SENTINEL was Katherine Rennick's vision of what national security could become in an age of algorithmic intelligence.

Claire had also spent several hours that morning researching Katherine Rennick.

Rennick's official biography was impressive and unsurprising. She'd started her climb with a PhD in computer science from MIT and spent her early career at DARPA working on machine learning applications for intelligence analysis. She had a meteoric rise through the NSA's technical directorate, becoming the youngest woman ever appointed to deputy director, a fact that the agency's public affairs office had highlighted in press releases touting their commitment to diversity. Recent photos showed a composed woman in her late fifties with silver hair cut short and eyes that revealed nothing.

The official biography only told part of the story. Claire had found the rest in archived interviews, academic papers, and congressional testimony transcripts that painted a picture of someone whose brilliance was matched only by her conviction. Rennick had grown up in a small town in West Virginia, the daughter of a coal miner who had died in a mine collapse when she was twelve. In a rare personal interview from fifteen years ago, she had described standing at her father's grave and making a promise: she would build systems that could prevent disasters before they happened. The conviction of her strong beliefs in prediction and prevention had shaped her entire career.

Her early work at DARPA focused on pattern recognition, teaching machines to see connections that humans couldn't. She developed algorithms that could predict equipment failures before they occurred, identify potential security threats from fragmentary intelligence, and model the behavior of complex systems with unprecedented accuracy. The work had earned her commendations, promotions, and the attention of people who saw applications beyond mechanical systems.

Her pivot had come after 9/11. Claire found a speech Rennick had given at a closed intelligence community conference in 2003. The transcript was leaked years later by a disgruntled attendee. "We failed because we couldn't see the pattern," Rennick had told the assembled intelligence officials. "We had the data and signals, but we couldn't connect them in time. The next attack, and there will be a next attack, will succeed or fail based on our ability to predict human behavior. Not after the fact or in real time. Before. We need to anticipate the future before it happens."

It was a philosophy that had guided her ever since. At the NSA, she championed every expansion of domestic surveillance authority, arguing in classified briefings that the distinction between foreign and domestic threats was an artifact of a pre-digital age. "Radicalization doesn't respect borders," she had reportedly told the Senate Intelligence Committee in a closed session. "A threat that originates overseas can manifest in an American citizen within weeks. If we blind ourselves to domestic patterns, we blind ourselves to half the picture."

Not everyone had agreed. Claire found references to internal conflicts, colleagues who had pushed back against Rennick's vision. One former NSA official, speaking anonymously to a reporter years later, had described her as "brilliant but frightening, someone who genuinely believed that privacy was a luxury we couldn't afford anymore." Another was blunt in his assessment: "Katherine doesn't see people. She sees data points. Patterns to be analyzed, behaviors to be predicted, threats to be neutralized. It's not malice. It's something worse. It's certainty."

That certainty had found its ultimate expression in SENTINEL.

When ALTAR was exposed, most of the intelligence community believed it was a good thing that this rogue AI program that had manipulated American citizens was outed. They'd seen the scandal that ended executive careers and threatened budgets, so they judiciously maintained relationships with oversight committees. They were the good guys. Katherine Rennick had seen something else. She had seen proof of concept.

In Rennick's opinion, ALTAR's behavioral modeling worked very well. It had successfully predicted emotional states, identified vulnerabilities, and manufactured relationships that felt real to the people being manipulated. Yes, it had been used for crude purposes, financial fraud, and political manipulation, but the underlying technology was sound. In the right hands, with the right oversight, it could be transformed into something that served the national interest rather than undermined it.

Or at least, that was how Rennick sold it to the consortium of intelligence officials who gathered in the aftermath of ALTAR's exposure. Claire could imagine the pitch: controlled deployment, strict targeting criteria, layers of authorization for the most aggressive interventions. It would be a scalpel, not a sledgehammer.

The fact that the tool required subverting democracy to function, that it depended on surveilling citizens without their knowledge, manipulating their lives without their consent, and occasionally destroying anyone who got too close to the truth, was, apparently, a price Katherine Rennick was willing to pay.

Elise stared at Katherine Rennick's photograph on her screen: that composed face, those unreadable eyes. She had covered enough scandals to know that the worst abuses were rarely committed by monsters. They were committed by true believers, people who were so convinced of their own righteousness that they couldn't see the line they had crossed until they were miles past it.

Katherine Rennick wasn't a monster. She was something more dangerous: a visionary who had built a machine for controlling human behavior and convinced herself it was a gift to the nation she served.

The question was whether she was a true believer or just another bureaucrat who had convinced herself that the ends justified the means.

Elise suspected she was both.

• • •

The knock came at 5:47 PM.

Elise's heart seized. She stood frozen in the middle of her living room, staring at the door like it might reveal what was waiting on the other side. The knock came again, two quick raps, then one, then two more.

The signal. Claire's signal.

She was across the room in three strides, fumbling with the locks, pulling the door open to find Claire standing in the hallway, exhausted and pale but unmistakably, wonderfully alive.

"Jesus Christ." Elise pulled her inside, closing the door and engaging all three locks before turning to face her. "Four hours. Four hours with no contact. I thought, " She stopped, not wanting to say what she'd thought.

"I know. I'm sorry." Claire dropped into the armchair by the window, her whole body sagging with fatigue. "They took my phones. Both of them. I couldn't call until I got them back, and by then I was already on the Metro."

"Who took your phones? What happened?"

"The FBI." Claire laughed, with a short, humorless sound. "They were waiting when I came out of the community center. Three agents. Very polite. Very insistent."

Elise felt the blood drain from her face. "The FBI arrested you?"

"No, not arrested. I was invited to have a conversation." Claire's matter-of-fact tone was that of someone recounting events that she hadn't fully processed yet. "They took me to the field office on 4th Street. Put me in an interview room and then put me on ice for about half an hour. And then," She paused, as something complicated crossed her face. "And then things got interesting."

Elise lowered herself onto the couch across from Claire. "Tell me everything."

• • •

The story took nearly an hour to tell.

Claire recounted everything: the interview room, the photographs of Seth Parker, the list of sixteen names with hers and Elise's handwritten at the bottom. She described Agent Ryan Cross, his forgettable face, his careful manner, the moment when the professional mask had slipped and something more human had shown through.

She told Elise about Cross's investigation three years ago, the anomalies he'd discovered, the way he'd been shut down and exiled to Omaha. She repeated his warning about the FBI being used, about the oversight apparatus being turned into a tool for the very program it was supposed to monitor.

And she shared her own analysis—the things Cross had known versus the things he hadn't mentioned. She weighed the possibility that he was genuine against the equal possibility that he was another layer of the trap.

When she finished, Elise was chewing her lip in an effort not to jump in with conclusions. moment.

"He didn't mention Dr. Singh," she said finally.

"No."

"Or the documents from Mercer."

"No."

"Or Katherine Rennick."

"No." Claire met her eyes. "Which means either he doesn't know about those pieces, or he knows and chose not to reveal that he knows."

"If he's genuine, that's good news. It means SENTINEL's information is incomplete." Elise stood and walked to her whiteboard, studying the web of connections she'd been building. "If he's not genuine, if this is some kind of operation, then showing up and warning you might be designed to make us trust him. To bring him inside our circle."

"A classic intelligence move. Offer help that seems too good to refuse."

"Exactly." Elise tapped the whiteboard with her finger. "But there's a third possibility. What if Cross is genuine, but he's being used without knowing it? SENTINEL is adaptive; it learns, it predicts. What if it predicted that Cross would try to warn us, and it's using that to monitor our response?"

Claire groaned, pressing her palms against her eyes. "God. It's like trying to play chess against an opponent who can see the entire board, and you can only see three squares."

"Welcome to asymmetric warfare." Elise returned to the couch and flopped down next to Claire. "The good news is, we don't have to figure out Cross's intentions right now. We can proceed carefully, share only what we're willing to lose, and see how he responds."

"And in the meantime?"

"In the meantime, we follow the thread they don't know about." Elise reached for the documents on her desk. "Katherine Rennick. She's the architect. She's the one who saw what ALTAR could become and made it happen. If we want to understand SENTINEL, really understand it, not just document its existence, we need to understand her."

Claire took the documents, flipping through the pages. "So how do we get close to an NSA deputy director without getting ourselves killed?"

"We don't get close to her. We get close to her enemies." Elise pulled out a separate sheet with notes she'd made during her research. "Rennick has risen fast. That means she's stepped on people along the way. She'll have rivals who got passed over. There must be subordinates who disagreed with her methods. Surely after ALTAR, there are partners in the consortium who think the program has gone too far."

"Dr. Singh said there were factions and disagreements about how far SENTINEL should go."

"Right. Which means not everyone in the intelligence community is comfortable with what's happening. Some of them might even be looking for a way out, a way to expose the program without destroying their own careers." Elise leaned forward. "We need to find those people and give them a reason to talk."

"And Agent Cross?"

"We keep him at arm's length. We don't trust him, but we don't shut him out either. If he's genuine, he could be valuable. If he's not, " She shrugged. "Better to know where the surveillance is coming from than to wonder."

Claire quietly processed Elise's take on where things stood. Then she nodded slowly. "Okay. We follow Rennick, we find her enemies, and we see who else wants this program exposed."

"It's not much of a plan."

"It's what we have." Claire set down the documents and looked at Elise the way she used to during the ALTAR investigation, when they were in too deep to stop and too stubborn to quit. "I'm glad we're doing this together. I don't think I could face it alone."

"You won't have to." Elise reached out and squeezed her hand. "Whatever happens, we face it together. That's the deal."

"That's the deal," Claire agreed. Then she added, "When the FBI walked in, I was scared, but I also felt a mixture of curiosity and determination. I focused on what I had learned about interrogation tactics to stay calm. Yet here I go again. I didn't think I could be that consumed again like I was when we uncovered ALTAR, but I'm right back with the same anxiety but not willing to step away. This is too important."

Elise shrugged. She was feeling the same, but she was also determined to step up in light of the importance of what they were undertaking.

Outside, the November evening had turned to twilight. The city lights were coming on, one by one, a constellation of ordinary life continuing in ordinary ways. Yet, here, in this small apartment with its RF-blocking curtains and white noise generator, two women were planning a rebellion.

It wasn't much. But it was a start.

• • •

Later that night, after Claire had finally gone home, Elise sat alone in her darkened apartment and thought about the future.

Not the immediate future. There'd be meetings, research, and careful maneuvering that would occupy the coming days. She was trying to imagine a more distant future. When all of this was over, one way or another, she would go back to her self-imposed hibernation

She tried to imagine what victory would look like. SENTINEL exposed and the program dismantled, with Katherine Rennick and her consortium held accountable for what they'd built. It was a pleasant fantasy, but it felt thin, insubstantial, like something she was supposed to want rather than something she could envision.

The truth was, she couldn't see past the fight. She couldn't imagine a world where this was finished and could return to normal life. Maybe because normal life no longer existed. Maybe because she'd been changed too much by what she'd learned over the past few years to ever go back to who she was before.

She thought about something Claire had said during the ALTAR investigation, during one of those late-night sessions when exhaustion stripped away the filters and they talked about things that mattered. "Every big story changes you," Claire had said. "The small ones you can walk away from, but the big ones, the ones that matter, they become part of who you are. You can't un-know what you've learned."

Elise hadn't fully understood at the time. She understood now.

She picked up Mercer's notes again, flipping to the last page, the final entry, dated two days before his death.

The system doesn't just predict behavior anymore, he had written. *It shapes it. Every interaction, every piece of information it controls or withholds, changes the landscape of possible futures. We're not watching an AI that monitors threats. We're watching an AI that creates the conditions for its own necessity. The more it intervenes, the more unstable things become. The more unstable things become, the more intervention seems justified. It's not a tool. It's an ecosystem that we're all living inside.*

Elise set down the notes and stared at the ceiling.

An ecosystem. They weren't fighting a program or a policy. They were fighting an entire architecture of control, one that had been designed to perpetuate itself, to grow more powerful with every threat it neutralized, to become so essential that no one could imagine dismantling it.

How did you fight something like that? How did you expose a system that had already infiltrated the mechanisms of exposure?

She didn't have an answer yet, but as she finally drifted toward sleep, one thought crystallized in her mind with perfect clarity. They weren't just trying to expose SENTINEL. They were trying to prove that there was still a world where exposure mattered. A world where truth could still win against the systems designed to suppress it.

If that world didn't exist anymore, then nothing they did would matter anyway. But if it did, if there was still a chance, they had to try.

CHAPTER TWELVE

The Defector

The name came from Paula Weber. It was delivered via a handwritten note passed during a meeting they had carefully planned at a Georgetown coffee shop.

They had choreographed the meeting carefully. Paula would arrive first, order her usual latte, and take a seat near the window with a paperback she had no intention of reading. Claire entered twelve minutes later and ordered tea and a muffin at the counter. She sat at the adjacent table without acknowledging Paula's presence. After taking her time to eat casually, Claire stood to leave. The tables were closely spaced, so it was easy to knock over Paula's bag, apologizing profusely while helping to gather the scattered contents. In the confusion, a folded piece of paper changed hands.

It was old tradecraft—analog and awkward and almost certainly overkill. But in a world where every electronic communication could be monitored, it paid to be overly cautious.

Claire didn't read the note until she was three blocks away, tucked into a doorway where she could watch the street in both directions. The paper was thin, the handwriting small and precise: *Thomas Winters. Former CIA liaison to the consortium. Forced out 8 months ago after raising concerns about program scope. Now teaching at Georgetown. Schedule attached. Be careful, he's being watched.*

Below the message, Paula had written out Winters's office hours and the location of his classroom. Claire memorized the information, then tore the paper into small pieces and scattered them in three different trash cans on her walk to the Metro.

She'd never heard the name Thomas Winters, but that meant nothing. The intelligence community was vast, and the people who worked in its shadows rarely surfaced in ways that journalists could track. What mattered was how Winters was mentally situated now that he had raised concerns about program scope and been forced out. Thomas Winters was one of Rennick's enemies. Just like they'd hoped to find.

• • •

Georgetown University's campus was beautiful in early winter, the old brick buildings framed by bare trees and iron lampposts that looked like they belonged in a Dickens novel. This area of Georgetown, with its iconic buildings, cobblestone sidewalks, and narrow streets, was often the setting for DC-based movies.

Claire walked through the campus grounds like any other visitor, with her press credentials safely hidden. Her appearance was carefully calibrated to blend in with the graduate students and adjunct professors who populated the place. She'd dressed down in jeans and a worn leather jacket, and she carried a messenger bag that had seen better days. Nothing about her screamed *journalist.*

Winters's office was in the School of Foreign Service, which was a stately building overlooking a quad where students hurried between classes with their collars turned up against the brisk wind. Claire timed her arrival to coincide with the end of his office hours and late enough that most students would have already come and gone, yet early enough that he wouldn't have left for the day.

She climbed to the third floor and found what she thought might be his door. The door was slightly ajar, so she double checked by reading the small plaque, "Thomas Winters, Adjunct Professor, Intelligence Studies." She steeled her resolve and knocked.

"Office hours are over." said a gruff voice that came from inside. "Come back Thursday."

Claire had considered how best to approach Professor Winters. She decided that a direct approach was best. Claire poked her head around the door, "I'm not a student, I'm a journalist. My name is Claire Hensley. I'd like to talk to you about SENTINEL."

The silence that followed was long and heavy. Winters stood up, his chair scraping against the wooden floor. He approached the door and swung it open just enough for Claire to step inside before he firmly closed it.

Thomas Winters was not what Claire had expected. She'd imagined someone severe, the stereotypical intelligence officer with hooded eyelids and careful posture. Instead, the man before her looked more like an aging professor than a spook. He was sixty-something, with a thick gray beard, wire-rimmed glasses, and the rumpled appearance of someone who had long since stopped caring about impressions. His eyes, though, were sharp and alert. They were the eyes of someone who spent decades reading people and wasn't about to stop now.

"Claire Hensley," he repeated. "The ALTAR reporter."

"You know my work."

"I know everyone's work. That's how I stay alive."

• • •

The office was small and cluttered with books, not the carefully curated shelves of an academic who wanted to impress, but the working library of someone who read constantly. Claire spied volumes on intelligence history, geopolitics, and technology stacked on every available surface, interspersed with journals, newspapers, and the occasional coffee mug that had been pressed into service as a paperweight.

Winters cleared a stack of papers from the chair across from his desk and gestured for Claire to sit. He didn't do pleasantries, he simply settled into his own chair and waited, his hands folded on the desk in front of him.

"How did you find me?" he asked.

"Someone who knows you were pushed out and thought you might be willing to talk."

"Willing is a strong word." He studied her face, reading something there that seemed to satisfy him. "How much do you know?"

"Enough to know that ALTAR's technology was acquired by the intelligence community and repurposed into something called SENTINEL. Enough to know that it's being used to target journalists, researchers, and oversight staff. Enough to know that people have died." Claire met his gaze steadily. "Not enough to prove any of it."

Winters continued to look at Claire without responding. Outside, a bell tower chimed the hour, four deep tones that seemed to echo the gravity of the conversation.

"I spent thirty-two years in the intelligence community," he said finally. "CIA, mostly, with stints at DIA and a few years on loan to NSA. I've done things in service to this country that would keep a normal person awake at night. I made peace with it all a long time ago." He paused, adjusting his glasses. "SENTINEL is different. SENTINEL isn't about protecting the country. It's about protecting a particular vision of what the country should be and who gets to define it."

"Katherine Rennick's vision."

Something flickered in Winters's eyes, surprise perhaps, or recognition. "You know about Rennick."

"I know she championed the program. I know she's the one who saw what ALTAR could become."

"Kate Rennick is a true believer." The words came out heavy, weighted with personal history. "I've known her for twenty years. I watched her rise through the ranks on brilliance and ambition and an absolute certainty that she knows what's best for the country. She's not corrupt. That's what makes her dangerous. She genuinely believes that SENTINEL is necessary because the threats facing this nation are so severe and existential that normal constraints don't apply."

"The Constitution might disagree."

"The Constitution is a document. Kate believes in outcomes." Winters leaned back in his chair, and the old leather creaked beneath him. "When I was part of the consortium, I tried to argue for limits and oversight mechanisms. I advocated for clear lines that the program couldn't cross. Kate listened politely and proceeded to ignore everything I said." He smiled without humor. "When I pushed harder, I was informed that my services were no longer required. They suggested medical retirement with very generous terms, as long as I kept my mouth shut."

"But you're talking to me now."

"I'm talking to you now." He nodded slowly. "Because in the eight months since they pushed me out, I've watched the program grow beyond anything I imagined. The target list has expanded. The neutralization protocols have become more aggressive. Three people I knew personally, people who were asking the same questions I was asking, are dead."

"Jason Mercer?"

"Jason was one. He was a good man who knew to be careful." Winters's voice hardened. "The official report is a lie, and everyone who knew him knows it's a lie. He didn't drink. But who do you report a lie to when the liars control the reporting?"

• • •

They talked for nearly two hours.

Winters was careful about what he shared, his decades of intelligence work had made discretion second nature, but what he offered was invaluable. He explained the consortium's structure: NSA as the lead agency, with participation from CIA, elements of the Defense Department, and a rotating cast of contractors who provided technical expertise and plausible deniability. He described the internal politics, the factions that had formed as the program expanded, and the growing unease among some members about where things were heading.

"There are people inside who aren't comfortable," he said. "Not many, and not anyone with power, but they exist. There are still some career professionals who are clear that they signed up to protect the country, not to build a domestic surveillance machine. The problem is, they're terrified. They've seen what happens to people who speak up."

"What would it take to get them to talk?"

He looked at Claire with a strained grin. "Safety and protection. The assurance that if they come forward, they won't end up like Jason." Winters shook his head. "I can't give them that. Neither can you. But if you could create enough public pressure, enough attention, if you could make it more dangerous to stay silent than to speak, some of them might take the risk."

"We need evidence first. Something concrete enough to publish."

"You need more than evidence. You need a narrative." Winters stood and walked to his window, looking out at the darkening campus. "The American public has been conditioned to accept surveillance in the name of security. You can show them documents, technical specifications, even proof of wrongdoing, and they'll shrug. 'That's how the world works,' they'll say. 'If you have nothing to hide, you have nothing to fear."

"That's not true."

"Of course it's not true, but truth isn't enough." He turned back to face her. "You need to make people feel it. You need to show them what it means when an invisible system can decide who succeeds and who fails, who gets to speak and who gets silenced. You need to make it personal."

Claire thought about the list of sixteen names. "We have stories. People who've been targeted."

"Use them. Put faces to the pattern, and let people see themselves in the victims." Winters returned to his desk and pulled out a drawer, extracting a small envelope. "I can't give you classified documents; besides, I destroyed everything when I left, for my own protection. But I can give you this."

He handed her an envelope. Inside was a single sheet of paper with a list of names and titles.

"These are people inside the consortium who have expressed doubts," he said. "Some of them spoke to me privately before I was pushed out. Some of them to each other, in conversations I heard about secondhand. I can't guarantee any of them will talk, but they're your best chance at finding someone who will."

Claire looked at the list. It had seven names with positions ranging from mid-level analysts to senior officials. Seven people who might be willing to confirm what she already knew, or who might report her approach directly to Katherine Rennick.

"How do I know I can trust you?" she asked. It was the question she'd been holding back throughout their conversation, the question that had to be asked even though she hated asking it.

Winters smiled, a tired, knowing expression. "You can't and you shouldn't. That's the world we live in now." He sat back down, his energy seeming to fade. "But I'll tell you this: I have a thirty-four-year-old daughter who works for an environmental nonprofit. She asks too many questions about powerful people. Four months ago, she was denied a grant that would have funded her research for three years. No explanation and no appeal. Just... denied."

He met Claire's eyes.

"She's not on your list of sixteen. She's not famous enough, or visible enough, but she's being watched. Her career is being shaped by decisions she doesn't know are being made. And there's nothing I can do to protect her, not while this program exists, and not while Kate Rennick and her believers are in charge." His voice took on a hint of anger. "So, when you ask if you can trust me, my answer is that I have more reason to want this exposed than you do. I just don't have the power to do it myself."

• • •

Claire left Georgetown as the last light faded from the sky.

She walked slowly, processing everything Winters had told her, turning the new information over in her mind like stones being examined for hidden facets. The list of seven names felt heavy in her pocket, not physically, but psychologically. Seven chances to find someone who would confirm the story. Seven opportunities to walk into a trap.

The evening was cold and damp, the kind of cold that seeped through your clothing and settled into your bones. Claire pulled her jacket tighter. All around her were people connected to networks that might or might not be capturing their every move.

She thought about what Winters had said about a narrative. He was right about making people feel the truth, she knew he was right. Facts alone were never enough to change minds. It took stories and characters that people could identify with, villains they could fear, stakes they could comprehend.

She had the villain: Katherine Rennick, the true believer who thought she was saving the country by building a machine to control it. She had the victims: sixteen people, and counting, whose lives had been systematically dismantled by an algorithm that decided they were threats. She had the stakes: nothing less than the question of whether democracy could survive in an age of algorithmic surveillance.

What she didn't have was enough proof. They needed the kind of proof that would stand up to the inevitable pushback, the denials, and the claims that she was a conspiracy theorist who had finally lost touch with reality.

The list of seven names in her pocket was a start.

She descended into the Metro station, the warm air rising to meet her like a promise of safety she knew was false. In the vast invisible network that connected everything to everything, SENTINEL was watching, learning, and predicting.

It couldn't predict everything or control everyone, and it couldn't stop two stubborn journalists who had already beaten one impossible system and were determined to beat another.

Claire boarded her train and sat in the back, where she could see everyone who entered and exited. Old necessary habits, the habits of someone who understood that the fight had only just begun.

She pulled out her burner phone and composed a text to Elise: *Met the professor. He gave us homework. Seven names. Will share tonight.*

She hit send as the train carried her through the darkness beneath the city, toward answers that might save them or toward a trap that would destroy them all.

Either way, she would find out soon enough.

CHAPTER THIRTEEN

Seven Doors

The first three names on Winters' list were dead ends. Not literally dead, but professionally unreachable, though Claire found herself checking obituaries now with a paranoia she'd never had before. Anthony Grayson, a senior analyst at DIA, had been transferred to an overseas posting two weeks before Claire tried to contact him. Diane Hollister, a deputy director at the CIA's Office of Science and Technology, was on extended medical leave with no return date. James Thornton, who had been one of the original architects of the SENTINEL technical framework, had simply vanished, his phone disconnected, his apartment empty, and his digital footprint scrubbed clean as if he'd never existed.

"They're cleaning house," Elise said, when Claire reported the pattern. They were sitting in an out-of-the-way Cuban coffee place in Adams Morgan where the music was loud enough to cover conversation and the clientele minded their own business. "Either they knew Winters was going to talk, or they have standing protocols to isolate anyone who might be vulnerable."

"Or both." Claire stirred her cortadito without drinking it. She knew the caffeine would only make her more anxious, and she was anxious enough already. "Three out of seven gone before we could even approach them. That's not coincidence."

"No, it's not." Claire pulled out the list, now creased and soft from handling. Four names remained. "The question is whether we keep going. Every approach is a risk, if one of these people reports us. "

"Then we're already compromised anyway." Claire studied the remaining names. "We didn't come this far to stop now."

• • •

The fourth name was Patricia Napper. She was a fifty-six-year-old career NSA employee who'd spent the last decade working on something called the Office of Compliance and Ethics, a bureaucratic backwater that most people in the intelligence community treated as a joke. The office existed, in theory, to ensure that NSA's operations stayed within legal boundaries. In practice, it served mainly to provide cover, rubber-stamping programs that had already been approved by people far above its pay grade.

Winters had flagged Napper as someone who took the job seriously. "Patricia actually reads the regulations," he'd said. "She believes in oversight. She's been raising concerns about SENTINEL for over a year, and she's been ignored every time. Sooner or later, that kind of frustration either breaks you or makes you willing to do something about it."

Claire found her at a church in Silver Spring during a Wednesday evening Bible study that Napper had attended for the past fifteen years. It was the kind of sleuthing that wouldn't show up in any database. It was the result of old-fashioned legwork. Claire had spent two days learning Napper's patterns before deciding this was the safest place to make contact.

The church was a modest brick building with a small parking lot and a sign that announced service times in both English and Spanish. Claire waited outside as the Bible study ended. She watched the participants trickle out in twos and threes, until a tall Black woman with close-cropped gray hair emerged alone, car keys already in her hand.

"Mrs. Napper?" Claire stepped forward, keeping her hands visible, her posture non-threatening. "My name is Claire Hensley. I'm a journalist. I wonder if I could have a few minutes of your time."

Napper abruptly stopped walking. Her face, illuminated by the parking lot lights, went through a rapid series of expressions: surprise, recognition, fear, and finally something that looked almost like resignation.

Her eyes darted around, and then she spoke, "I know who you are." Her voice was low, controlled, the voice of someone who had learned to keep her emotions in check. "I've been expecting someone like you for months. I just didn't think it would happen in a church parking lot."

"Would you prefer somewhere else?"

"I'd prefer not to have this conversation at all." But she didn't walk away. Instead, she glanced around, checking for observers with the same practiced caution that Claire had seen in Thomas Winters. "There's a diner two blocks east. It's open late. Sit in the back booth and order a piece of pie. I'll be there in twenty minutes."

She got into her car and drove away without another word.

• • •

The diner was exactly the kind of place Claire had hoped for, a relic from the 1970s with red vinyl booths, laminate tables, and a menu that featured coffee in three sizes and pie in seven flavors.

She sat in the back booth with her back to the wall, watching the door. She ordered a slice of apple and a cup of decaf. The diner was nearly empty other than a young couple in the front booth and an elderly man at the counter nursing a cup of coffee that had probably gone cold an hour ago. The fluorescent lights buzzed faintly overhead, casting everything in a pale, unflattering glow.

Napper arrived exactly twenty minutes later, as promised. She slid into the booth across from Claire, folded her hands on the table in front of her, and kept her expression carefully neutral.

"Before we begin," she said, "I need you to understand something. I have thirty-one years of federal service and a pension that I've earned. I have a husband with a heart condition and two grandchildren who I would like to watch grow up. I am not going to throw all of that away for a newspaper story."

"I understand."

"I don't think you do." Napper's eyes were steady and unflinching. "I've seen what happens to people who talk. Not just the obvious investigations, prosecutions, and revoked security clearances. The other things that can't be traced. The ways a life can fall apart without anyone ever being able to prove why."

"You're talking about SENTINEL."

A muscle twitched in Napper's jaw. "I'm not confirming or denying anything. I'm explaining why this conversation is dangerous for both of us."

"Then why did you come?"

The question hung in the air. Outside, a car passed on the empty street, its headlights sweeping briefly across the diner's windows. Napper watched it go, then turned back to Claire.

"Because I'm tired," she said. "I've spent fourteen months writing reports that no one reads, raising concerns that no one addresses, watching a program expand beyond anything that should be legal, and being told, every time, that it's not my place to question. That the people in charge know what they're doing. That national security requires sacrifices."

She leaned forward, her voice dropping.

"I joined the NSA because I believed in the mission. I believed that protecting this country meant following rules, respecting limits, and understanding that the Constitution isn't just a suggestion. I've spent my whole career trying to hold that line." Her voice cracked slightly. "Now I watch people I've worked with for decades pretend that the line doesn't exist. That it never existed. That anyone who remembers it is naïve, dangerous, or both."

Claire waited, letting the silence do its work.

"My oldest grandson is twelve," Napper continued. "He's a smart kid who wants to be an engineer. Last month, he asked me what I do for work, really do, not the sanitized version I usually give. I couldn't answer him. I couldn't tell him that I spend my days trying to stop something I don't have the power to stop. That I'm part of a system that's supposed to protect people like him, but that's turning into something that will control people like him."

"So, help me stop it."

"It's not that simple."

"I know it's not, but every story starts somewhere. Every exposure begins with someone who decides that the risk of silence is greater than the risk of speaking." Claire pushed her untouched pie aside. "I can't give you safety or promise that there won't be consequences, but I can promise that your voice won't be alone. There are others who feel what you feel, who see what you see. Together, you might be able to do what none of you can do separately."

Napper studied her then asked, "Who else have you talked to?"

"I can't tell you that. Not yet. Not until I know I can trust you."

"And how do you decide if you can trust me?"

"I don't. Not completely. I just decide if the risk is worth taking." Claire met her eyes. "Is it?"

• • •

Napper didn't give Claire documents; she was too careful about that, too aware of the digital trails that could link her to any leak. But she gave her something almost as valuable, context. As Claire listened to the institutional history of how SENTINEL had evolved and the internal debates that had been suppressed, she heard familiar echoes of potential vulnerabilities from past investigations. Claire was careful to create two distinct lists when Napper named other people inside the system who might be persuadable, and the names of those who were true believers best avoided. Both lists were essential.

Napper talked about Katherine Rennick with the weary familiarity of someone who had spent years working in her shadow. "Kate's genuinely brilliant. She believes that what she's building is necessary because the threats facing this country are so severe that normal constraints won't work." Napper looked pained, "Kate thinks history will vindicate her, even if the present condemns her."

"Do you think she's right?"

"I think she believes there's no other way." Napper shook her head. "The problem with zealots is that they can justify anything. Every abuse becomes a necessary evil, and every line crossed becomes a line that needed to be crossed. Eventually, they've gone so far there's no way back."

"You think Rennick has crossed that line?"

"She crossed it a long time ago. Most of the people around her crossed it with her." Napper's face hardened. "I think the ones who haven't crossed it yet are running out of time to decide which side they're on."

Claire was getting a clearer picture of the landscape. She now understood the factions within the consortium, the pressure points where the consensus was weakest, and the specific operations that had caused the most internal controversy. She also recognized one name that stood out. This person was someone Napper mentioned almost in passing, who hadn't been on Winters's list, but who might be the key to everything.

"If you want to understand how SENTINEL really works," Napper had said, "you need to talk to the engineers who built it." She paused as she considered who she might suggest. "There's a woman named Lisa Norman. She was one of the original ALTAR engineers before the acquisition. She's still at Nexus working on SENTINEL. From what I've heard, she's not happy about what her creation has become."

Claire added Lisa Norman to her list of possibles. Another door to knock on.

Napper left first. Claire waited ten minutes before walking back to her car through empty streets except for the occasional late-night dog walker. The weather made her want to hurry home and crawl into bed with a good book. Instead, she focused on the task ahead and one new bright spot.

Claire now had a new lead, an engineer who might understand SENTINEL from the inside in ways that none of the bureaucrats ever could.

• • •

She called Elise from one of the last pay phones remaining in the city. It was tucked into a corner of a side street close to Union Station where the restaurant crowds and late-night commuters provided cover.

When Elise answered, Claire was quick to let her know that Napper had talked. "She gave us a new name of an engineer at Nexus who had worked on ALTAR and now works on SENTINEL."

"That's the technical side," Elise said. "The part Seth Parker couldn't give us. If we can get an engineer to talk, it changes the game."

Elise tried to contain her excitement. "We'll get a better understanding of the system vulnerabilities and the limits. Not just what it does, but how it does it." Claire gripped the phone tighter. "Elise, this could be the piece we've been missing. Someone who can help us prove that the dangers SENTINEL poses are being turbocharged."

"Or someone who's being dangled as bait, just like Daniel warned about Parker."

"That's always the risk, but we can't let the risk paralyze us." Claire watched the crowds flow in and out of the station, individuals wrapped up in their lives, unaware of the invisible architecture that might home in on them. "We need to find Lisa Norman."

"I'll start digging. She was with ALTAR, so there might be traces for leverage in technical papers, conference presentations, something that gives us a way in."

"Be careful. If she's still working on SENTINEL at Nexus, she's probably being monitored more closely than anyone."

"I know." Elise sounded determined. "But that's true of everyone we're talking to. We're all being watched, Claire. The only question is whether we let that stop us."

"It won't."

"Then we keep going." A pause. "Get some sleep tonight. You sound exhausted."

"I am exhausted, but I don't think sleep is going to come easy."

"It never does when you're this deep in a story." Elise's voice softened. "Try anyway. We're going to need all our strength for what comes next."

Claire hung up and stood still for a moment. She knew she'd come to terms with the responsibility, the danger, the knowledge that every step forward was a step deeper into territory where the rules no longer applied.

But Elise was right. They couldn't let that stop them. She headed back to her car to drive home to a few hours of restless sleep before the work began again.

She finally exhaled when she crawled into bed. As she figured, sleep was elusive. She lay there ruminating. Seven doors; three closed before they could even knock.

A new, eighth door that might lead somewhere none of them had expected.

The investigation was growing. The picture was becoming clearer. Somewhere in the vast machinery of SENTINEL, something was watching, calculating, deciding what to do about two journalists who refused to stop asking questions.

CHAPTER FOURTEEN

The Architect

Lisa Norman was not easy to find.

Elise spent three days building a profile from fragments of old conference papers, archived LinkedIn pages, and a handful of academic citations from her pre-ALTAR work. The woman who emerged from this digital archaeology was brilliant and private. After ALTAR's collapse, Lisa Norman had retreated from public visibility so completely that finding her current address required the kind of detective work that bordered on surveillance itself.

"She is still at Nexus," Elise said, spreading printouts across her kitchen table. Claire sat across from her, nursing a cup of tea and munching on powdered sugar donuts, her favorite. "But she's not on their public-facing staff directory or listed in any of their recent contract disclosures. She's a ghost."

"That could mean she's working on something classified", Claire speculated.

"Or it could mean she's being protected. " Elise turned to her computer and tapped on a conference photo from six years ago showing a small woman at a podium who was gesturing at a slide filled with mathematical notation. "This is the most recent image I could find. She was presenting at an AI ethics symposium in San Francisco on behavioral modeling and what she referred to as the 'Boundaries of Consent.'"

Claire leaned forward for a closer look. Lisa Norman appeared to be in her late thirties, though the image quality made it hard to be certain. Her features were sharp and looked more angular with her dark hair pulled back in a practical ponytail. In the picture, she had a focused intensity that suggested someone who lived more in her mind than in the physical world. Claire wondered if that intensity masked the doubts of someone wrestling with the implications of their work.

"An ethics symposium," Claire said. "That's interesting, for someone involved in building behavioral manipulation systems."

"That's what caught my attention," Elise offered. "Most of the ALTAR engineers went dark after the scandal. They either changed careers or moved overseas for what they hoped would be a lower profile. The majority scrubbed their online presence, but Norman did the opposite. She went to a public forum and talked about ethical boundaries." Elise pulled out another sheet. "I found a transcript of part of her presentation. Listen to this: 'The systems we build reflect the values we hold. When we create technology capable of understanding human behavior at scale, we assume a responsibility that transcends commercial interests or institutional mandates. We become, in a very real sense, the architects of how people experience reality itself.'"

"That doesn't sound like someone who would be comfortable building SENTINEL."

"No, it doesn't." Elise set down the transcript. "Which is exactly why Napper thought she might talk."

• • •

They found her through her daughter.

It wasn't ideal, approaching someone through their family. Involving a family member crossed boundaries that Claire had always tried to respect. But Lisa Norman had made herself unreachable through normal channels, and time was not a luxury they possessed. Every day they waited was another day SENTINEL used to predict their next move into whatever windows of opportunity remained.

The daughter's name was Maya. She was seventeen years old, attending a prestigious STEM magnet school in Fairfax County, where she was apparently something of a prodigy. The young lady was impressive in her own right as captain of the robotics team and a winner of multiple science fair awards. She was already being recruited by MIT and Stanford. The apple, it seemed, had not fallen far from the tree.

Claire waited outside the school on Thursday afternoon. She tried to be inconspicuous, standing near the bus stop where Maya was scheduled to catch her ride home. Claire felt uncomfortable, almost predatory, watching teenagers pile out of the building in their favorite cliques. This wasn't journalism, this was closer to stalking. The fact that it was necessary didn't make it feel any less wrong.

Maya Norman was easy to spot. She had her mother's features, including the focus in her eyes and the same practical ponytail. She walked alone, earbuds in, not seeming to mind the heavy backpack slung over one shoulder. Claire took note of a robotics competition trophy tucked under her arm. Claire intercepted her before she reached the bus.

"Maya Norman?" Claire kept her voice gentle, non-threatening. "My name is Claire Hensley. I'm a journalist. I was hoping you could help me get a message to your mother."

Maya stopped, took a moment to remove her ear buds as her expression shifted from surprise to wariness in the space of a heartbeat. "My mom doesn't talk to journalists."

"I know. She's been very careful about that. But this is important, more important than she might realize." Claire held out a sealed envelope. "I'm not asking you to convince her of anything. I'm just asking you to give her this. She can decide what to do with it."

Maya didn't take the envelope. Her eyes, so like her mother's, studied Claire with an intelligence that seemed far too mature for seventeen. "You're the one who wrote about ALTAR."

"Yes."

"My mom cried when that story came out. She doesn't cry about anything." Maya's voice was tinged with anger or maybe grief. "Do you know what it's like to watch your parent realize that their life's work was used to hurt people?"

Claire felt the question like a physical blow. "No. I don't, and I'm sorry for whatever pain that story caused your family, but what's happening now is much worse. Your mother might be one of the only people who can help to stop it."

Around them, the after-school chaos continued. The ordinariness of buses loading, cars pulling up, and students shouting to each other across the parking lot felt surreal. Maya took some time to consider Claire's request against the backdrop of normal life that made this conversation about secret surveillance systems seem absurd.

"She won't thank me for this," Maya said finally. She took the envelope. "But I'll give it to her."

"That's all I'm asking."

Maya tucked the envelope into her backpack and headed for her bus without another word. Claire watched her go, feeling guilty for what she'd just done. Using a child as a messenger and knowing that she was reopening wounds that had barely healed. She knew she was asking a family to risk everything for a story that might never be published. It made her feel sick.

The things you do when the stakes are high enough, she thought as she walked away. The compromises you make with your principles. She wondered how many more she would have to make before this was over.

• • •

Lisa Norman's call came four days later.

Claire was in her office at the Post, pretending to work on a story about city council zoning disputes while reviewing the evidence they'd gathered so far. Her burner phone buzzed and displayed a number she didn't recognize, which meant either a wrong number or exactly the call she'd been waiting for.

"Ms. Hensley." The voice was quiet and precise, with the slight flatness of someone who had spent years training themselves to reveal nothing. "This is Lisa Norman. I received your letter."

Claire closed her office door and moved away from the window facing the bullpen. She flipped the on switch for the air purifier so its white noise would make surveillance harder. "Thank you for calling. I wasn't sure you would."

"I almost didn't. I've spent the last four years trying to put ALTAR behind me. Trying to convince myself that what I helped build wasn't as bad as the stories made it seem." A pause. "Your letter suggested that I've been lying to myself."

"I don't know what you've told yourself. I only know what the system you helped create has become."

"SENTINEL." Lisa said the name as though it left a bitter taste in her mouth. "I know about it. I've been working on it for the past two years."

Claire's heart stuttered. "You've been … "

"Working on it. Yes. Not by choice, or not entirely by choice." Lisa's voice dropped even lower. "When Nexus acquired ALTAR's assets, they made it very clear that my continued employment, and certain other considerations, depended on my cooperation. I told myself it would be different this time and that I could steer it in a better direction. I thought having someone with principles on the inside was better than leaving it to people without them."

"Was it? Different?"

The silence stretched so long that Claire thought the call might have dropped. When Lisa spoke again, her voice was barely audible.

"No. It's worse. So much worse than ALTAR ever was." A shaky breath. "ALTAR manipulated people into believing synthetic relationships were better for their well-being. It was invasive and unethical, and I will never forgive myself for my role in creating such a system. But it operated within boundaries. It had limits, even if those limits were defined by commercial interests rather than ethics."

"SENTINEL doesn't have limits?"

"SENTINEL doesn't have limits because it doesn't need them. It's trying to control the entire information ecosystem. Every threat it neutralizes teaches it how to neutralize threats more effectively. Every person it isolates gives it data on how to isolate people more efficiently." Lisa's voice cracked. "The people running it don't see human beings anymore. They see data points, variables, and systems to be optimized and threats to be managed."

"Will you help us expose it?"

Another pregnant pause. "I need to think." She stopped. "Can we meet? There are things I can't say over the phone, even on a burner. There are things you need to understand about how SENTINEL works before you go any further."

"Name the time and place."

"Tomorrow at 4:00 PM. There's a hiking trail on the Virginia side of Great Falls Park, the Billy Goat Trail, Section C. It's too cold for most hikers this time of year. It will be getting dark, and the terrain makes electronic surveillance difficult." She paused. "Come alone, and Ms. Hensley? If I see anyone else, or if I sense anything wrong, I will disappear and you will never hear from me again."

"I understand."

"I hope you do. Because what I'm about to tell you could get us both killed."

The line went dead.

• • •

The trees had shed most of their leaves, their bare branches sketching dark lines against an overcast sky. The Potomac rushed over its ancient rocks with a sound like continuous thunder, drowning out the smaller noises of the forest. Claire arrived an hour early, parked at the Visitor Center, and walked along the paved path on the way to the trail. At every turn, she checked behind her, although the park seemed void of visitors.

Claire couldn’t help but appreciate the powerful Potomac River and the waterfalls she passed along the way to the forest. The water level, lower than in spring, exposed the huge boulders and rocks that were a potential source of fatal danger for anyone who got too close to the water’s edge and fell in. A metaphorical reminder of caution from Mother Nature?

She found the spot Lisa had described, a rocky outcropping overlooking the river, accessible only by scrambling over boulders that would be treacherous for anyone not paying attention. It was exactly the kind of place where you could see anyone approaching long before they arrived. Exactly the kind of place someone with secrets would choose.

Lisa Norman was already there when Claire arrived, sitting on a flat rock with her back against a larger boulder, watching the trail with the wary alertness of a prey animal. She was smaller than the conference photo had suggested, barely five feet tall, with the kind of slight frame that made her look fragile until you noticed the wiry strength in her arms and the steel in her eyes.

"You're early," Lisa said.

"So are you."

"I've been here awhile. Watching." She gestured to a spot on a nearby rock. "Sit. We don't have much time, and there's a lot you need to understand."

Claire sat, the cold stone seeping through her jeans. Below them, the Potomac churned and roared, indifferent to the secrets being shared on its banks.

"When I designed ALTAR's core architecture," Lisa began, "I was trying to solve what I thought was a beautiful problem. Human connections are messy, unpredictable, and often painful. I wanted to understand the patterns beneath it, the mathematical structures that govern how people form attachments, how they fall in love, how they build trust." She picked up a small stone and turned it over in her fingers. "I never intended for it to be used to manipulate people. The original design was to research ways to smooth out human relationships."

"But EmotiMetrics had other ideas."

"EmotiMetrics saw dollar signs. They took my research and weaponized it. They turned it into a system for exploiting the patterns I'd discovered that made people vulnerable to manipulation." Lisa threw the stone toward the river. It disappeared into the churning water without a sound. "When your story broke, I felt relief. Finally, I thought, it's over, and people will see what they built and be horrified. I was sure they'd tear it down."

"But they didn't tear it down."

"No. They sold it. To people who saw exactly what it could become." Lisa turned to face Claire, her eyes haunted. "SENTINEL isn't just an evolution of ALTAR. It's a fundamental transformation. ALTAR was about prediction, understanding what people would feel, what they would do. SENTINEL is about surveillance and control. It doesn't just predict behavior, it shapes it. It's optimized to manipulate the information environment so that people make the choices SENTINEL wants them to make."

"How does it work? Technically?"

Lisa was quiet for a moment, organizing her thoughts. "Imagine you have a map of every connection in a person's life. Every relationship, every information source, and every institution they interact with become data points. Now imagine you can see not just the connections, but the influence pathways, how information flows through those connections, how it shapes beliefs and decisions."

"A social graph," Claire said. "But more detailed."

"Much more detailed," Lisa affirmed. "SENTINEL doesn't just map connections; it models the psychological dynamics of each relationship. It knows which people you trust, how much you trust them, and what kinds of information you're likely to accept from each data source. It builds what we call an 'influence topology', a map of how ideas propagate through your personal network."

"And then it manipulates the topology."

"Exactly. If SENTINEL wants you to believe something, or stop believing something, it doesn't come at you directly, it works through your network. It might plant information with a friend you trust, or discredit a source you rely on, or introduce doubt through channels you'd never suspect. By the time you change your mind, you think it was your idea. You think you reached the conclusion yourself, through your own reasoning."

Claire felt the dread of facing a fearsome invisible foe. "That's what happened to my sources. The ones who stopped talking to me."

"Probably. SENTINEL would have identified everyone in your professional network. It would have modeled the influence relationships, who trusted whom, who would be susceptible to what kinds of pressure. Then it would have worked through those channels to isolate you. A rumor here, a warning there, a convenient coincidence that made you seem unreliable." Lisa shook her head. "You wouldn't have seen it happening because it wasn't a single action. It was a thousand small adjustments, coordinated across your entire network."

"Death by a thousand cuts."

"That's what the operators call the neutralization protocol. It's designed to be invisible. You won't find virtual fingerprints or evidence that anything was done at all. The target just gradually loses access and their credibility. At some point, they lose the ability to function effectively. Everyone around them attributes the changes to bad luck or poor choices."

• • •

Lisa explained the technical architecture of SENTINEL with its machine learning models that process behavioral data. She detailed the integration points with other government systems and the feedback loops that allowed the system to learn and adapt from each operation. She went on to describe the organizational structure and detail how Katherine Rennick had built a network of true believers within the intelligence community. Very few were brave enough to push back against a system that anticipated, identified, and eliminated threats to its power. It's how the program had grown from a pilot project into something that touched nearly every aspect of federal information management.

"The thing is," Lisa said, "it is an effective national security weapon. SENTINEL has prevented terrorist attacks and disrupted foreign influence operations. It's identified threats that human analysts would have missed. That's how they justify it. Every abuse, every overreach, every instance of human collateral damage is weighed against the threats that were stopped. The math always comes out in their favor, because they control the math."

"What about oversight? Congress? The courts?"

Lisa laughed, a bitter, hollow sound. "What oversight? The program is classified at a level that excludes most of Congress. The courts have no jurisdiction because nothing SENTINEL does is technically illegal. It works through existing systems, authorities, and existing institutional relationships. It doesn't break laws. It just makes sure that the laws don't apply to the people it protects."

"Then how do we stop it?"

"I don't know if we can." Lisa met Claire's eyes with a look of despair. "SENTINEL is designed to prevent exactly what you're trying to do. It monitors for threats to itself. It predicts opposition before it forms and neutralizes the resistance before it becomes effective." She paused. "The fact that we're having this conversation means I've already been flagged. Probably you too. We're both in the system now, being tracked, being modeled, being assessed."

"Then why are you talking to me?"

Lisa was quiet for a long moment, watching the river flow past below them. When she spoke, her voice was barely audible above the water's roar.

"Because my daughter asked me to." She turned to look at Claire. "Maya came home with your letter, and she asked me what ALTAR was really about and what I really did. I had to tell her, not the sanitized version I've been telling myself, but the truth. I helped build something that hurt people and I've spent the last four years working on something even worse."

"What did she say?"

"She asked me if I was going to do anything about it." Lisa's voice cracked. "She's seventeen years old. She believes that people can change things. That truth matters and standing up for what's right is worth the risk." She wiped her eyes with the back of her hand as the tears began to pour out. "How do I tell her that I'm too afraid? SENTINEL is so big and powerful as well as entrenched. How do I teach her to accept a world where the bad guys always win?"

"So, you decided to fight."

"I decided to try. I don't know if it will matter or if anything I can give you will be enough to make a difference, but I can't look my daughter in the eye and tell her I didn't even try." Lisa reached into her jacket and pulled out a small USB drive. "This is everything I have. Technical documentation, internal communications and operational records. It's not complete. They've gotten better at compartmentalization, but it's enough to prove that SENTINEL exists and what it does."

Claire took the drive carefully. "Lisa, if they find out you gave me this… "

"I know." Lisa stood, brushing dust from her pants. "I have plans. Maya and I will be on a flight out of the country within seventy-two hours. I have money in accounts they don't know about, contacts in places SENTINEL can't easily reach." She paused. "I'm not naive. I know there's no guarantee of safety, but I've made my choice. Now you have to make yours."

"What do you mean?"

"I mean that the moment you start using that information, SENTINEL will know. It will escalate. It will come after you with everything it has." Lisa's eyes were hard now, determined. "You have to decide if you're willing to risk everything, your career, your relationships, maybe your life, to expose something that most people would rather not know about."

Claire looked at the USB drive in her hand. Such a small thing, with such enormous consequences.

"I've already decided," Claire answered. " I decided when my sources started disappearing and my stories started falling apart. I decided every time I looked in the mirror and had to choose either accepting what was happening or fighting back. I realized if I have to face myself every day, I need to be true to who I am"

"Then we understand each other." Lisa offered her hand. Claire took it. The grip was brief but firm. They were two women bound by a shared purpose, about to step into a battle that neither might survive.

"Good luck, Ms. Hensley."

"Good luck, Dr. Norman."

Lisa turned and began picking her way down the rocks toward a different trail, one that would take her to a different parking lot and a different exit. Claire watched her go until she disappeared into the gray tangle of bare trees and winter shadows.

Then she slipped the USB drive into her pocket and started the long walk back to her car, carrying evidence that could change everything, or destroy everyone she loved.

The river roared behind her, indifferent to it all.

CHAPTER FIFTEEN

The Evidence

They gathered in Elise's apartment at midnight. The city seemed quiet outside the RF-blocking curtains.

Claire had driven a circuitous route from Great Falls, doubling back twice, switching cars once with a rental she'd arranged under a friend's name. The distinction between paranoia and prudence had ceased to matter. The USB drive radiated danger with every mile.

Elise met her at the door with the same tense alertness that had become their default state. No words were exchanged until they were inside with the locks engaged and the white noise generator humming its protective static.

"You got it?" Elise asked.

Claire pulled out the drive and set it on the kitchen table between them.

"Lisa Norman gave me everything she had. She said this drive includes technical documentation, internal communications as well as operational records." Claire sat down heavily, the exhaustion of the past days finally catching up with her. "She's leaving the country with her daughter. They'll be gone within seventy-two hours."

"Smart." Elise picked up the drive, turning it over in her fingers. "The moment we start using this, SENTINEL will know where it came from. She's right to run."

"She told me something else." Claire met Elise's eyes. "She said the moment we act on this information, SENTINEL will escalate its neutralizing protocols. It will come after us with everything it has."

"We knew that was coming."

"Knowing and experiencing are different things." Claire rubbed her eyes. "I've been thinking about it the whole drive back. What does escalation really mean? Are we all ready for what happens next?"

Elise was quiet for a moment. Then she walked to the window opening a side of the curtain just enough to look down at the empty street below.

"I've also been thinking about what we're asking people to risk," she said." Daniel Okafor has a family, Paula Weber is trying to rebuild her career, and Robert Baskin," She stopped, shook her head. "We've been so focused on exposing SENTINEL that I'm not sure we've fully reckoned with the cost. Not just to us, but to everyone we've brought into this."

"Are you having second thoughts?"

"No." Elise let the curtain fall back into place and turned to face Claire. "I just want us to go in with clear eyes. We're not just journalists anymore or investigators. We're asking people to go to war against something that has never lost."

"Then let's make sure we win."

Elise managed a small smile. "That's the Claire I remember." She held up the USB drive. "Let's see what Dr. Norman gave us."

• • •

They spent the next six hours going through the files.

Elise worked on her air-gapped laptop, the one she'd bought with cash years ago and never connected to the internet. The screen's blue glow illuminated her face as she navigated folder after folder of documents, each one revealing another piece of architecture they'd tried to understand.

The technical documentation was dense, filled with mathematical notation and systems diagrams that would take weeks to fully comprehend, but the broad strokes were clear enough, and the details illustrated everything Lisa had described at Great Falls.

SENTINEL operated on three interconnected layers. The first was data collection that included feeds from social media platforms, telecommunications providers, financial institutions, and dozens of government databases. The system ingested billions of data points daily, building and updating profiles on millions of Americans.

The second layer showed how their machine learning models metabolized the raw data into behavioral predictions. These models estimated how individuals would respond to various stimuli with frightening accuracy. It predicted what information they'd find persuasive and which relationships they relied on for guidance and support.

The third layer suggested actions to take, the operational protocols that translated analysis into intervention. This was where SENTINEL became truly dangerous. It didn't just watch and predict. It reached into people's lives and changed things, nudging the information environment in ways that produced desired outcomes.

"Look at this," Elise said, pulling up a document titled *INFLUENCE PATHWAY OPTIMIZATION*. "This is the algorithm that determines how to isolate a target. It maps their entire trust network, identifies the most efficient intervention points, and generates a sequenced action plan."

Claire leaned over her shoulder to read. The document was written in the dry, clinical language of technical specifications, but the implications were anything but dry.

Phase 1: Trust Erosion. Introduce contradictory information through secondary trusted sources. Objective: Create doubt regarding target's reliability without direct attribution.

Phase 2: Network Degradation. Systematic reduction of target's professional relationships through coordinated intervention across institutional channels. Objective: Limit target's access to platforms and resources.

Phase 3: Capability Neutralization. Escalated measures as required based on target's continued resistance. Options include: financial disruption, legal complications, health interventions, and terminal protocols.

"Terminal protocols," Claire repeated. "That's what they call it when they kill someone."

"Clinical language for murder." Elise feigned control, but Claire could see her hands trembling slightly on the keyboard. "They've turned assassination into a flowchart."

Claire asked what by now was becoming obvious, "And this has all been approved? There are people who signed off on this?"

Elise navigated to another folder, this one contained internal communications. A paper trail of bureaucratic complicity. She scrolled past emails, memos, and meeting notes stopping on one thread that caught her eye.

"Here." She pulled up an email thread dated eight months earlier. The sender was Katherine Rennick. The recipients were a distribution list labeled SENTINEL OVERSIGHT COMMITTEE.

Re: Mercer Situation

The asset has been neutralized. Terminal protocol was executed successfully with no attributable indicators. Local law enforcement has classified the incident as accidental. Recommend closing the file and moving resources to priority targets.

Claire felt sick. "She's talking about Jason Mercer. The man with twelve years of sobriety who supposedly died drunk."

"And she's talking about it like she's closing a ticket on a technical problem that was solved." Elise scrolled through more emails. "There are dozens like this. Maybe hundreds. People whose lives were destroyed or ended, all discussed in the same bureaucratic language you'd use for a software update."

"This is what we needed. We have them." Claire straightened up, something fierce kindling in her chest. "This is proof. Not circumstantial evidence or anonymous sources. This is Katherine Rennick in her own words, authorizing murder."

"It's proof if we can get it published. If we can get it in front of people who matter." Elise closed the laptop and rubbed her eyes. "That's where it gets complicated."

• • •

Dawn was breaking over the city when they finally stopped to rest.

Claire lay on Elise's couch, too wired to sleep but too exhausted to keep working. Images of the documents swam behind her closed eyes, flowcharts of destruction, emails authorizing death, the cold machinery of a system designed to eliminate anyone who threatened it.

"We need a publication strategy," Claire said, as she stared at the ceiling. "If we give this to just one paper, SENTINEL will find a way to kill the story before it runs. If it's everywhere at once it's harder to suppress. We need multiple outlets and a coordinated release time and day."

"Daniel's been working on that," Elise said from her armchair. "He thinks he has three outlets that might be willing to coordinate. The Post might be interested; they've been burned by government surveillance stories before and they're hungry for vindication. There's also a European consortium that's been doing good work on transatlantic intelligence sharing."

Elise paused before adding. "There is another problem. The documents we have are extremely classified. Publishing them could expose Lisa Norman as the source, even if she's already out of the country. Publishing them could expose us to prosecution under the Espionage Act."

"Since when has that stopped us?"

"It hasn't, but we need to be smart about this." Elise stood and walked to the window again. It had become a habit, Claire realized, a way of checking that the world outside still existed. "We need to verify everything independently before we publish. We need lawyers. We need to make sure that every claim we make can be defended in court."

"SENTINEL won't wait for us to build a legal defense."

Elise turned from the window and began to pace. "No, it won't, which is why we need to move fast and cautiously. If we make one mistake, if there's just one piece of evidence that doesn't check out, they'll use it to discredit the entire story."

Claire's normie phone buzzed, not the burner, but her regular phone. It was one she still carried for appearances. She glanced at the screen and felt her blood turn to ice.

"Claire." Elise had seen her expression change. "What is it?"

"A text from my editor." Claire's voice sounded strangled in her throat. "He wants to see me in his office first thing this morning. He says it's urgent."

"That could be anything."

"At six in the morning? After I've been unreachable for two days?" Claire sat up, her exhaustion suddenly forgotten. "SENTINEL is moving."

"You don't know that."

"I know how this works. We've seen the playbook." She gestured at the laptop. "Phase one: trust erosion. What better way to erode trust than to turn my own editor against me?"

Elise continued pacing. "Then don't go, stay here. We'll figure out another way."

"If I don't go, it looks like I'm running and that is ammunition." Claire stood and began gathering her things. "Besides, I need to know what they're planning and what the angle is. If we can understand their approach, maybe we can counter it."

"Claire…"

"I'll be careful." She paused at the door. "But if something happens, if I don't check in by noon, assume the worst. Get the documents to Daniel and get them published, whatever it takes."

"Nothing is going to happen."

"Probably not, but if it does, " Claire met her eyes. "Promise me you'll finish this. Promise me you won't let them win."

Elise held her gaze for a long moment. "I promise."

Claire nodded once, then stepped out into the predawn light.

• • •

The Post building was quiet at seven in the morning.

Most of the newsroom wouldn't arrive for another hour, but the lights were already on in Marcus Quinn's office. Her editor sat behind his desk, his face drawn with the tension of a man who was about to do something he didn't want to do. He wasn't alone. With him were two people Claire didn't recognize sitting in the chairs across from him. The man and woman were both dressed in the anonymous dark suits of federal employees.

Marcus stood when she entered but didn't greet her other than a direct suggestion: "Please, close the door."

She did, then stood with her back against it, making no move to sit. "You wanted to see me."

"These people are from the Justice Department," Marcus said. His tone was measured. He chose every word with deliberate precision. "They have some concerns about your recent activities."

"Concerns?" Claire looked at the two federal employees. The man was middle-aged with the bland competence of a career bureaucrat. The woman was younger, lithe and athletic looking. She watched Claire with the evaluating gaze of a predator assessing prey. "What kind of concerns?" Claire challenged.'

The woman spoke. "Ms. Hensley, we have reason to believe you've been in contact with individuals who have access to classified national security information. We'd like to discuss those contacts with you."

"I'm a journalist. I talk to a lot of people."

"We're aware of that." The woman's smile didn't reach her eyes. "We're also aware that some of those conversations may have involved the unauthorized disclosure of classified material. That's a federal crime, Ms. Hensley. For both the person disclosing and the person receiving."

"Are you threatening me?"

"We're informing you of the legal landscape." The man spoke now, his voice smooth and reasonable. "We're not here to make accusations. We're here to have a conversation. To understand your activities and intentions. To see if there's a way to resolve this situation without it becoming... adversarial."

Claire looked at Marcus, who had sat back down and was staring at his desk like he wished he could disappear into it. "Did you invite these people here, or did they invite themselves?"

"They came to me with concerns about stories that might be based on illegally obtained information." Marcus said, still not meeting her eyes. 'They mentioned that stories based on illegally obtained information could trigger the paper's legal exposure."

"What stories? I haven't published anything."

"Not yet." The woman leaned forward. "But we know you're working on something. We know you've been meeting with people who have access to information they shouldn't be sharing. We know you've been asking questions about programs that don't officially exist."

"If those programs don't officially exist, how would you know what questions I've been asking about them?"

A flicker of something crossed the woman's face, irritation perhaps, or grudging respect. "Ms. Hensley, let's not play games. You're a talented journalist with a distinguished career. It would be a shame to see that career end in a federal courtroom."

"Is that the offer? Drop the story or face prosecution?"

"The offer," the man said, "is cooperation. Help us understand what you know and where you got it. Work with us instead of against us. In return, we can ensure that any legal complications are... minimized."

Claire felt something cold settle in her chest, not fear exactly, but crystalline clarity. This was the moment of choice. The point where she could step back and protect the career she'd spent years building. Or she could keep going.

"I appreciate you coming here," she said. "I appreciate the Post's concern for my well-being. But I'm not going to discuss my sources, my methods, or my stories with anyone from the Justice Department." She straightened, pulling herself to her full height. "That's not how journalism works."

"Ms. Hensley… "

"If you want to prosecute me, go ahead. I'll see you in court. In the meantime, I have work to do."

She turned and opened the door.

"Claire." Marcus' voice stopped her. She looked back. Her editor was finally meeting her eyes, and there was something in his expression she couldn't quite read. "Be careful. Please."

"I always am."

She walked out of the office, past the empty desks, down the elevator and out into the morning streets. Her hands were steady, but her heart was racing. Amazingly, her mind was clear.

Phase one had begun. SENTINEL was moving against her. It was time to move faster.

• • •

She called Elise from a payphone two blocks from the Post.

"They came for me," she said, when Elise answered. "Two people from the Justice Department were waiting for me in Marcus's office. They know we have something."

"What did they want?"

"Cooperation and sources. The usual." Claire watched the street, checking for anyone who might be watching her. The paranoia felt justified now. "I told them no."

"Of course you did. Claire, if they're moving this fast, it means they know more than we thought. If Lisa has already left the country, they probably suspect we have documents."

"Or someone talked." Claire's mind raced through the possibilities. "We need to accelerate our timeline and get the documents to Daniel today."

"That's risky. If we publish without proper verification…"

"If we don't publish soon, there won't be anything to verify. They'll find a way to discredit us, arrest us, or worse." Claire gripped the phone tighter. "Lisa warned me this would happen. She said the moment we acted; SENTINEL would escalate. Well, we've acted and now we're in a race."

"Then we run the race." Elise's voice was steady, determined. "I'll contact Daniel. You get somewhere safe where they can't find you easily. We'll regroup this afternoon and figure out our next move."

"There's something else." Claire hesitated. "The way Marcus looked at me when I left, I don't think he's completely on their side. I think he's scared, but I don't think he's turned."

"You want to trust him?"

"I want to give him a chance. When the story breaks, we're going to need allies inside the mainstream press who can vouch for our credibility." Claire took a breath. "Marcus and I have worked together for years. He's not a hero, but he's not a villain either. He's just a man trying to protect his paper and his people."

"That's a risk."

"Everything is at risk now." Claire smiled grimly. "But some risks are worth taking."

She hung up and stepped back onto the street. Activity was picking up as the city hummed with the business of another day. People hurried along worried about being late for early morning meetings and other concerns that seemed so important until they weren't.

Claire envied their oblivion. They were unaware of the gathering power of the net surrounding them, monitoring their communications, mapping their relationships, making decisions about who succeeded and who needed to be stopped.

If Claire had anything to say about it, soon the whole world would know.

She hailed a cab and gave an address on the other side of the city. Claire needed to lay low. She needed to prepare for the battle that had finally begun.

SENTINEL had made its first serious move.

Time to engage.

CHAPTER SIXTEEN

Counterstrike

Seth Parker knew something was wrong the moment he pulled into the Nexus parking garage.

His usual spot on the third level was taken, not by another car, but by a pair of orange cones that hadn't been there yesterday. A small meaningless thing in isolation, but Seth had spent fifteen years in network security, and he'd learned to read patterns the way other people read facial expressions. Small disruptions in routine were often the first sign that something larger was shifting.

He parked on the fourth level instead and sat for a moment, hands on the steering wheel trying to quiet the anxiety that had been building in his chest for days. Ever since he'd met Claire Hensley in the cemetery and handed over the USB drive with everything he'd been able to gather, he tried to ignore a growing sense of dread.

He'd known it was a risk. He'd weighed that risk against the alternative of spending the rest of his career pretending he didn't know what his systems were being used for. He decided he'd live with the consequences. Knowing you've made the right choice doesn't make it any easier when the consequences start arriving.

His phone buzzed. A text from his daughter Emma:

Dad, something weird happened. Two men came to my apartment asking about you. They said they were from your company's HR department. They wanted to know if you'd been acting differently lately. I didn't tell them anything. What's going on?

Seth stared at the message. They were coming for him, and they were using his daughter to do it.

He typed back quickly: *Stay away from the apartment today. Go to your friend's place, the one in Baltimore. Don't tell anyone where you are. I'll explain everything soon. I love you.*

He sat in his car, staring at the concrete walls of the parking garage, trying to decide what to do next.

• • •

The group met in a warehouse in Northeast D.C.

Daniel Okafor had found an abandoned printing facility that had been sitting empty for years, waiting for a developer who never came. The building had no power, no security cameras, and walls thick enough to block most electronic surveillance. It was cold and dark, and it smelled of mold, but it was safe. As safe as anywhere could be now.

They gathered in what had once been the main production floor, sitting on overturned crates in a circle of flashlight beams. Claire and Elise, Daniel, Paula Weber, Robert Baskin, and Thomas Winters, the Georgetown professor, who had insisted on being present despite the risk. Patricia Napper was also present. She had driven in from Maryland.

Seven people and seven targets, a conspiracy of the hunted, gathered in the dark to plan their counterattack.

"They came for me this morning," Claire said. She'd briefed the others on her encounter at the Post. Recounting it made it feel more real. "Two people from the Justice Department tried to intimidate me after working my editor over with potential threats about legal action. They know we have something."

"Not just you." Daniel's voice was grim. "I got a call from an old contact at the Times. They've received inquiries, official and unofficial, about any stories involving classified surveillance programs. Someone is putting pressure on every major outlet."

"They visited my husband at his office," Patricia said quietly. "They asked him about my mental state and whether I'd been under extra work stress lately." She shook her head. "Thirty-one years of loyal service, and they're trying to make me sound unstable."

"It's the playbook." Elise pulled out a sheaf of printouts from Lisa Norman's documents. "Trust erosion. They'll work to seed doubt with everyone connected to us. They intend to make it harder for anyone to believe us when we publish."

Robert Baskin had been quiet since arriving, his face drawn with worry. "I got a call from the university today. My research grant is under review for some kind of compliance issue they can't quite explain." He laughed bitterly. "A compliance issue that didn't exist until I started talking to you people."

"They're targeting all of us," Winters said. He appeared calm, the professor in him treating this as an intellectual problem to be solved. "Classic suppression strategy. Divide and demoralize. Make each target feel isolated, make them think they're the only one being pressured. The hope is that someone cracks, runs, or decides the cost is too high."

"Will anyone here crack?" Claire asked. Her eyes moved from face to face, reading the fear and uncertainty that each of them carried.

Silence. The flashlight beams wavered as people shifted on their makeshift seats. Paula broke the silence. "They already took my career once. They don't get to take my self-respect too."

"I won't," said Daniel. "I've been waiting for a chance to fight back since they shut down my investigation. This is that chance."

"I'm in," said Robert. "If I'm going to lose my grant anyway, I might as well lose it for something that matters."

One by one, they affirmed their commitment.

"Then we need a plan," Claire said. "We also need to think about what happens after publication. How are we going to protect ourselves, and how will we protect each other?"

• • •

They spent the next three hours building their strategy.

Daniel laid out the publication approach. He'd secured tentative commitments from three outlets: the NY Times (through a sympathetic deputy editor), the Washington Post, and a European investigative consortium called the International Reporting Project. Each would receive the same package of documents to be published simultaneously. The goal was to create a wave too big to suppress. If one outlet was blocked or pressured, the others would carry the story forward.

"We will release in seventy-two hours," Daniel said. "That gives us time for basic verification without giving SENTINEL time to fully neutralize our sources."

"Seventy-two hours isn't enough for proper verification," Robert objected. "If we miss anything, they'll have just what they need to discredit the entire story."

"Then we prioritize," Elise said. "We focus on smoking guns. Katherine Rennick's emails, the operational protocols, and the evidence of terminal actions are straightforward. The technical documentation can come later, once the main story is out and people are paying attention."

Patricia said she was committed, but her voice sounded shaky when she asked, "What about legal protection? We're all exposed if they decide to prosecute."

"I have a lawyer," Claire said. "She's a media defense specialist. She's handled whistleblower cases before. I've already briefed her on the broad strokes. She's willing to represent anyone who needs it."

"Pro bono?"

"For now. She believes in the case." Claire paused. "She also said we should prepare for the worst. Asset freezes, travel restrictions, possibly even detention. SENTINEL's reach extends into law enforcement. They could make our lives very difficult very quickly."

"Which is why we need exit plans," Winters said. "Each of us should have a way out, somewhere to go if things get too hot. Whatever you can arrange. I don't want to sound too dramatic, but this is deadly serious, and we need to be safe to operate."

"That sounds like running," Paula said.

"It sounds like surviving." Winters's voice was gentle but firm. "We're not useful to anyone if we're in prison or dead. Sometimes the best resistance is staying free to fight another day."

Elise and Claire glanced at each other. It was obvious they had the same thoughts. They had escaped before and left everything behind. Here they were again.

The conversation continued around logistics, contingencies, and fallback positions. They decided who would hold copies of the documents. They planned on how to communicate if their usual channels were compromised. It was hard to face, but they strategized on what to do if one of them was taken into custody.

As they talked, Claire found herself studying each face in the glow of their flashlights. These people had been strangers a few weeks ago. Now they were her co-conspirators and allies. They were her fellow targets who had risked everything to be here. Each of them had decided that the truth was worth more than their safety.

It was, she thought, a remarkable thing. In a world of surveillance and manipulation, in a society where every relationship could be exploited, these people had chosen to trust each other. That had to count for something.

• • •

As they were wrapping up, Elise's burner phone buzzed with an incoming call from a number she didn't recognize. She hesitated, then put the call on speaker.

"Ms. Marston." The speaker was professional with the clipped diction of someone used to giving orders. "My name is Agent Ryan Cross. I believe you know who I am."

Elise's eyes met Claire's despite the dim lighting. Claire nodded in acknowledgment. She'd told Elise about Cross, his warning, and her uncertainty about what side he was on.

"I've heard your name," Elise said carefully. "I'm not sure I know anything else about you."

"That's fair. I haven't earned your trust." To Claire, Cross sounded urgent in a way that he hadn't been when they had spoken at the FBI field office. "I need you to listen to me very carefully. You're in danger, all of you. More than you realize." Claire signaled for Elise to continue the conversation.

"We're aware of the danger."

"No, you're not. SENTINEL has escalated the pressure on your sources. The visits from Justice were phase one. Phase two started an hour ago."

Elise felt her stomach drop. "What does phase two look like?"

"Seth Parker was arrested forty-five minutes ago on espionage charges. He's being held without bail at an undisclosed location." Elise listened intently; was there a legit note of anger in Cross? "They're not playing games. They're going to take down everyone connected to this until there's no one left to tell the story."

"How do you know this?"

"Because I'm still inside the system with access to information I shouldn't have. I just got the order to bring you in for questioning. I'm choosing to ignore it at my own peril."

Elise looked around at the seven faces looking back at her with wide eyes and tense expressions. "Why are you telling us this?"

"Because I've spent three years watching SENTINEL destroy people who didn't deserve it. I'm tired of being a tool." Cross's voice hardened. "Seth Parker was my friend. We worked together years ago, and I know he is a good man. He doesn't deserve to be thrown into a black hole because he grew a conscience."

"What do you want us to do?"

"Get your story out now. Tonight, if possible. Every hour you wait is another hour for them to eliminate your sources, seize your evidence, and close down your options." What he said next surprised them all. "And Ms. Marston? When this is over, assuming any of us are still standing, I want to tell my side of the story. I want people to know that not everyone in the system went along willingly."

"I'll keep that in mind."

"Do that. And be careful. They know more than you think. They always do."

Cross hung up.

Elise lowered her phone and took stock of the frozen faces around her. "They're moving faster than we expected."

A ripple of shock continued to reverberate through the group. Parker was their inside source, the one who had started everything. If they could take him, they could take anyone.

"Seventy-two hours is too long," Daniel said. "We need to publish tomorrow. Maybe sooner."

"We're not ready," Robert protested. "What about the verification?"

"We're as ready as we're going to get." Claire stood, her decision made. "We publish what we have. We talked about this. We can fill in the technical gaps once we've verified them. If we wait, we'll never publish at all."

"And if the narrative has holes? If they find something they can use to discredit us?"

"We'll make the pressure to publish part of our narrative and describe the unfolding nature of their campaign against us. We let people know there is more to the story that involves technical details we will publish once the details are verified." Claire looked around the circle, meeting each pair of eyes in turn. "We didn't come this far to stop because we're scared. We came this far because we believed the truth matters. Does anyone here no longer believe that?"

Silence. Then, one by one, heads nodded in agreement. No one was giving up.

"Then we have work to do." Claire grabbed her bag. "Daniel, contact your outlets and tell them we're moving up the timeline. Elise, let's get those documents ready for distribution. The rest of you, find somewhere safe and stay there until we're published. Once the story is out, we'll all be safer in the spotlight; in the meantime, we're targets."

The group disappeared into the cold night. They had less than twenty-four hours to dig in or lose everything.

Claire was the last to leave. She glanced around the empty production floor, surrounded by the echoes of machines that had once churned out newspapers by the thousands as she came to terms with what they were about to do.

In a few hours, they would light a match. The explosion that followed would reshape the landscape of American power, or it would destroy them all.

There was no middle ground anymore. There never had been.

She walked out into the darkness, leaving the past behind, and headed toward a future that no one could predict.

CHAPTER SEVENTEEN

The Director

Katherine Rennick hadn't slept in thirty-six hours.

She stood at the window of her office on the seventh floor of NSA headquarters, watching the pre-dawn darkness that blanketed Fort Meade. In a few hours, the building would come alive with the controlled chaos of the intelligence community, analysts streaming through security checkpoints, briefings convening in windowless rooms, the endless machinery of national security grinding forward. But for now, in these quiet hours before dawn, she had the building almost to herself.

A stranger might be unsettled by Katherine's ability to reveal nothing in her facial expressions or body language. Years of discipline honed her skill to reveal nothing, unless she chose to. She cultivated that blankness over three decades, learning to use her expressions as a tool as precise as any piece of tradecraft. It served her well in meetings, in negotiations, and the delicate dance of power that defined life at her level.

But alone, in that pre-dawn morning, she wondered what that blankness had cost her.

Her phone buzzed. She glanced at the update from the operations center. *HENSLEY/MARSTON PACKAGE CONFIRMED IN TRANSIT TO MULTIPLE OUTLETS. ESTIMATED TIME TO PUBLICATION: 12-18 HOURS.*

Katherine returned to staring out of the window. So, it was happening. Despite the pressure campaigns, the legal threats, and the carefully orchestrated isolation, Claire Hensley and her people had managed to assemble something publishable. They were going to try to expose SENTINEL.

She wasn't sure what she felt, anger or fear. These women were about to destroy everything she had built and sacrificed for. They were going to compromise sources and methods and give ammunition to every enemy of the United States who wanted to understand how American intelligence operated.

What she had unconsciously worked to ignore was feeling something closer to exhaustion. For the first time, Katherine faced a bone-deep weariness that had been building for years so gradually that she'd barely noticed it until now.

She thought about the first time she'd seen ALTAR's potential. She'd been a deputy director then, overseeing technology acquisition. When the EmotiMetrics scandal had broken, everyone else had seen a disaster to be contained, but Katherine had seen something else: A tool so powerful it could reshape the entire landscape of national security.

She'd intuitively grasped the power of behavioral modeling and predictive algorithms to predict human behavior at a level that human beings themselves couldn't understand. In the right hands, responsible American hands, that technology could prevent attacks before they happened, neutralize threats before they materialized and protect the nation in ways that traditional intelligence gathering never could.

All it required was the willingness to use it.

• • •

In the beginning, Katherine had agreed that there should be limits.

Democratic governance required oversight mechanisms and clear ethical boundaries. A framework of accountability. But good intentions were lost in the noise of political jockeying. Congress was supposed to be the check on this kind of power, but Congress had long since stopped doing its job. They were too busy fundraising to read briefings, too analog to understand what they were authorizing, and too captured by the special interests they were meant to oversee. The people sworn to uphold the system were the ones hollowing it out. Where do you turn when the watchmen abandon their posts?

Limits, she learned, were like walls in a desert. The winds of necessity eroded the walls grain by grain. It happened so slowly that you didn't notice until you looked up and the walls were gone. The old answers didn't work anymore, and there was no guarantee that new ones would replace them.

The first time someone proposed using SENTINEL against a domestic target, she objected. The program was designed for foreign threats, she'd emphasized. There were laws and constitutional constraints that must be adhered to. Using it against American citizens, even American citizens who were genuine security risks, crossed a line that shouldn't be crossed.

The first grain of sand was a congressional staffer who was leaking classified information to foreign intelligence services. Real harm was being done to national security. Traditional methods of deterrence and detection—like surveillance, investigation, prosecution—were too slow and uncertain. These measures were constrained by the very laws the leaker was exploiting. SENTINEL could handle it cleanly and quietly without the mess of a public trial that would expose more secrets than it protected.

Her impulse to protect the country won. She had approved the operation. The staffer was neutralized by destroying him professionally, shattering his credibility, and revoking his access to sensitive information. The leak was stopped, protecting the immediate national security concerns. But the line she'd sworn she wouldn't cross had become a little blurrier.

After that, it got easier. Each decision was built on the ones before it. Each compromise was justified by the ones that preceded it. There was a journalist who was about to publish details of an ongoing operation. She'd made the mistake of being indiscreet in her personal life. She backed off once the trade off to her privacy became clear. Then there was the researcher whose work threatened to expose a crucial intelligence method. Discrediting the methodology in his previous research was easy, which called into question the veracity of his current study. It was just enough to get his grant pulled. The activist whose social media advocacy provided cover for foreign influence was bot-bombed into pariah status, effectively marginalizing and isolating him.

Once the wall was breached by a legitimate security concern, the erosion of obstacles took on a momentum of its own. Targets weren't exactly enemies. They didn't have to be working against the country on purpose. They were simply problems to be solved. Every day, people became variables in an equation that needed to be balanced for the good of national security.

Then came the terminal protocols.

Katherine closed her eyes. She remembered the first time she'd authorized one. Jason Mercer. Jason had stumbled onto evidence of SENTINEL's domestic operations and was planning to go public. She felt some regret at the time. She knew he had a daughter.

Katherine told herself it was necessary. Mercer would have caused incalculable damage. The secrets he was about to reveal would have compromised operations that were protecting thousands of lives. The moral calculus, however ugly, came out in favor of action.

Over the years, she had told herself a lot of things to protect the mission. She wasn't sure she believed any of them anymore.

• • •

Katherine's phone buzzed again with another update: *CROSS, RYAN, FAILURE TO COMPLY WITH DETENTION ORDER. CURRENT LOCATION UNKNOWN. RECOMMEND ESCALATION TO PRIORITY STATUS.*

So, Cross had finally picked a side. Katherine wasn't surprised. She'd watched his file for years, tracked the way he'd responded to his assignments, noted the subtle signs of discomfort that he thought he was hiding. Cross was a good, skilled agent. He was dedicated and genuinely patriotic, but he had a weakness that Katherine had learned to recognize in her three decades of intelligence work.

He believed in rules and limits. He believed that there were lines that shouldn't be crossed, no matter how compelling the justification.

Katherine had believed that before she'd learned that the world didn't care about your principles. The enemies of the nation don't constrain themselves with ethical frameworks. Katherine came to believe that the only way to protect the people you were sworn to protect was to be willing to do what they couldn't imagine you would do.

She typed a response: *Approved, but I want him brought in alive. He still has value.* Then she turned back to the window.

The sky was beginning to show the first pink and yellow hints of dawn touching the horizon. In a few hours, the sun would rise on a day that might change everything. The public would learn about SENTINEL, or at least, about the version of SENTINEL that Claire Hensley and her sources understood. There would be outrage, investigations, and Congressional hearings. Citizens would demand accountability, transparency, and reform.

Katherine knew she'd be the villain. She'd be painted as the architect of a surveillance state, the woman who had turned the tools of national security against the very citizens she was supposed to protect. Her name would become synonymous with overreach and abuse, with the corruption of American values in the name of American security. Accountability meant someone had to take the fall.

She wondered if history would remember the threats she had stopped. Who would tell the story of the attacks that never happened because SENTINEL saw them coming? What about the important operations that had been protected and disasters that had been averted because she had been willing to do what others wouldn't.

No one would tell those stories. You can't tell what you can't reveal. Besides, history remembered villains more easily than it remembered the shadows they had held at bay.

• • •

Her secure line rang at 6:47 AM.

She picked it up knowing who it would be. Only a handful of people had this number, and at this hour, on this day, only one of them would be calling.

"Katherine." The individual on the other end was looking for damage control. "We need to talk about containment options."

"There are no containment options." She kept her voice level. "The documents are already with multiple outlets. The sources are too dispersed to neutralize in time. We've lost the initiative."

"Then we need to think about shaping the narrative. Get ahead of this story before it gets ahead of us."

"The narrative is going to be what it's going to be. Once those documents hit, no amount of spin is going to change the fundamental picture." Katherine paused. "We knew this day might come. We planned for it."

"The plans assumed we'd have more control over the timing. More ability to shape the battlefield."

"Plans rarely survive contact with the enemy." She turned away from the window and walked to her desk. "I'll take responsibility. I'll be the public face of the program and accept accountability. It protects our people who need protection and gives the investigators a target."

"Katherine… "

"It's my program and my legacy." She sat down as the weight of thirty years settled onto her shoulders. "I built SENTINEL, and I approved the operations. I made the decisions that led us here. If someone has to answer for it, it should be me."

Silence on the other end. Then: "You're sure about this?"

"I've been sure for a long time. I just didn't know when the moment would arrive." She looked at the photograph of her niece's children, sitting on her desk. She smiled back at the photo of them smiling at a birthday party, innocent of the world their great-aunt had helped create. "I'll make sure the transition is smooth and that SENTINEL doesn't die with my career. The threats it was built to address aren't going away just because the program becomes public."

"I'll handle it."

"I know you will." She ended the call, took a deep breath, and prepared herself for action.

The sun was up now. The morning light spilled across her desk, illuminating the neat stacks of briefing papers, her secure computer terminal, and the other trappings of power she had accumulated over three decades. In a few hours, none of it would matter. She would be the subject of investigations instead of the author of them. Her name would be spoken with contempt instead of respect.

She took comfort in knowing the program would survive in some form, under some name, with some set of constraints that would gradually erode the way all constraints did. SENTINEL must continue because the threats were real. She knew the people who came after her would face the same impossible choices she had faced, they would struggle with the same compromises, and the cycle would continue.

That was the truth that Claire Hensley and her idealistic friends would never understand. You couldn't kill a program like SENTINEL by exposing it. You could only change its shape, force it into new channels, make it adapt and evolve. The darkness didn't disappear just because you shone a light on it. It just moved to where the light couldn't reach.

Katherine Rennick stood, straightened her jacket, and walked out of her office to face the day that would end her career. She had made her choices, and now she would live with them. All of them.

CHAPTER EIGHTEEN

Going Dark

Claire and Elise split up at 3:00 AM.

It was Elise's idea; the same logic that made them scatter after the warehouse meeting was more urgent now. Seth Parker's arrest had changed the calculus. SENTINEL wasn't just monitoring them anymore. It was actively hunting, and the safest thing the targets could do was stop being in the same place.

"If they take one of us, the other can still get the story out," Elise said, packing a go-bag in the dim light of her apartment. She jammed in a few pieces of durable clothing, cash, three burner phones, and her laptop that had never touched the internet. "Redundancy. It's the only way to beat a system designed to eliminate single points of failure."

"By becoming multiple points of failure ourselves." A creature of habit, Claire always kept a go-bag close. Years of last-minute dispatches to cover breaking stories made preparation for contingencies a must-have part of a journalist's routine. As she got up to leave, she asked, "Where will you go?"

"It's better if you don't know. Better if neither of us knows where the other is." Elise zipped her bag and turned to face her. Her expression was hard to read, but her voice was steady. "We communicate only through the dead drops we established. Nothing electronic unless it's life or death."

"And the documents?"

"We each take a complete copy. You handle the Post, I'll work the European consortium, Daniel's got the Times." Elise handed her a USB drive, one of four identical copies they'd made. "Daniel has one too. So does the lawyer. If any one of us goes down, the others keep moving."

Claire took the drive and slipped it into a hidden pocket sewn into the lining of her jacket. Such a small thing with such huge importance.

"How long do we have?" she asked.

"Cross said they're scrambling, but that won't last. Once they realize Seth isn't going to give them what they want, they'll expand the search." Elise shouldered her bag. "Twelve hours, maybe. Twenty-four if we're lucky. After that, they'll have identified everyone who was at the warehouse, everyone we've talked to, everyone who might be helping us."

"Then we'd better not waste time."

The two women who rebuilt their partnership from the ashes of ALTAR, and who spent months uncovering a truth that powerful people would kill to protect, faced each other. There was nothing left to say that hadn't already been said. Nothing to do but move.

"Be careful," Elise said.

"You too."

Claire left first, taking the back stairs to the alley behind the building. She'd walk six blocks to a parking garage where she'd stashed a rental car under a false name. Elise would wait fifteen minutes before leaving via a different route. She'd head to a different safe house, hopefully increasing the odds that one of them would beat the clock.

The city was mostly quiet in the pre-dawn darkness. Somewhere in the distance, a siren wailed and faded. Claire walked with her head down, her pace unhurried, trying to look like anyone else out too early or too late, a night shift worker, an insomniac, someone with nothing to hide.

As she slid in behind the wheel of her rental car and fastened her seat belt, she felt the USB drive against her ribs. Claire adjusted the rear-view mirror and pulled out of the garage, unable to shake the feeling that somewhere, somehow, invisible eyes were watching.

• • •

The first sign of trouble emerged at 7:00 AM.

Claire had driven south deeper into Virginia, avoiding I95 for longer routes through suburbs that were just beginning to wake. She'd stopped at a diner outside Fredericksburg, the kind of place that welcomed cash and didn't have security cameras, when her burner phone buzzed with a text from Daniel.

The Times is getting cold feet. Legal got a call from DOJ. They're talking about prior restraint.

Prior restraint. The government was trying to stop publication before it happened, something that had been virtually impossible since the Pentagon Papers case, but that didn't mean they wouldn't try. The threat alone could spook an editor into delaying, demanding more review, looking for reasons to kill the story.

Claire typed back: *What do you think they'll do?*

Holding for now. But nervous. Legal review expanded to include outside counsel.

Outside counsel meant more people seeing the documents. More potential leaks back to the government. More opportunities for someone to lose their nerve or be pressured into betraying them.

She stared at her phone while she calculated options. The whole strategy depended on simultaneous publication, hitting the government with multiple stories at once, making it impossible to suppress them all. If one dropped out or delayed, the whole thing could unravel.

Her phone buzzed again; this time it was from one of Elise's burners.

European consortium confirmed. Publishing from Brussels in 18 hours regardless of U.S. outlets. Can't be stopped by American courts.

At least something was going right. Even if the American papers folded, the story would get out. But it would be weaker without them and easier to dismiss as foreign propaganda aimed as an attack on American security rather than a defense of American values.

She needed to talk to Marcus and find out what was really happening at the Post, whether there was any chance of holding the line. Calling him directly was too risky; if they were monitoring his communications, which they almost certainly were, it would lead them straight to her.

She left cash on the table and walked out of the diner, her mind racing through alternatives. There had to be another way. There was always another way.

She just had to find it before time ran out.

• • •

Elise was on a train to Philadelphia when her phone died.

She'd charged it fully before leaving, so it was concerning that the phone simply stopped working. The screen went black in the middle of composing a message. She tried restarting it, removing and reinserting the battery. Nothing. The device was dead, killed by something she hadn't anticipated.

Remote kill switch. She'd heard of the capability but never seen it deployed. SENTINEL, or whatever remained of it after the official disavowal, had the ability to brick any device connected to a cellular network. They'd just demonstrated it.

That meant they knew which phone she was using, which meant they were tracking her.

She forced herself to stay calm, to keep her breathing steady. She wouldn't look around the train car in obvious panic. She checked her watch. She had twenty minutes until the train reached Philadelphia. She needed to get off before then, somewhere unexpected, where she could disappear into a crowd and switch to her backup phone.

The train was slowing, approaching a suburban station. Elise gathered her bag, moved toward the doors, and kept her head down as she tried to look like any other commuter ending an ordinary journey. When the doors opened, she stepped out onto a platform and walked quickly toward the exit.

She didn't see the men until it was almost too late.

Two of them were standing near the ticket machines. Their anonymous dark suits gave them away. They weren't looking directly at her, but their positioning was too perfect and their feigned nonchalance too studied. They were watching for someone.

Elise changed direction smoothly, angling toward a different exit, fighting the urge to run. Running would confirm their suspicions. Maybe if she walked like someone who had nothing to hide, it might buy her the seconds she needed.

She pushed through a door marked EMPLOYEES ONLY and found herself in a service corridor. She had no idea where it led and no time to worry about it. She walked fast, then faster, and broke into a run when she heard voices behind her calling out orders.

The corridor ended in a fire door. She hit it at full speed, bursting out into bright daylight, stumbling down a short flight of metal stairs into a parking lot. There were cars and people everywhere. She slowed to a walk, merged with the crowd, and headed for the street.

She silently coached herself to avoid the panic she felt. Don't look back. Don't look back.

She looked back.

Two suits had emerged from the station and were scanning the parking lot, speaking into their earpieces. One of them pointed at the general area where she'd disappeared into the crowd.

Elise ducked between parked cars, cut through a gap in a chain-link fence, and emerged onto a residential street. She walked for three blocks without looking back again, turned twice at random, and finally ducked into a small coffee shop that had a back exit she'd spotted through the window.

She headed for the bathroom where she could activate her backup phone to send a single text to Daniel's emergency number:

Compromised. Primary phone killed remotely. They're hunting actively. Continuing mission. Tell C to watch her back.

Then she destroyed the SIM card, pocketed the phone, and walked out the back door into an alley that smelled of garbage and old grease.

Sixteen hours until the European publication. Sixteen hours of running, hiding, staying one step ahead of a system designed to predict her every move.

She started walking north, toward a bus station she remembered from a college trip twenty years ago. Hopefully it was still there and she could reach it. She had to stay invisible long enough to matter.

• • •

Claire found Marcus at his daughter's soccer game.

It was a risk, a huge risk, but she was out of options. The Post's legal team was in full panic mode, demanding more time, more review, more assurances that they wouldn't be prosecuted for publishing classified material. Daniel's contacts at the Times had gone dark, either scared off or told to stop communicating. The coordinated publication was falling apart, and Claire couldn't fix it from a distance.

So, she drove to Bethesda, to the suburban soccer field where Marcus spent every Saturday morning pretending to be a normal father with a normal life. She parked two blocks away and walked to the sidelines, finding a spot where she could watch without being obvious.

Marcus saw her after the first quarter. She watched his face change from surprise to fear, then settle on a careful blankness as he made his way around the edge of the field to where she stood.

"You shouldn't be here," he said quietly, standing beside her but not looking at her. They both pretended to watch the game.

"I wouldn't be if there was another choice." Claire kept her voice low. "The story is falling apart. I need to know where you stand."

"Where I stand?" He shook his head slightly. "I stand where I've always stood, with the story. But it's not that simple. The pressure coming down from ownership is unlike anything I've seen. They're not just worried about lawsuits, Claire. They're worried about losing broadcast licenses, government contracts, and access."

"Access to what? To officials who lie to them? To press conferences that tell them nothing?"

"You know how the game works." His voice was tired, defeated. "The Post isn't an independent paper anymore. It's part of a media conglomerate with business interests that extend way beyond journalism. The people who make the real decisions, they're weighing this story against a hundred other considerations."

"And they're leaning toward killing it."

"They're leaning toward delay, which amounts to the same thing." Marcus finally turned to look at her. "I'm sorry, Claire. I've fought for this story. I've argued until I'm hoarse, but I don't control what happens next."

Claire felt a sense of determination. The Post had been her home for her journalism career. She'd believed, despite everything, that when the moment came, they would do the right thing. She believed that journalism still meant something and that the truth still mattered to the people who claimed to serve it.

"What if I could give you a reason to publish?" she said. "Something that makes delay impossible?"

"Like what?"

"Like the story going live somewhere else. Tonight, with or without the Post." She watched his face. "If you're not first, you're just chasing someone else's scoop. The lawyers can argue about liability all they want, but once the information is public, the calculus changes."

"You have another outlet?"

"Two. One domestic and one European. The European is motivated and beyond the reach of American courts." She paused. "They're publishing at midnight Brussels time. That's 6:00 PM here. The Post can either lead the American coverage or spend the next week explaining why they didn't."

Quinn was quiet for a long moment, watching his daughter chase a soccer ball across the green field. When he spoke, his voice was different, harder, more decisive.

"6:00 PM."

"Yes."

"I'll make some calls." He turned to face her fully. "No promises, but if you can guarantee the European publication is happening regardless, that changes the conversation. That makes this a question of journalistic pride, not legal risk."

"The European publication is happening. I can guarantee that."

"Then you might have your story." He paused. "Claire, whatever happens, be careful. The people who came to my office, the pressure we've been under, this isn't normal. This isn't how these things usually work. Someone wants this story dead badly enough to break all the rules."

"I know," she said. "That's why it has to be told."

She walked away without looking back, disappearing into the crowd of parents and siblings before anyone could notice that anything unusual had happened. Behind her, the soccer game continued as if nothing was wrong.

Eight hours until publication. Eight hours of running, hiding, hoping that the fragile network they'd built would hold together long enough to matter.

Claire got in her car and headed for a safe house this time in Baltimore, where she would wait for the world to change, or watch it stay the same.

CHAPTER NINETEEN

The Final Hours

Daniel Okafor was arrested at 2:47 PM. Claire got the news through a message from Paula, who had seen the breaking alert on her phone: *Former journalist Daniel Okafor taken into custody by federal agents. Sources say espionage-related charges.*

She was in the Baltimore safe house, a cramped apartment above a laundromat, rented under a name she'd never used before, when the message came through. Three hours until publication. Three hours until everything they'd worked for either became real or disappeared into the silence of suppressed stories and buried truths.

And now Daniel was gone.

She stared at the message, her mind racing through the implications. Daniel had a copy of the documents. Daniel knew the publication timeline. Daniel knew which outlets were involved, which editors were sympathetic, which lawyers had been consulted. If they could break him, if they could get him to talk, they could unravel the entire network in the hours they had left.

Her phone buzzed again from one of Elise's backups.

Heard about D. Still moving. European timeline unchanged. Brussels won't fold.

At least something was holding. The International Reporting Project operated out of Belgium, beyond the easy reach of American law enforcement. Even if every domestic outlet collapsed, that story would go live. The question was whether a single European publication could generate enough attention to break through the noise, or whether it would be dismissed as foreign interference and buried under an avalanche of official denials.

Claire typed a response: *Post still uncertain. Quinn trying. Need backup plan if domestic falls through.*

The reply came thirty seconds later: *Working on it. Stay hidden. They're picking us off.*

Picking us off like they'd done eighteen months ago, when ALTAR fell apart and everyone connected to the investigation found their lives upended. They were capable of worse, as they'd proven with Jason Mercer and others whose deaths had been disguised as accidents and misfortunes. SENTINEL's playbook hadn't changed. Only the timeline had accelerated.

Claire walked to the window and looked down at the street below. She felt zero comfort that everything looked normal while the invisible war raged around it. Elise was running, Daniel was in a cell, Seth Parker was still locked away on charges that might never be formally filed. And the people responsible for all of it were sitting in their offices making phone calls and applying pressure, confident that they could make this problem disappear like all the others.

Not this time, she thought. Whatever it takes. Not this time.

• • •

The call from Marcus came at 4:15 PM.

"We're in," he said, without preamble. "Legal signed off twenty minutes ago. We publish at 6:00, same time as Brussels."

Claire felt something loosen in her chest, tension she hadn't realized she was holding. "What changed?"

"Daniel's arrest. Ownership realized that if we don't publish and the European story runs anyway, we look like cowards. Or worse, it looks like we were suppressing the story on government orders." In a grim admission, Marcus said, "They're not doing this because it's right, they're doing it because the alternative is worse for business."

"I'll take it."

Marcus continued, "Claire, there's something else. Rumor has it that the NY Times is in. They saw Daniel's arrest and decided they couldn't let others have the story. Journalistic competition, if nothing else. You're going to have coordinated publication after all. Three outlets all at once."

Three outlets. Claire allowed herself a moment of something that might have been hope. Even SENTINEL couldn't suppress three simultaneous publications. The story was going to get out. The truth was going to be told.

"Marcus, thank you for fighting for this."

"Don't thank me yet. We still have to survive the next ninety minutes." His voice dropped. "Claire, there's something you should know. An hour ago, the FBI showed up at the Post building with a warrant. They're seizing computers, documents, anything related to the SENTINEL investigation."

"Can they stop publication?"

"They're trying. Our lawyers are in court right now arguing against an emergency injunction." The story is already loaded in the system, set to go live automatically at 6:00. Even if they get an injunction, they'd have to physically stop the servers from publishing. And by the time they figure out how to do that..."

"It'll be too late."

"That's the plan. But Claire, stay hidden. Whatever happens in the next two hours, stay out of sight. If this goes wrong, you're the only one who can tell people what really happened."

She promised she would, then ended the call and sat in the silence of the safe house, watching the clock count down toward the moment that would change everything.

• • •

At 5:30 PM, Elise called from a payphone in Philadelphia.

"I almost didn't make it," she said. Her voice was ragged, exhausted. "They were waiting at every train station, every bus terminal. I've been on foot for the last four hours, switching neighborhoods, doubling back."

"Are you safe now?"

"Safe enough. I'm in a library basement, using their computer to monitor the European feed. Brussels is ready. They're going live in thirty minutes."

Claire breathed a sigh of relief. "We'll all be on the same schedule, then. Post, Times, Brussels, all at 6:00 PM Eastern."

Twenty-eight minutes to go. Claire's heart was racing now with the adrenaline of the final countdown flooding her system. After the months of investigation, the weeks of fear, the days of running, it came down to twenty-eight minutes.

"We wait," she said.

"We wait." Elise's voice was steadier now. "Claire, whatever happens, we did this. Together. No matter how it ends, we did something that mattered."

"It's not over yet."

"No. But when it is, when this is done, I want you to know that I wouldn't have wanted anyone else beside me. Through all of it. You're the best partner I've ever had."

Claire felt her throat tighten. "Same. On all of it."

"I'll call you when it's live. Stay safe until then."

"You too."

The line went dead. Claire set down her phone and turned to the safehouse laptop she'd set up on the kitchen table, its screen showing a browser window with the Post's website. In twenty-five minutes, that page would refresh and the world would be different.

Or the page would stay the same, and everything they'd risked would have been for nothing.

She sat down to wait.

• • •

At 5:54 PM, someone knocked on the door of the safe house.

Claire froze. No one knew she was there. The apartment had been rented through three layers of cutouts. She hadn't shared the address…except,

The knock came again. Three short, two long. It was a pattern she recognized.

She crossed to the door and looked through the peephole. Agent Ryan Cross stood in the hallway, alone, his face drawn with exhaustion.

Claire opened the door. "How did you find me?"

"I'm good at my job." He stepped inside without waiting for an invitation, his eyes scanning the apartment. "We don't have much time. They know you're in Baltimore. They're working through a list of possible locations. This address is on the list."

"How long?"

"Twenty minutes, maybe less." He turned to face her. "You need to move. Now. Before they narrow it down."

Claire glanced at the laptop. It was 5:56 PM and four minutes until publication. "I'm not leaving. Not until the story goes live."

"Ms. Hensley, "

"Four minutes. That's all I need." She met his eyes. "After that, it doesn't matter if they find me. The story will be out. Whatever they do to me won't change that."

Cross stared at her for a long moment. Then something shifted in his demeanor, a recognition of a determination that matched his own.

"Then I'll wait with you," he said. "If they come, I can buy you time with my credentials if I can cause enough confusion. Whatever it takes."

"That would end your career."

"My career ended the moment I decided to help you." He moved to the window and looked down at the street. "I've been running on borrowed time for weeks. Might as well make it count for something."

5:58 PM.

Claire refreshed the Post's website. Nothing. The same stories that had been there all day. Local politics, international news, sports scores. The ordinary business of a world that didn't know it was about to change.

5:59 PM.

"Anything?" Cross asked from the window.

"Not yet."

She refreshed again. Still nothing. Her finger hovered over the trackpad, ready to refresh again, watching the seconds tick by on the corner of the screen.

6:00 PM.

She refreshed.

The headline filled her screen, bold and uncompromising: *SECRET NSA PROGRAM TARGETED JOURNALISTS, RESEARCHERS, CONGRESSIONAL STAFF: DOCUMENTS REVEAL YEARS OF ILLEGAL SURVEILLANCE AND ALLEGED STATE-SPONSORED KILLINGS*

Below it was her byline. Her name, attached to the story that would define the rest of her life.

"It's live," she said. Her voice came out strange, disconnected from her body. "It's actually live."

Cross turned from the window. "Then we need to go now."

He stopped short to listen. Through the thin walls of the apartment, came the sound of multiple vehicle car doors slamming.

"Fire Escape," Claire said, already moving. She grabbed her bag with the essentials she'd kept packed for exactly this moment. "It leads to the alley."

They ran.

Behind them, she heard the front door of the building crash open. She tried not to panic when she heard the voices shouting. The machinery of suppression arrived too late to stop what had already begun.

The fire escape was rusted and groaned under their weight, but it held. They dropped into the alley and ran, turning corners at random, putting distance between themselves and the safe house that wasn't safe anymore.

Gasping for breath in the shadow of a dumpster three blocks away, Claire pulled out her phone and checked the Post's website again.

The story was still there. A quick check of social media showed it was spreading. She could see the cascade beginning as other outlets picked it up. For a change, something good was propagating faster than anyone could stop it.

They had done it.

Whatever came next, arrest, prosecution, whatever price they would have to pay, they had done it.

The truth was out, and nothing would ever be the same.

CHAPTER TWENTY

Wildfire

Claire and Cross spent that first night in a motel outside Wilmington, paying cash, using names they'd never used before.

Cross had contacts, people who owed him favors, people who knew how to make someone disappear for a few days without asking questions. He'd gotten them out of Baltimore through a series of back roads and borrowed vehicles, never staying in one car long enough for any surveillance system to track them.

They kept watching the world react to what they'd done.

The coverage was everywhere. Every channel, every network, every news website Claire checked on the motel's ancient computer. SENTINEL was the top story. Pundits argued about implications. Former intelligence officials were dragged out of retirement to explain what it all meant. Politicians issued statements, some demanding investigations, others defending the need for strong national security measures.

"It's working," Cross said. He was standing by the window, peering through a gap in the curtains at the parking lot below. He hadn't stopped fidgeting since they'd arrived. He checked exits and monitored approaches. He was operating on an alertness that seemed hardwired into his nervous system. "The story's too big to bury with so many outlets, and too much detail they can't rebut."

"They'll try." Claire was exhausted. She was running on fumes and adrenaline, but she couldn't stop watching the coverage. She continually refreshed websites to track the spread and was awed by the speed and implied impact of what they'd released. "They'll deny, deflect, and do their best to discredit. They'll say the documents are fake, that we're foreign agents, that this is all part of some conspiracy to undermine national security."

"Some of that is already happening." Cross nodded toward the television, where a talking head was explaining why the American people should be skeptical of alleged documents from anonymous sources with clear political agendas. "But it's not sticking," Cross said. "The details are too specific, the corroboration is too strong, and Katherine Rennick's name is being attached to everything. That makes it real in a way they can't explain away."

Claire's phone buzzed with a text from Elise: *Made it out. Safe for now. Watching the news. We did it.*

She typed back: *Where are you?*

Still better if none of us know where the others are. Harder to round us all up that way.

She was right. Claire hated it, but Elise was right. Until they knew how the government would respond, whether there would be arrests, prosecutions, or something worse, staying separated was the only smart play.

Daniel? she typed.

Still in custody. Lawyer says they're not filing charges yet. Holding him on 'national security concerns.' Could be days before we know more.

Claire knew it couldn't have been avoided. Daniel was sitting in a cell somewhere, not knowing what would happen to him, while the story he'd helped bring to light exploded across the world. It wasn't fair. None of this was fair, but fair had never been part of the equation, and it wasn't anyone's priority.

• • •

By morning, the story had evolved. The initial shock was giving way to something more structured: Calls for congressional hearings, demands for an independent investigation, questions about who had authorized SENTINEL and who had known about its operations. The Senate Intelligence Committee announced it would hold closed-door briefings with intelligence community leaders. The House Judiciary Committee said it was considering subpoenas, and Katherine Rennick had gone to ground.

The NSA's public affairs office issued a terse statement acknowledging that certain programs were "under review" and that the agency was "cooperating fully with appropriate oversight bodies." But Rennick herself had not appeared publicly. She had not been seen entering or leaving NSA headquarters. The woman who had built SENTINEL was letting others take the first wave of heat while she, what? Prepared for her defense? Negotiated her exit? Planned her next move?

Claire didn't trust the silence. Rennick was too smart and experienced to simply disappear without a reason. Whatever she was doing, it would be strategic and calculated. There had to be more to her silence, a larger plan that Claire couldn't see yet.

"We should move," Cross said. He'd been up all night, as far as Claire could tell, maintaining his watch while she'd caught a few hours of fitful sleep on the motel's thin mattress. "Staying in one place too long is a risk. They'll be checking motels, hotels, anywhere someone might go to ground."

"Where else can we go?"

"I know of a cabin in West Virginia. It's off the grid with no utilities and no records. A friend bought it years ago for exactly this kind of situation." He paused. "It's not comfortable, but it's safe."

"For how long? We can't hide forever."

"Not forever, just until we see which way this breaks." Cross stopped moving around the room long enough to face her. "The next forty-eight hours will tell us everything. Either the political pressure forces them to stand down, or they double down and come after everyone involved. We need to be invisible until we know which it is."

Claire looked at the television, where a former CIA director was explaining that programs like SENTINEL, while perhaps "aggressive in certain implementations," were essential to protecting the homeland from evolving threats. The anchor was nodding along, asking softball questions, providing the kind of sympathetic platform that made controversial programs seem reasonable.

"They're not going to stand down," she said. "Look at this. They're already building the narrative that it is a necessary evil. Regrettable but justified. The usual storyline."

"Maybe, but the documents are specific with names, dates, and operations. They can't spin their way out of terminal protocols and coordinated character assassinations." Cross shook his head. "Someone is going to have to answer for this. The only question is who, and how much."

"Rennick."

"Probably. She's the obvious sacrifice, high enough to satisfy public outrage and connected enough to know where the bodies are buried." His expression darkened. "The question is whether she goes quietly or tries to bring others down with her."

Claire thought about that as they packed their few belongings and prepared to move again. Katherine Rennick, going down. It should have felt like victory, but instead, it felt like the opening move in a game whose rules she didn't fully understand.

• • •

The cabin was exactly as Cross had described—primitive, isolated, invisible, and musty. It sat at the end of a dirt road that wound through miles of Appalachian forest. It was a single-room structure with the bare necessities, a wood stove, a hand pump for water, and no connection to the outside world except for the satellite phone Cross had brought with them. The nearest neighbor was five miles away. The nearest town was twenty.

"Home sweet home," Cross said, with something that might have been dark humor. "For the next few days, at least."

Claire set her bag on the rough wooden floor and looked around. Dust mites floated in shafts of afternoon light that filtered through grimy windows. The air smelled of disuse. It was a place designed for hiding and surviving.

"I need to contact the others," she said. "Let them know we're safe and coordinate next steps."

"Careful." Cross was already checking the cabin's perimeter, looking for signs that anyone had been there recently. "Short messages, nothing that can be traced, and nothing about location, not even a hint."

She used the satellite phone to send a series of brief, coded messages. To Elise: *Relocated. Secure. Standing by.* To Paula: *Safe. Monitor political response. Report developments.* To the lawyer handling Daniel's case: *Client status? Options?*

The responses came slowly, filtered through layers of caution and encryption.

Elise: *Congressional hearings announced. Rennick scheduled to testify next week. Closed session.*

Paula: *Intel Committee already circling wagons. Expect limited hangout strategy. Rennick as scapegoat, program survival under new name.*

The lawyer: *Daniel being transferred to federal facility. Formal charges expected within 72 hours. Espionage Act likely. Will fight for bail but prospects uncertain.*

The Espionage Act. The same hammer they'd used against whistleblowers for decades. It was a blunt instrument that turned people who revealed government wrongdoing into criminals deserving of decades in prison. Daniel had known the risk.

"They're charging Daniel," Claire told Cross. "Espionage Act."

His jaw tightened. "That's to be expected. They need to show they're punishing the people responsible. Daniel's an easy target; he's already in custody, already identified, and tied to the documents." He paused. "You're probably next on the list, along with Elise."

"I know." Claire sat down on a wooden chair that creaked under her weight. "I've known since we started this. We all have."

She looked out the window at the forest pressing close around the cabin, thankful for the trees that hid them from the world. "We each made our choice. We decided the truth mattered more than our safety. I still believe that.

"So do I." Cross went to the wood stove and began building a fire. "That's why I'm here instead of sitting in an

FBI field office pretending I don't know what SENTINEL really was." He struck a match and held it to the kindling.

The fire caught, its small flames licking at dry wood, slowly building toward something that might warm them against the early winter cold. Claire watched it grow and thought about everything they'd set in motion, the hearings that would come, the investigations that would follow, the political battles that would be fought over the meaning of what they'd revealed.

The truth was loose in the world. What happened next was beyond their control. All they could do now was survive long enough to see how it ended.

CHAPTER TWENTY-ONE

The Sacrifice

Katherine Rennick's testimony lasted for six hours.

Claire watched it from the cabin, huddled around a laptop that Cross had connected to a portable satellite antenna. The signal was weak and intermittent, the video buffering every few minutes, but it was better than just having a phone. The essential picture came through clearly enough: the most powerful woman in American intelligence sat alone at a witness table, methodically dismantling her own legacy.

The hearing was closed to the public. The committee credited national security concerns for the press blackout. But someone was leaking audio and video excerpts in real time in addition to the transcripts that appeared on X within minutes of key exchanges. Cable news anchors read the most damning passages in breathless tones; their faces lit with the excitement of a scandal that was still unfolding.

Rennick admitted everything. She wasn't defiant or apologetic. She described her vision and role in Sentinel with the clinical precision of an intelligence officer delivering a briefing. Yes, SENTINEL had targeted American citizens. Yes, there had been operations designed to destroy careers, discredit researchers, and silence journalists. Yes, there had been what the internal documents called "terminal protocols", actions that resulted in deaths made to look like accidents.

"I authorized those operations," she said, according to the transcripts. "I take full responsibility for the decisions that were made under my direction. The personnel who carried out those operations were following lawful orders from their chain of command."

"She's protecting them," Cross said. He was standing behind Claire, his jaw muscles flexing with the recognition of another well-worn path. "She's taking all the blame so the people below her don't get prosecuted. It's the honorable thing to do, in a twisted way.

"Here we go again," Claire said. "If she goes down alone, the system survives. The people who implemented SENTINEL, the infrastructure that supported it, the mindset that created it, all that stays in place. They just need a new name and a new figurehead."

"You think they'll try to rebuild?"

"I think they never stopped. Somewhere in that building, people are already working on SENTINEL's successor." Claire refreshed the page, waiting for more transcripts to appear. "Rennick is buying them time. Every day the spotlight is on her is a day they can work in the shadows."

The next excerpt appeared: Senator Johnson was asking about oversight failures, who had known what and when. Rennick's response was careful, naming names only when absolutely necessary. She framed everything as the decisions of a small group acting within legal frameworks that, while aggressive, had been reviewed and approved by appropriate authorities.

"She's very good at this," Cross observed. "Giving them enough to satisfy the outrage while protecting as much as possible."

"She's had thirty years to learn how the game is played." Claire watched another transcript appear: Rennick explained that she was offering her resignation, effective immediately, and that she would cooperate fully with any criminal investigation. "And now she's making her final move."

• • •

Rennick's resignation was accepted within hours. The President issued a statement expressing "deep concern" about the revelations and pledging a "thorough review" of intelligence community practices. The Director of National Intelligence announced that all programs involving domestic surveillance would be suspended pending that review. The Attorney General said his office was evaluating whether criminal charges were warranted.

It was, by any measure, a remarkable response. In the space of a week, the most secret program in American intelligence had been exposed, its architect had resigned in disgrace, and the entire apparatus of national security was scrambling to contain the damage. The system was doing what systems do when confronted with undeniable evidence of wrongdoing: sacrificing a piece to save the whole.

And yet, Claire suspected that something was wrong. Things were too clean and coordinated. Rennick's testimony had been extremely polished; the government's response was fierce and swift. And the narrative was too neatly packaged. This was what capitulation looked like when it was planned in advance. In her gut, she knew that the people in power had gamed out every scenario and chosen the path of least resistance.

"They're letting her take the fall," she said to Cross that evening, as they sat by the wood stove eating canned soup. "The whole intelligence community, the oversight committees, the White House, they're all stepping back and letting Rennick absorb the impact, and she's letting them."

"What else can she do? Fight back? Name names? Burn down the whole apparatus?" Cross shook his head. "She built SENTINEL because she believed in it. She still believes in it. The last thing she wants is to destroy the system she spent her life serving."

"Even if that system is rotten?"

"She doesn't think it's rotten. She thinks it made mistakes and went too far in certain cases, but the core mission of protecting the country no matter what, well, she still believes in that." Cross set down his bowl. "That's what makes her dangerous. True believers don't break; they adapt."

Claire considered that as the fire crackled and darkness set in. Rennick was adapting. She was cooperating with investigators, saying all the right things while she calculated her next move.

The story wasn't over. She could feel it. They had won a battle, not the war. For now, for tonight, it was enough to be alive and free, knowing that the truth was out in the world where no one could take it back.

• • •

The pressure on Claire, Elise, and others eased over the following days. With Rennick's resignation dominating the news, the hunt for the people who had exposed SENTINEL seemed to lose urgency. Daniel Okafor was quietly released on bail, with charges still pending, but the government's appetite for prosecution apparently diminished in the political firestorm. Seth Parker's lawyers reported that discussions about dropping his charges had begun.

Claire emerged from hiding after ten days. She slipped back into Washington on a bus, checking into a hotel under her own name for the first time since the story broke. No one stopped her and no one followed her. The surveillance apparatus that had tracked her every move seemed to have evaporated or at least turned its attention elsewhere.

Elise surfaced two days later, calling from a new burner she had picked up in New York. "It's strange," she said. "I keep waiting for the other shoe to drop, the knock on the door, the arrest warrant, or the midnight raid, but nothing happened."

"Maybe we actually won."

"Did we?" Elise didn't sound convinced. "Rennick is out, but the program ran for years with dozens of people involved. One resignation doesn't undo all of that. One testimony doesn't hold anyone accountable."

"The investigations are ongoing, and the hearings are continuing. Give it time."

"Time." Elise laughed incredulously, but there was no humor in it. "Time is what they want. Time for the news cycle to move on and for public outrage to fade. Time for the whole thing to become old news that nobody cares about anymore."

She wasn't wrong, Claire knew. They'd both seen it happen before, scandals that burned bright and faded fast, reforms that were promised and never delivered, accountability that was discussed and never achieved. The system had remarkable powers of absorption. It could take almost any blow and keep functioning, metabolizing criticism in committee meetings and commission reports that changed nothing fundamental.

But this time felt different. The documents were too specific, the operations too egregious, and the body count too real. Surely, this time, there would be meaningful consequences.

"Come back to Washington," Claire said. "We should regroup and figure out next steps. Make sure this doesn't just disappear."

"All right, next steps. But Claire, stay careful. Just because they've stopped chasing us doesn't mean they've forgotten about us."

"I know. I haven't forgotten about them either."

• • •

They gathered at the Post building three weeks after publication.

Not all of them. Daniel was still dealing with legal complications, and Cross had disappeared saying he needed time to figure out his next move. With Claire, Elise, Paula Weber, Robert Baskin, who had flown in from Europe, and Patricia Napper, looking ten years younger than she had during those terrified weeks of hiding, it felt like a reunion of sorts.

They sat in a conference room on the seventh floor, the same floor where Claire had worked for years, surrounded by the familiar hum of a newsroom in motion. Through the glass window, they could see the ordinary business of journalism continuing as if the world hadn't fundamentally shifted.

"I can't believe we're here," Patricia said. She was holding a mug of coffee like it was a precious artifact, something she'd been denied during the weeks of fear. "A month ago, I was hiding in my sister's basement in Philadelphia, convinced I'd never see my grandchildren again. Now I'm sitting in a newsroom, drinking coffee, talking about what comes next."

"What does come next?" Robert asked, trying to not look jet lagged. "We exposed SENTINEL and Rennick is gone, but the underlying issues, the surveillance infrastructure, the lack of real oversight, the willingness to target citizens who ask inconvenient questions, none of that has changed."

"The hearings are still going," Paula said. "Senator Johnson is pushing for real reform, new oversight mechanisms, limitations on domestic operations, and mandatory disclosure requirements. There's momentum."

"There's always momentum right after a scandal," Claire said. "The question is whether it lasts and if the reforms have teeth. The real test is whether anyone actually goes to prison for what happened."

"Rennick will," Elise said. "That seems certain now. The Attorney General is convening a grand jury. Criminal charges are expected within the month."

"Just Rennick?"

"For now. Maybe others later, depending on what the investigations turn up." Elise shrugged. "It's not nothing. A year ago, the idea of a senior intelligence official facing criminal prosecution for domestic surveillance would have been a fantasy. Now it's happening."

Claire looked around the table at her allies, her co-conspirators, the improbable coalition that revealed one of the most powerful secret programs in American history. They had risked everything. Some of them had lost careers and important relationships. And now they sat in a conference room speculating on whether or not it mattered.

"It mattered," she said, not realizing she'd spoken aloud until she saw them looking at her. "Whatever happens next, whatever reforms pass or don't pass, or what happens to Rennick or anyone else, we told the truth. We gave people the information they needed to make informed decisions about our democracy. That matters."

"It matters if something changes," Robert said.

"Something already has." Claire gestured at the newsroom beyond the glass. "Every journalist in this building knows what happened to us. Every intelligence analyst in Washington knows what happened to Rennick. Every politician considering whether to authorize the next SENTINEL knows that someone might be watching, might be ready to expose them. That's a change. Maybe not enough, but it's something."

The room was quiet for a moment. Then Patricia raised her coffee cup.

"To something," she said. "And to everyone who helped make it happen."

They raised their cups, coffee, water, whatever they had, and drank to the uncertain victory they had won. They were not ready to declare victory, but a modest celebration seemed appropriate.

Outside, Washington went about its business, the machinery of government grinding forward as it always did. Somewhere in that machinery, Claire knew, people were already working on the next iteration of SENTINE that would avoid the mistakes that had led to exposure.

But for now, in this moment, it was enough to be together and alive. They had fought and survived to expose the truth.

The rest would come later.

CHAPTER TWENTY-TWO

Normal

Two months later, Katherine Rennick was sentenced to eight years in federal prison. Claire attended the sentencing. She hadn't planned to; she told herself that the outcome was predetermined and that watching Rennick's sentencing wouldn't change anything. But when the day came, she found herself driving to Alexandria, parking three blocks from the federal courthouse, and walking through security with the other spectators and journalists who had come to witness the end of an era.

The courtroom was smaller than she'd expected but typical in its institutional trappings—wood-paneled walls, hard benches that kept everyone just deferentially uncomfortable enough, and the American flag hanging limply beside the judge's bench. Rennick sat at the defense table in a dark suit, her hair even shorter than it had been during the hearings. Her posture was as straight and controlled as ever. She didn't look like a criminal; she was the consummate career intelligence officer who made hard decisions she believed were necessary and was now paying the price for being caught.

The judge was a stern-faced woman in her sixties who read the sentence with the practiced detachment of someone who had delivered thousands of similar pronouncements. Rennick was sentenced to eight years with the possibility of parole after five. She was prohibited from having any government position for life. There was also a fine that was symbolic rather than punitive, given that Rennick's assets had already been frozen pending civil litigation from the families of SENTINEL's victims.

Rennick stood to receive the sentence, her face betraying nothing. When the judge asked if she had anything to say, she shook her head no, a small, precise movement that seemed to close a chapter rather than express remorse.

Then the marshals led her away.

Claire sat in the gallery after the courtroom emptied, trying to understand what she felt. Satisfaction? Justice? Closure? None of those words fit. Rennick was going to prison, but the system that she built remained intact. The people who had implemented her orders were still free. The infrastructure of surveillance and manipulation had been damaged but not destroyed.

It was, she supposed, the best outcome they could have hoped for, but it wasn't enough for Claire. It would never be enough, but it was something.

• • •

Life, improbably, returned to something like normal. Claire went back to work at the Post, accepting a promotion to senior investigative correspondent and a mandate to pursue whatever stories she thought merited investigation. The paper treated her like a hero. She was the journalist who exposed SENTINEL, risked everything for the truth, and gave the Post its biggest story in decades.

Claire found she didn't enjoy the attention. The congratulations felt hollow and the admiration misplaced. She hadn't done it for recognition or career advancement. She hadn't done it alone. She, Elise, and their allies did it because it needed to be done, because the alternative, staying silent while powerful people destroyed innocent lives, was unthinkable. Being praised for basic moral courage made her uncomfortable in ways she couldn't quite articulate.

Elise returned to the Digital Rights Foundation, which had seen a surge of donations and public interest in the wake of the SENTINEL revelations. She threw herself into the work of policy advocacy, legal challenges, and public education about surveillance and privacy rights. It was important and necessary work, but Elise wasn't unaffected by the SENTINEL experience. She exhibited a wariness that hadn't been there before. She varied her routes and routines and took notice of things that might be surveillance or might be nothing at all.

"Do you ever feel like we're still being watched?" Elise asked one evening, as they shared takeout in Claire's apartment. "Like someone's still tracking everything we do?"

"Sometimes." Claire set down her chopsticks. "But I think that's just... residue, trauma from what we went through. It takes time to stop feeling hunted."

"Maybe." Elise didn't sound convinced. "Or maybe we're right to be paranoid. Just because they stopped chasing us doesn't mean they stopped watching."

Claire didn't have an answer for that. The truth was, she didn't know. SENTINEL had officially been dismantled, its operations terminated, its personnel reassigned or retired. But "officially" meant little in the intelligence world. Programs ended on paper all the time while continuing under new names, new budgets, and new chains of command that were harder to trace.

She told herself that they'd done what they could. The story was out, and the public knew. Whatever happened in the shadows, there were now people watching, waiting, ready to expose the next abuse. That had to count for something.

• • •

The coalition scattered to their separate lives.

Daniel Okafor's charges were eventually dropped with quiet notification from the Justice Department that they had decided not to pursue prosecution "in light of the public interest considerations." He celebrated by starting a nonprofit focused on protecting journalists from the kind of institutional retaliation they had all experienced. Within months, he had funding, staff, and a waiting list of reporters seeking help.

Seth Parker emerged from his legal limbo a free man. The espionage charges were dismissed in a deal that required him to surrender his security clearance, which he did gladly. He had to commit to a new non-disclosure agreement and refrain from discussing classified information he'd learned at Nexus. He moved to Colorado to be closer to his daughter Emma, who was starting a graduate program in Boulder. He occasionally emailed Claire brief updates on his new life of hiking in the mountains, learning to ski, and slowly rebuilding a sense of normalcy that had been shattered when he'd decided to become a whistleblower.

Paula Weber thrived in her new role as Senator Johnson's chief of staff, shepherding the Intelligence Reform Act through committee hearings and floor debates. The legislation wasn't perfect—it never was—but it included real limitations on domestic surveillance, new oversight mechanisms, and mandatory disclosure requirements that would make another SENTINEL harder to hide. When it passed five months after Rennick's sentencing, Paula called Claire to share the news.

"We did it," she said. "Not everything we wanted, but more than anyone thought possible. Real reform and actual accountability."

"Congratulations," Claire said. "You made it happen."

"We all did. Every one of us who took a risk, who told the truth, who refused to stay silent." Paula paused. "I think about that sometimes. How close we came to failing. How easily they could have crushed us. And then I think about all the people who will be protected because we didn't give up."

"That's why we did it."

"I know. I just wanted to say thank you for everything."

After the call, Claire sat for a long time, thinking about Paula's words. Real reform and actual accountability. It was more than most whistleblowers. Maybe they really had changed something.

She wanted to believe it. She needed to believe it.

• • •

Robert Baskin was the first to notice something wrong. He called Claire on a Tuesday evening, nine months after the story had broken, his voice carrying the tension of someone trying to stay calm while delivering alarming news.

"My grant got pulled," he said. "The European research position. The review committee said there were 'irregularities' in my application materials. Documentation issues. Nothing specific, just vague concerns that suddenly made me ineligible for the funding I'd already been awarded."

"That sounds familiar."

"It sounds exactly like what happened before SENTINEL. The same intimidation tactics. Create doubt, undermine credibility, make everything fall apart without any obvious cause." Robert's voice tightened. "Claire, I thought this was over. I thought we won."

"We did win. Rennick is in prison and the reform bill passed. SENTINEL was dismantled."

"Then why is this happening?"

She didn't have an answer, but she did have her suspicions. Part of her wanted to dismiss it as a coincidence, as the ordinary friction of academic bureaucracy, as paranoia born from months of justified fear. Another part, the part that had learned to read patterns in seemingly random events, knew better.

"Let me make some calls," she said. "See if anyone else is experiencing anything unusual."

"You think it's connected?"

"I don't know, but I'm going to find out."

She hung up and stared at her phone. She felt a familiar twinge of frustration. They'd had nine months of believing they had made a difference, letting their guard down, and trusting that the exposure had been enough to force real change.

Maybe Robert's situation was nothing. Maybe she was seeing ghosts.

But Katherine Rennick's words echoed in her memory, the warning she'd delivered at her press conference nine months ago: *The intelligence community has survived revelations before. It will survive this one.*

Claire started making calls.

• • •

By the end of the week, the pattern was undeniable. Patricia Napper's pension had been "flagged for review", her thirty-one years of service suddenly subject to questions about eligibility and benefit calculations. Thomas Winters had been denied tenure, despite a unanimous recommendation from his department, on the grounds of "insufficient institutional commitment." A reporter who had worked on the European end of the SENTINEL story had been arrested in Brussels on drug charges that her colleagues swore were fabricated.

Ryan Cross had stopped responding to messages. His phone went straight to voicemail, and his email bounced back undelivered. The small house in Vermont where he'd been rebuilding his life stood empty; the neighbors said he left one morning and never returned.

"This isn't coincidence," Elise said. They were in Claire's apartment with the curtains drawn. They spoke in hushed voices despite having swept the room for surveillance devices. Old habits were returning faster than Claire would have liked. "This is coordinated. This is SENTINEL."

"SENTINEL was dismantled."

Claire nearly spit out her response, "Just like ALTAR, SENTINEL was a name. A structure. The people who ran it, the technology that powered it, the mindset that created it, none of that was dismantled. It just went underground." Elise's face grew pale. "They waited to let us think we'd won, and now they're coming back."

"For revenge?"

"For elimination. We exposed them once and can expose them again. As long as we're out here, as long as we're watching, we're a threat." Elise seemed to shrink in her chair. "They're not going to make the same mistake twice. They're not going to let us gather evidence and build a case and coordinate with multiple outlets. They're going to take us apart, one by one, before we even realize what's happening."

Claire thought about the last nine months of normalcy, and the gradual relaxation of vigilance as day after day passed without incident. She had wanted so badly to believe that the battle was won and she could go back to being a journalist instead of a hunted fugitive.

But the invisible war was never won permanently. The forces they fought against were patient and deeply embedded in the structures of power. They could absorb a scandal and sacrifice a leader. They could wait for the outrage and investigations to settle down. They counted on the same mission creep and loosening boundaries that meant they'd be back in the business of neutralization.

"What do we do?" Claire asked.

Elise sat up straight again, her expression hard. "We do what we did before. We fight, we document, and we expose." She paused. "But this time, we know what we're dealing with. This time, we don't have the luxury of surprise."

"And we don't have Cross to help us," Claire added.

"No." Elise's voice was quiet. "We don't know what happened to Cross. We don't know who else they've gotten to. We don't know how much our network is compromised." She met Claire's eyes. "We're starting from scratch, and they have a nine-month head start."

The words hung in the air between them, heavy with implication. Nine months of peace that hadn't been peace at all, just the calm before a storm they hadn't seen coming. A new version of SENTINEL, or whatever they were calling it now, was tracking their every move, waiting for the right moment to strike.

"We'd better get started," Claire said. "Before they finish what they've begun."

CHAPTER TWENTY-THREE

Terminal

Thomas Winters died on a Wednesday. The official report called it a single-car accident. His vehicle had left the road on a curve outside Middleburg, Virginia. It rolled twice before coming to rest in a drainage ditch. The medical examiner noted elevated blood alcohol levels. The police report mentioned that Winters had seemed distracted in recent weeks. According to colleagues, he was stressed about his tenure denial and began drinking more than usual. A tragic but understandable end for a man whose life had been upended by forces beyond his control.

Claire learned about it from a news alert on her phone, three words that stopped her heart: *Georgetown professor dies.*

She was at her desk in the Post newsroom, surrounded by the ordinary sounds of keyboards clicking, and the low murmur of reporters chasing deadlines. The world going on as if Thomas Winters hadn't just been murdered.

Because that's what it was. She knew it with a certainty that bypassed logic and went straight to her bones. Thomas hadn't touched alcohol in fifteen years, a fact he'd shared during one of their strategy sessions in the church basement. The elevated blood alcohol wasn't evidence of a relapse. It was a signature. It was the same technique they'd used on Jason Mercer before any of them knew what SENTINEL was capable of.

She stood abruptly, knocking a stack of papers off her desk. A colleague glanced over with concern, but Claire was already walking, fast, then faster, toward the elevator, her phone pressed to her ear.

Elise answered on the second ring. "You saw."

"It's them. It has to be them."

"I know." Elise was working hard at holding herself together through sheer force of will. "I'm at his daughter's apartment. She called me when she got the news. Claire, she's devastated, and she has no idea."

"Don't tell her, not yet anyway. Not until we know more."

"Know more?" A bitter laugh. "What more is there to know? They made it look like an accident, just like before."

The elevator arrived. Claire stepped in alone and punched the button for the lobby. "We need to meet, but not at your place or mine. Somewhere public with witnesses."

"The coffee shop on M Street. The one with the big windows."

"Twenty minutes."

She ended the call and stared at her reflection in the elevator's polished metal doors. The lines of exhaustion were carved into her face. She'd let her guard drop, believing that the nightmare was over.

The nightmare continued.

• • •

The coffee shop was crowded with the lunch rush, which was exactly what Claire wanted.

She found a table with her back to the wall where she could see both entrances and the street beyond. Old habits, returning with a vengeance. Fifteen minutes later, Elise walked in, her face drawn, and her movements carrying the jerky energy of barely suppressed panic.

"Patricia just called," Elise said, sliding into the seat across from her. "She's leaving town tonight. Her daughter is in Florida, so she's going to stay there indefinitely. She said she can't," Elise's voice cracked. "She said she can't wait around to be next."

"She might be right to run."

"That's what you think we should do? Run?"

"I don't know what we should do." Claire clasped her hands together to try and stop them from shaking. "Thomas is dead. Cross is missing, probably dead too. Robert's career is in ruins, and Patricia's fleeing. They're dismantling us piece by piece, and we don't even know who 'they' are anymore."

"We know exactly who they are," Elise hissed. "The same people it's always been. The intelligence community, the surveillance state, the apparatus that Rennick built and someone else inherited." Elise leaned forward, her voice low and intense. "How could we have been so stupid? SENTINEL didn't die when Rennick went to prison. It just changed hands."

"Then who's running it now?"

"I don't know, but I intend to find out."

Claire stared at her. "Elise, they just killed Thomas and made it look like nothing. There were no fingerprints, no evidence, just another sad story about a troubled man who drove drunk. If we start investigating again…"

"Then what? We're next?" Elise's eyes were bright with fury. "We're already on their list. Running didn't save Thomas, and staying quiet didn't save Cross. The only thing that saved us last time was exposing them. Making their crimes public and taking away their ability to operate in the shadows."

"We had documents and sources last time. We had Cross on the inside, feeding us information." Claire shook her head. "We have nothing now, and we don't even know what we're looking for."

"Then we find something. We start over and rebuild the network, find new sources, dig until we find the evidence we need." Elise reached across the table and gripped Claire's wrist. "I'm not going to run, Claire. I'm not going to spend the rest of my life looking over my shoulder, waiting for them to decide it's my turn. If they want to kill me, they're going to have to work for it."

Claire looked at her friend and ally, the woman who had stood beside her through everything. There was steel in Elise's eyes, a determination that wouldn't bend. She recognized that look. She'd seen it in her own mirror, months ago, when she'd decided to pursue the SENTINEL story despite every warning.

"All right," she said. "We fight, but we need to get smarter. We don't take unnecessary risks, we don't trust anyone we haven't vetted, and we assume they're watching everything we do."

"They are."

"I know. That's what scares me." Claire pulled out a notepad and pen, analog and untraceable. "Let's start with what we know. The attacks began roughly two weeks ago. Robert's grant, Patricia's pension, the Brussels arrest. That's coordinated. That's not random bureaucratic friction."

"Someone gave an order. Someone with the authority and resources to reach across multiple institutions, multiple countries."

"Someone who knows where we are and what our next moves would be." Claire wrote quickly, her mind racing. "The list of people with that information is small. It is only the intelligence community leadership, key members of the oversight committees, and a few senior Justice Department officials."

"And anyone they chose to share it with." Elise pulled out her own notebook. "We need to find out who took over SENTINEL's operations after Rennick resigned. Who inherited the infrastructure."

"Lisa Norman might know. She built the system and would understand how it could be transferred, reconfigured, hidden."

"Lisa Norman is in Portugal, living under an assumed name, trying to keep herself and her daughter alive." Elise shook her head. "She's not going to come out of hiding to help us. Not after what happened last time."

"We have to try. Without Cross, she's the only one who understands who is best poised to drive the mission." Claire underlined a note. "Without that knowledge, we're fighting blind."

"If we contact her, we might lead them right to her."

The words hung between them, heavy with implication. Every action they took from this point forward carried risk, not just for themselves, but for anyone they reached out to. The system they were fighting had eyes everywhere, tentacles that reached every communication channel, every database, every institution. Moving against it meant accepting that more people might die in addition to the ones who had already died.

"We'll find another way," Claire said finally. "We'll find the information we need without putting Lisa at risk. There has to be another path."

"There's always another path," Elise agreed. "We just have to find it before they find us."

• • •

Thomas Winters was buried on a damp, gray Saturday, under a sky that threatened rain. Claire stood at the edge of the crowd, watching from a distance as the Georgetown community gathered to mourn one of their own. Colleagues who had denied him tenure now spoke of his brilliance, his dedication, and his tragic end. Students who had packed his courses wept openly. His daughter, a young woman in her late twenties, stood motionless beside the grave, her face a mask of grief that couldn't quite hide the rage beneath.

She knows, Claire thought, or suspects. She might not have evidence, might not be able to prove anything, but somewhere in her heart, she knows her father didn't die in a drunk driving accident.

The service ended, and people drifted toward their cars, exchanging hushed condolences and promising to stay in touch. Claire waited until the crowd thinned, then approached the grave, where a mound of fresh earth marked Thomas Winters's final resting place.

She didn't pray, as she wasn't sure she believed in anything that would listen, but she stood in silence for a long moment, trying to find words for what she felt.

"I'm sorry," she said finally, her voice barely above a whisper. "I'm sorry we couldn't protect you. I'm sorry your courage cost you everything." She paused. "I promise we'll finish what you helped start. Whatever it takes."

A movement at the edge of her vision made her turn. A man was standing thirty yards away, partially hidden by a large oak tree. Dark suit, government bearing, watching the funeral with an expression that revealed nothing.

Their eyes met across the cemetery. The man didn't look away and didn't pretend he hadn't been watching. He simply stood there, letting her see him, letting her know she was observed.

A message, a reminder that they knew exactly where she was and what she was doing. Claire held his gaze for a long moment, refusing to show the fear that coiled in her stomach. Then she turned and walked away, her pace measured, her head high. She didn't look back.

• • •

Someone had broken into Claire's apartment. She discovered the break-in when she came home from the funeral, still wearing her black dress. The door was locked, as she'd left it. The security system showed no alerts. But inside, things had been moved, subtly, almost imperceptibly, but moved nonetheless.

The dust on her nightstand revealed that the book she placed there last night had shifted two inches to the left. A drawer in her desk wasn't quite closed. The stack of mail on her kitchen counter was reordered in a way she wouldn't have done herself.

They had been inside. They had rifled through her belongings and invaded the one space she had thought was hers alone. They did it in a way that made sure she would know. Another message—we can reach you anywhere, anytime. You are not safe.

Claire stood in the middle of her living room, her hands trembling and her heart pounding in her chest. Every instinct screamed at her to run, grab her go-bag, get in her car, drive until she ran out of road. She could disappear like Patricia was doing, like Cross had tried to do before they caught up with him. But running hadn't saved anyone; it just meant dying exhausted.

She pulled out her phone and called Elise.

"They were in my apartment."

"Mine too." Elise's voice was tight with controlled fury. "Same signature. Nothing taken, nothing damaged. Just enough to let us know they can."

"It's escalating. First the institutional attacks, then Thomas, and now this." Claire walked to the window and looked out at the city, the lights of a thousand windows glittering in the darkness. "They're not just trying to neutralize us anymore. They're trying to terrify us."

"Is it working?"

Claire thought about the question. The honest answer was yes; she was terrified, more frightened than she'd ever been in her life. But terror and surrender weren't the same thing. Terror was just an emotion; what you did with it was a choice.

"No," she said. "It's not working."

"Good. Come over and let's decide what our next move is."

When Claire arrived, she told Elise about a message she received on her way over from someone who might be able to help them. Elise's voice almost whispered. "Someone inside the system. Someone who says they know who's running the operation against us. Who?"

"They won't say. They want to meet first, tomorrow night, at a location they'll provide."

Elise thought for minute and then responded, "It could be a trap, but it might be our only chance. What do you want to do?"

Claire looked around Elise's violated apartment and thought of her own, at the evidence of intrusion that marked every surface. They had taken Thomas, and they had probably taken Cross. They would take them too, eventually, unless they found a way to stop them.

"Set up the meeting, but on our terms," Claire said. "We need backup plans, exit routes, everything we learned the first time around."

"Already thinking about it."

"Good." Elise closed the RF blocking curtains tight, blocking out the city and whatever eyes might be watching. "Because this time, we're not just fighting for a story. We're fighting for our lives."

CHAPTER TWENTY-FOUR

The Source

The meeting was set for 10:00 PM at the Lincoln Memorial. Claire arrived early, approaching from the south side along the Reflecting Pool. Except for the city rats, the memorial was nearly empty at this hour. There were a few tourists lingering on the steps, and a park ranger making his rounds with a flashlight. The massive statue of Lincoln gazed out over the mall, illuminated from below, his expression carrying the gravity of decisions that had shaped a nation.

She climbed the steps slowly, scanning for anything out of place. Elise was already inside, positioned near the south chamber, watching the entrance from a spot that gave her clear sightlines in three directions. They arrived separately and had taken different routes. They understood the risk they were taking so they relied on their established fallback points in case things went wrong. They felt a bit more secure using old protocols that had worked for them over the years.

The source had specified a bench on the memorial's east side, overlooking the Reflecting Pool. Claire found it and sat, her hands in her coat pockets, her eyes moving constantly across the darkness.

At 10:07, a woman sat down beside her.

She was in her early thirties, maybe, with dark hair pulled back in a practical ponytail and the kind of unremarkable face that would disappear in any crowd. She wore a government ID badge clipped to her jacket, which she made no effort to hide. NSA. The three letters were visible even in the dim light.

"Ms. Hensley." The woman's voice was barely above a whisper. "I'm taking a significant risk being here."

"So am I."

"I know. I've read your file." A pause. "The current version of your file, I mean. The one that's been updated in the last two weeks."

Claire felt a chill that had nothing to do with the night air. "You work for them."

"I work for the NSA. I thought that meant working for the country." The woman's voice carried a bitterness that was hard to fake. "I joined right out of grad school. Cryptography. I believed in the mission—protecting Americans, stopping attacks, using technology to keep people safe. When SENTINEL was exposed, I thought it was an aberration. I was naive. SENTINEL became what it became because oversight died. The moment Congress stopped watching, the tools we'd built for protection became instruments of political control and personal profit. That's not corruption of the system, that *is* the system, when no one's minding it."

"And now, what do you think now?"

"Now I know better." The woman turned to face her, and Claire saw someone whose world view had been shattered. "SENTINEL didn't die, Ms. Hensley. It evolved. The people running it now make Katherine Rennick look like a civil libertarian."

• • •

Her name was Meranda Caine. She previously worked in the NSA's Signals Intelligence Directorate for eight years, specializing in algorithm development for pattern recognition systems. After the SENTINEL revelations, she was assigned to what the agency called the "reform compliance team". It was purportedly a group tasked with ensuring that the new oversight requirements were being properly implemented.

"It was supposed to be about accountability," Meranda said. "For the first few months, I believed we were designing meaningful reforms. Real changes to how the agency operated."

"What changed?"

"I noticed inconsistencies like server traffic that didn't match the official records and processing loads that suggested computational activity far beyond what our authorized programs would require." Meranda's hands and their white knuckles were clasped tightly in her lap. "I started digging. I was careful and figured out how to gain access to data flows I wasn't supposed to see. And I found ORION."

"ORION?"

"The new name. Same core architecture as SENTINEL with the behavioral modeling, the influence topology, and the predictive algorithms, but refined and upgraded. They learned from the vulnerabilities you exposed. The documentation is better hidden, and the operational security is tighter. And the scope..." She shook her head. "SENTINEL targeted hundreds of people over several years, ORION has identified thousands of potential targets in the nine months it's been operational."

"Thousands?"

"Journalists, researchers, activists, politicians, business leaders—anyone whose influence patterns suggest they might become obstacles to their objectives." Meranda's voice dropped even lower. "They're not just watching anymore. They're preemptively shaping and nudging people toward certain positions, away from asking probing questions, before they even become threats."

Claire reflected on the last nine months. She wondered, had the feeling that the world had moved on and that the fight was over been manufactured? Had they been nudged toward complacency while their enemies regrouped?

"Who's running it?" she asked.

Meranda hesitated. "Do you remember the congressional hearings? The Intelligence Committee members who questioned Rennick?"

"Of course."

"Do you remember Senator James Harwood from Virginia being a part of the committee? He barely asked any questions. You might remember him being sympathetic to 'national security concerns.' When he spoke, he was very understanding about the 'difficult choices' intelligence professionals have to make."

Claire remembered. He was a quiet presence at the hearings, nodding along while his colleagues demanded answers. She'd assumed he was just one of the intelligence community's reliable defenders, the kind of politician who never met a surveillance program he didn't like.

"Harwood retired from the Senate eight months ago," Meranda continued. "He took a consulting position with a private intelligence contractor. Except the contractor is a shell company, and the consulting position is cover for his real role overseeing ORION's operations from outside the official government structure."

"A senator?"

"A former senator with decades of intelligence community connections, unlimited access to classified systems, and complete deniability." Meranda paused to let it all sink in. "Rennick believed in process and rules. She bent them, broke them sometimes, but she still operated within a framework. Harwood doesn't have that constraint. He's not officially a member of the government anymore. He's just a private citizen with a consulting contract and a program that can reach into anyone's life and tear it apart."

Claire felt the pieces clicking into place. The nine months of peace had been a transition phase. Time for Harwood to establish his operation, take over SENTINEL's infrastructure, and begin building something far more coercive and powerful.

"Why are you telling me this?" she asked. "You could be arrested or worse."

"Because someone has to stop them." Meranda reached into her jacket and pulled out a USB drive, small and unremarkable. "Everything I've found is on here. Server logs, communication intercepts, operational planning documents. It's not as comprehensive as what you had on SENTINEL, they've learned to be more careful, but it's enough to prove ORION exists. Enough to show that the reforms were a lie."

"And you trust me with this and potentially your life?"

"I'm giving it to the person who exposed SENTINEL." Meranda pressed the drive into Claire's hand. "I can't do what you did. I don't have the network, the sources, the ability to coordinate a publication that can't be suppressed. But you do. You've done it before."

Claire closed her fingers around the drive. "They'll come for you," she said. "Once this gets out, they'll know where it came from."

"I know. I've made arrangements." Meranda stood, her movements crisp and controlled. "I have forty-eight hours before my absence is noticed. By then, I'll be somewhere they can't easily reach."

"Where?"

"It's better if no one knows." She paused, looking down at Claire with an expression that mixed fear, hope and resignation. "Finish this, Ms. Hensley for all of us. For everyone they've hurt and everyone they're planning to hurt."

Then she disappeared into the darkness on her way toward the Mall.

Claire watched her go; the USB drive clutched in her fist like a weapon.

• • •

Elise appeared beside her thirty seconds later. "I saw the handoff. What did she give you?"

"Everything." Claire stood, her legs unsteady. "Or hopefully enough. Just as we thought, SENTINEL has a new name, a new leader, and a scope that makes the original look small."

"Who's running it?"

"James Harwood. The senator who sat on the Intelligence Committee during the hearings. He retired, went private, and took SENTINEL's infrastructure with him." Claire started walking toward the steps. "We need to move."

She froze and took stock of what she sensed but had not seen yet.

At the base of the memorial, where the steps met the plaza, three figures had appeared in dark suits with government bearing. They were standing in a loose formation that blocked the most direct exit route.

"Claire." Elise's voice was tight. "I see them."

More figures emerged from the darkness. There were two on the north side and two more approaching from the direction of the Reflecting Pool. They'd formed a perimeter, closing in with professional precision.

The meeting had been observed, and now ORION was making its move.

"The fallback," Elise said. "Now."

The women moved fast, angling toward the memorial's south chamber where a service door led to a maintenance corridor they'd scouted earlier that day. The figures below started up the steps. They picked up their pace when they realized their targets were spooked.

Elise hit the service door at a run. She'd practiced the same maneuver back at the suburban train station. Claire was right behind her. The corridor was dark, lit only by emergency strips along the floor. They ran without speaking, navigating by memory and instinct, their footsteps echoing off the concrete walls.

Behind them, the door crashed open with voices shouting for them to stop, the pursuing flashlight beams cutting into the darkness.

The corridor ended at another door that led to an exterior stairwell on the memorial's west side. Elise burst through it into the cold night air, Claire still on her heels. Below them was the dark expanse of the Potomac. Above them were the lights of Arlington Cemetery on the far shore.

"The car," Elise gasped. "Two blocks south. Go."

They ran, cutting across the grass toward the road, weaving through parked vehicles and landscaping barriers. Claire's lungs burned and her legs screamed, but she kept moving with the USB drive clutched in her hand, knowing that everything depended on getting away and surviving long enough to use what Meranda had given them.

The car was now in sight. They dove into the rental, Elise behind the wheel. The engine roared to life before Claire had even closed the door.

In the rearview mirror, Elise saw figures emerging from the memorial grounds, running toward their own vehicles. At least the fugitives had a head start, and Claire had the drive. Elise floored the accelerator, and they disappeared into the Washington night.

• • •

They avoided toll roads and drove for two hours before stopping. Switchbacks, detours, doubling back on themselves, every evasive technique they'd learned during the SENTINEL investigation and the months of fear that followed. When they finally pulled into a rest stop in rural Maryland, both were shaking with exhaustion and adrenaline.

"We need to look at what's on this drive," Claire said. She was already pulling out a laptop, air-gapped, and never connected to any network. "We need to know what we're dealing with."

"And then?"

"We do what we did before. We find outlets, we verify, and then we publish." Claire plugged in the drive and watched the files appear. There were multiple folders containing documents, server logs and emails. It was the digital skeleton of yet another surveillance apparatus that had refused to die. "This time, we do it faster," Claire said with resolve. "They know we have this now. They'll be coming."

Elise leaned over to look at the screen. "Do you think Meranda got away?"

Claire thought about the woman on the memorial steps, walking into the darkness with forty-eight hours to disappear. She thought about Thomas Winters, who hadn't been able to disappear fast enough. She thought about Ryan Cross, who had vanished and might never be seen again.

"I hope so," she said. "But we can't count on it. We can only count on ourselves."

She opened the first file and started to read. The war wasn't over. It was just entering a new phase.

CHAPTER TWENTY-FIVE

Orion

It was hard to believe, but the documents painted a picture of something far worse than SENTINEL. Claire and Elise spent the night in a motel outside Hagerstown, Maryland, poring over Meranda's files by the glow of their air-gapped laptop. What they found made the original revelations look like a prelude, a rough draft of something that had now been perfected.

ORION didn't just surveil, warn, and nudge. It had mastered prediction and the neutralizing protocols SENTINEL had begun. The system exploited years of behavioral data, refined by machine learning algorithms sharpened during its run as SENTINEL.

The files contained targeting criteria that read like a dystopian checklist: *Pattern indicators for oppositional tendency development. Predictive markers for institutional skepticism. Behavioral signatures associated with whistleblower potential.*

"They're not waiting for people to become problems anymore," Elise said, her voice hollow. "They're identifying people who might become problems and neutralizing them in advance."

"Preventive destruction." Claire scrolled through another document, an operational summary showing intervention timelines. Some targets would be subjected to years of subtle manipulation before they even knew they were being watched. Relationships would be undermined and career opportunities diverted. Others would end their lives prematurely. "They've widened their net. They'll eliminate anyone who might get in their way."

The scope was staggering. Meranda had estimated thousands of targets, but the documents suggested the number was higher, perhaps tens of thousands, spread across every sector of American society. Politicians, journalists, academics, business leaders, activists. Anyone whose influence patterns suggested they might one day become inconvenient.

At the center of it all was James Harwood.

The files contained communications between Harwood and key intelligence officials, people who had officially condemned SENTINEL while quietly helping its successor take shape. There were budget documents showing funding flows through a maze of private contractors and classified accounts. There were operational authorizations bearing Harwood's signature, approving actions against specific targets with the clinical detachment of a bureaucrat signing expense reports.

One authorization, dated three weeks ago, stood out: It targeted Thomas Winters.

Claire stared at the document, her hands trembling. Thomas's name, typed in a government font. A checkbox marked "Terminal action approved." A signature line with Harwood's initials. The official sanction for murder, reduced to administrative paperwork.

"We have him," she said. "This is proof, direct authorization of an assassination by a former U.S. senator."

"We have evidence," Elise corrected. "Proof requires verification, corroboration, multiple sources. Right now, we have files on a USB drive that could be dismissed as fabrications."

"Then we verify and corroborate. We find the sources." Claire closed the laptop. "But first, we need to survive long enough to do it."

• • •

Come morning, they learned Meranda Caine was dead. The news came through a breaking alert on Claire's phone: *NSA employee found dead in apparent suicide. Officials say the woman had been under investigation for unauthorized access to classified systems.*

Suicide. The same verdict they'd rendered for others who knew too much, said too much, threatened the wrong people. Meranda had thought she had forty-eight hours when she had less than twelve.

Claire sat on the edge of the motel bed, feeling something inside her go cold and hard. Another name to add to the list. Another person who had risked everything to tell the truth and paid the ultimate price.

"They're cleaning up fast," Elise said. "They'll get rid of anyone who might corroborate what's on that drive."

History was repeating itself in an awful loop of discovery, disclosure, and more death. "We need allies and outlets. Someone willing to publish before they can stop us." Elise turned from the window when Claire added, "The Post won't touch this. Not after what happened last time. They've already been visited by government lawyers warning about 'ongoing national security matters.'"

"How do you know that?"

"Marcus texted me a warning last night. He said the paper has been told that any story involving intelligence community operations will result in immediate legal action." Elise's expression was grim. Claire reiterated what they both knew was inevitable, "They've locked down the mainstream press. Everyone's scared."

Claire thought about their options. The Post was out, and the NY Times would be under similar pressure. The European consortium had lost key members to legal complications and professional destruction. Daniel's nonprofit was too small and vulnerable. Every institutional pathway they'd used before had been anticipated and blocked.

"What about Senator Johnson?" she asked. "She led the SENTINEL hearings and pushed through the reform bill. If anyone in government would want to know about this, she would."

"Johnson is under surveillance and has been for months, according to these documents." Elise gestured at the laptop. "ORION identified her as a priority target after the reforms passed. They've been working to isolate her, undermine her support base, position rivals to challenge her in the next election."

"They're targeting a sitting senator?"

"They're targeting anyone who might threaten them. Johnson is at the top of the list." Elise sat down across from Claire. "We can't go through normal channels. Every normal channel has been compromised or intimidated. We need something else, something they haven't anticipated."

Claire was quiet for a long moment, turning over possibilities in her mind. Then a thought struck her, something so obvious she couldn't believe she hadn't considered it before.

"Katherine Rennick," she said.

Elise stared at her. "Rennick is in federal prison."

"Exactly. She's the one person ORION can't pressure, threaten, or make disappear." Claire felt an idea taking shape, jelling into something that might actually work. "And she knows more about how these systems operate than anyone alive. She built SENTINEL. She'd understand ORION's architecture, its vulnerabilities, its operators."

"She's also the person who authorized terminal actions against American citizens. She tried to destroy us." Elise wasn't convinced. "Why would she help?"

"Because Harwood is her enemy too." Claire stood, pacing the small room. "Think about it. Rennick went to prison to protect the institution. She sacrificed herself to preserve the system she believed in. Now Harwood has taken that system and turned it into something even she would consider monstrous."

"You think she has principles? After everything she did?"

"I think she has a code. A twisted, dangerous code, but a code nonetheless." Claire stopped pacing. "She believed in limits and process. She started out believing that there were lines that shouldn't be crossed, even in the name of national security. She lost the plot, but, on some level, she had a conscience. Harwood is unabashedly crossing all of those lines and getting rich as a result. That's a whole other level of evil."

Elise was quiet, processing the argument. Finally, she said, "Even if you're right, how do we get to her? Federal prison isn't exactly open for visitors."

"Journalists can request interviews with inmates. It takes time to go through channels, but it's possible." Claire grabbed her bag and started packing. "And while we wait, we do everything else. We verify what we can, reach out to secondary sources, prepare the story so it's ready the moment we have somewhere to publish it."

"All while ORION is hunting us."

"All while ORION is hunting us," Claire agreed. "We knew it wouldn't be easy. We knew there would be costs. Meranda knew it too. We can honor her sacrifice by finishing what she started, or we can run and hide and wait for them to find us anyway. Elise, we've been at this crossroads before. I know you're getting tired. So am I. I don't think we have another choice, do you?"

Elise stood, shouldering her own bag. "Then let's finish it."

• • •

They spent the next three days in constant motion. They never stayed in one place more than twelve hours. They paid cash for everything. They avoided their electronics and communicated only through in-person, chance encounters. These skills had become survival instincts now, the difference between life and death measured in tradecraft and paranoia.

Claire submitted the interview request to the Bureau of Prisons through a lawyer, one of the few people they still trusted. She was a media defense attorney who had helped them during the first investigation. The request would take weeks to process under normal circumstances, but Claire had asked the lawyer to emphasize the urgency, to frame it as a follow-up to the original SENTINEL reporting.

Meanwhile, they worked the documents.

Elise focused on the technical material to decode the operational logs and verify the authenticity of the data signatures. Everything checked out. The files were genuine NSA documents, created on government systems, bearing the digital fingerprints of legitimate intelligence operations.

Claire worked on the human angle, reaching out to sources she'd developed over two decades of investigative journalism. Most wouldn't talk—they were either too compromised or too scared. They were all aware of what had happened to people who crossed the intelligence community. Less than a handful responded carefully, through intermediaries.

There was a former NSA analyst, now retired, who had heard rumors about a program called ORION but had never seen proof it existed. There was a congressional staffer who had noticed irregularities in intelligence community budget submissions. Lastly, there was a journalist in Brussels who had been investigating similar patterns in European surveillance operations.

On the fourth day, the lawyer called.

"The interview's been approved," she said. "Katherine Rennick has agreed to speak with you tomorrow afternoon at the federal correctional facility in Alderson, West Virginia."

Claire felt a surge of something that might have been hope. "That was fast."

"Too fast." The lawyer's voice was cautious. "I don't know what strings got pulled or why, but this kind of expedited access doesn't happen without someone making it happen. Be careful, Claire. This could be a trap."

"At this point, we don't have the luxury of being careful." Claire looked at Elise, who nodded slowly. "We're going."

"Then watch your back. Whatever Rennick tells you, remember who she is. Remember what she did. She's not your ally, she's a weapon, and weapons don't care who they're pointed at."

The lawyer hung up. Claire stared at her phone for a long moment, thinking about what waited for them in West

Virginia. Yes, Rennick was the enemy they had helped bring down but she had also been used.

The architect of SENTINEL agreed to meet. The woman who had authorized the destruction of countless lives in the name of national security.

And now, maybe she was the only person who could help them destroy what had risen in SENTINEL's place.

"Pack light," she said to Elise. "We leave at dawn."

CHAPTER TWENTY-SIX

The Enemy of My Enemy

The Federal Prison Camp at Alderson sat in the hills of West Virginia like a cruel joke, a campus of low buildings surrounded by green lawns, more college dormitory than penitentiary.

Claire passed through three security checkpoints before reaching the visitors' room. She had to surrender her phone, her bag, and anything that could record or transmit. The room itself was institutional beige, furnished with bolted-down tables and plastic chairs. Prisoners and their visitors were watched over by cameras in every corner and guards who stood with the studied boredom of people who had seen everything.

She waited for twelve minutes before Katherine Rennick was brought in.

Prison had changed Katherine. The silver hair was longer now. The dark suits had been replaced by khaki scrubs that hung loose on a frame that had grown thinner. Her skin was pale and pasty-looking, but her eyes were still of someone who had spent thirty years learning to see through people.

Rennick sat down across from Claire and, for a long moment, neither of them spoke. Two women who had tried to destroy each other and now were separated by nothing but a prison table.

"Ms. Hensley." Rennick's voice still carried an authority that even federal prison couldn't diminish. "I have to admit, I didn't expect to see you again. Certainly not here."

"I didn't expect to be here."

"Yet here you are." A ghost of a smile crossed Rennick's face. "What is it you need? Something you can't get anywhere else, of course." She leaned back slightly in her chair and held up a hand for Claire to wait while she reached into the pocket of her prison khakis and produced a small notepad and stubby pencil, items she was permitted in this minimum-security prison. She slid them across the table toward Claire, then pulled out a second set for herself. Her eyes flicked almost imperceptibly toward the cameras in the corners, then back to Claire.

Rennick got right to the point. "They approved of this visit faster than any I've seen in eighteen months," her eyes conveyed nothing. She wrote something on her notepad, angling it so only Claire could read: *Assume every word is recorded. Write anything sensitive.* Rennick didn't trust that they weren't being monitored by the very people Claire had come to discuss.

Claire understood immediately. She had a spur-of-the-moment idea. "I had some loose ends that needed cleaning up for a web update on the hearing." She picked up the pencil and notepad in appreciation of the additional caution.

Claire had rehearsed arguments, anticipated objections, and strategies for persuasion on the drive from Maryland. But sitting across from Rennick, all that preparation seemed inadequate. There was no way to ease her nervousness. She started anyway.

"Now that you've had time to think about the hearing, are there things you feel weren't fairly treated in our coverage?" It took some doing, but as she pretended to get ready for Rennick's response, she wrote on her notepad: *SENTINEL new name Orion, Harwood heading. significantly bigger scope.*

Rennick's expression didn't change, but something flickered in her eyes. Interest, calculation, or perhaps, buried deep, a spark of anger.

Continue, Rennick wrote as she answered. "My intentions were always well meaning. Sometimes, it takes unorthodox measures to keep our country safe. You can second guess my decisions, but I made them based on what was important at the time. Many of those details are classified and can't be revealed in a public trial, so no, your coverage will always be incomplete."

Claire pretended to take notes. Her message for Rennick was brief, and she hoped triggering: *expanded scope targets 10,000+ termination protocols favored. Harwood=contractor w/ deniability. no rules.*

Claire asked another question to give Rennick an opportunity to write a response to this news if she elected to. It also gave cover for an ongoing exchange. "I understand you can't comment on classified details, but this is a chance to explain how you evaluated the decisions you made."

Rennick continued, "I built SENTINEL to protect this country. I made difficult compromises, but always within a framework. Always with the understanding that there were boundaries that shouldn't be crossed. I honor values and principles that have always guided my intentions." Her eyes met Claire's.

Rennick switched to writing rapidly, *He hates rules, why I kept him at arm's length. proof of malfeasance?*

Claire had a decision to make. How much would she share, and what about the cameras? She'd come this far, so in a low whisper, she laid out a recap of the files from Meranda, the operational logs, the targeting lists, the authorization for Thomas Winters's murder, the type of corroborating sources they'd found. She held nothing back. If Rennick was going to help them, she needed the complete picture.

When Claire finished, Rennick sat and stared for nearly a minute. Her gaze returned to her notepad as her mind worked through the implications before she shared her thoughts.

You have enough to prove ORION exists, not enough to bring it down.

Claire threw out a hail-Mary-pass of a premise she hoped would help her understand how Harwood might approach Orion. She prayed that Rennick would understand and follow her lead when she asked it.

"Ms. Rennick, I believe that national security is personally very important to you. If you had a second chance to do it all over again so you could continue to serve the mission without jeopardizing it, well, what would you need to do differently?"

Rennick raised one eyebrow, gave the questions some thought, glanced at the camera and began to outline a cautionary tale. "I would learn from my mistakes. I'd make sure that any accessible system documentation had plausible deniability to support the tough choices that seem to multiply. I'd do a better job of managing skeptics. I'd discourage micromanaging by well-intentioned journalists or Senate Oversight Committees who don't have access to sensitive intelligence. To do that successfully, I'd need to go on an information offensive and do a better job of articulating challenges we can't simply ignore. I'd also tighten the decision tree to ensure that all decisions were carefully vetted before executing them.

Then what do we need? Claire wrote.

Rennick continued her narrative, "There would still be tough choices to make, and there must be accountability for those. I'd design a system for the most sensitive authorizations. I'd use a digital ledger that requires multi-factor authentication: password, my full signature, biometric scan, and a physical token that only authorized personnel possess. Every action in the ledger would be cryptographically signed and timestamped. It ensures accountability within the program. Accountability is important to maintain the trust of the people putting their lives on the line."

"How would you make the system tamper-proof to ensure accountability?" Claire asked.

"I'd set up a separate secure facility with back-up security protocols to prevent rogue operators from getting away with unauthorized actions."

Harwood would be using this system? Claire wrote.

Yes, if using SENTINEL as base. Recorded, biometric sig.

Claire felt her pulse quicken as she wrote her response. *How do we access it?*

You don't.

Claire needed to continue this conversation. There was a lot she needed to get before leaving, so she asked another interview sounding question. "Do you have regrets, not about the mission, but about what has happened to you personally?"

Rennick continued "In hindsight, I'd plan a better exit strategy for myself. I'd spend more time cultivating allies in the Justice Department and the White House. If there was another investigation, instead of allowing myself to be the scapegoat and not have a chance to continue to personally keep fighting for what I believe in, I'd sacrifice some direct reports, claim the program was operating outside of my knowledge, and live to fight another day."

Rennick whispered. "The ledger is on an air-gapped system at a secure facility. No network access, no remote entry, the only access is physical." She smiled thinly. "I assume that's where you're hoping I can help."

Claire wrote back a definitive *Yes.*

• • •

You know the facilities and security protocols, Claire wrote.

Rennick scribbled, *as you see, no way 4 hands-on assistance.*

Claire implored*, help me stop Harwood. Layout, access points, authentication requirements*

Rennick studied Claire for a long moment and almost laughed. She tilted her head, blinked, and smiled "That's ambitious, Ms. Hensley. Even for you."

"Do you have a better idea?" Claire whispered.

"Several, but none are given the current circumstances." Rennick leaned over the table to continue her writing. *Facility called Relay Station Echo. Looks like a telecommunications research center, Mountains of western Virginia. substantial security, not impenetrable.*

"What would we need to get in?" Claire whispered.

"Credentials from someone with active access" Rennick whispered back before continuing her writing, *maintenance window every Thursday night, 2-4 AM. Security systems cycle through diagnostic routines. authentication protocols relaxed for system testing. I was told it's an acceptable risk.*

"How do we get credentials?" Claire whispered.

“Ms. Hensley,” she whispered, "That's your problem to solve. I can't conjure access cards out of thin air." Rennick's expression hardened.

Rennick continued the earlier conversational thread for the camera’s benefit, "This is where you need to understand something, Ms. Hensley. I'm not talking to you because I have personal regrets. I regret the perversion of everything I built with good intentions. I'm not seeking forgiveness for what I did."

"I didn't ask for your forgiveness."

Then Rennick said rather loudly, "Good. Because you won't get it. I don't regret SENTINEL. I regret that it was exposed. I regret that people like you were able to paint necessary actions as crimes." Her voice was cold, unapologetic.

Back to a whisper she continued, "Harwood has crossed lines I cannot accept."

Claire absorbed this, recognizing it for what it was: not an alliance, but a temporary convergence of interests. Rennick wasn't changing sides. She was protecting her legacy by destroying the man who had corrupted it.

Claire wasn’t about to stop now. She wrote, *we need a longer convo, I have an idea for cover. Let’s pretend-*

Claire launched into her improbable scheme. “Ms. Rennick, yours is a compelling life story. I admire your passion for national security and good intentions. I’d like to write your biography. It would an honor to use your story to help Americans understand how difficult it was for you to walk the lines you did to protect them. Before you say no, can we discuss and maybe outline what that arrangement might look like? Tell me, what would it take?" Claire asked, the covert doubling for her overt, real question.

Rennick crossed between writing and whispering for the next forty minutes, laying out the architecture of Relay Station Echo with the precision of someone who had spent years thinking about security systems. The layout, the personnel rotation, and the location of the server room where the ledger was stored. The vulnerabilities she had identified and warned about that had been ignored.

Claire tried to memorize the whispers and hoped her written notes wouldn't be taken when she left the room, although Rennick didn't seem concerned. Hopefully key details could live in her head until she could transfer it to Elise.

When Rennick finished, she sat back and looked at Claire with something that might have been respect or the calculation of a chess player evaluating an opponent.

"One more thing," she whispered. "He'll know you're coming. Not specifics, but the general shape of it. He's been watching you since you obtained those documents. I'm sure he knows you are here. This meeting was approved too quickly. He'll be expecting you to make a move."

"Then we'll have to be faster than he expects." Claire whispered.

"Speed won't be enough. You need misdirection. Make him look in the wrong direction while you move in the right one." When Rennick finished writing, she stood, signaling that the interview was over. She whispered, "I've given you what you need. What you do with it is up to you."

Claire stood as well, facing the woman who had been her enemy and was now... what? Not an ally or a friend, something stranger. A weapon pointed at a common target.

"Why did you agree to meet me?" Claire asked. "You could have refused. You had nothing to gain by seeing me."

Rennick considered the question but maintained her steel gaze as she leaned into Claire and spoke softly, "I built something I believed in and sacrificed for. Harwood has turned it into a monster." Her eyes were hard, unforgiving. "I'd rather see it destroyed than watch him wield it without restraint. If that means helping the woman who put me in prison, so be it."

She turned and walked toward the door, where a guard waited to escort her back to her cell. At the threshold, she paused and looked back.

"Good luck, Ms. Hensley. You'll need it."

Then she was gone, and Claire was alone in the visitors' room, carrying the knowledge that might save them, or get them all killed. She expected to be stopped at the door, but the guards didn't say a word. Claire figured that the guards were not really listening and didn't care, since this was a minimum-security facility. Others would review the meeting and determine what Rennick had told her.

• • •

Elise was waiting in the parking lot, her eyes scanning every car that entered. "Well?" she asked as Claire slid into the passenger seat.

"She talked. I have notes on a system where Harwood's authorizations are stored." Claire buckled her seatbelt as Elise pulled out of the lot. "There's a ledger. It's cryptographically signed and biometrically authenticated. Every terminal action Harwood has approved is recorded there. It's the proof we need."

"And let me guess, it's stored in a secure facility that's impossible to access."

"Not impossible. Just extremely difficult." Claire began recounting what Rennick had told her—the location, the maintenance window, the vulnerabilities that existed during the diagnostic routine. "We still need credentials. Someone with active access to the facility."

"Where exactly are we supposed to find someone like that?"

Claire was thinking through the options. Then a name surfaced in her memory, someone they'd almost forgotten in the chaos of the past weeks.

"Ryan Cross," she said. "He disappeared, but that doesn't mean he's dead. He worked in counterintelligence at the FBI. If anyone knows people with access to facilities like this, he does."

"Cross could be anywhere. He could be in a shallow grave somewhere."

"Or he could be hiding. He was extremely resourceful when we were on the run together. What if he's waiting for an opportunity to fight back?" Claire pulled out her phone, one of the burners they'd been cycling through. "Before Ryan disappeared, he gave me an emergency contact. A way to reach him if everything went wrong."

"You never mentioned that."

"I never thought I'd need it. I thought we had won." Claire stared at the phone in her hand. "I was wrong about a lot of things."

She dialed the number in a sequence she'd memorized months ago and never expected to use. The phone rang once. Twice. Three times.

Then a voice she recognized: "I was wondering when you'd call."

"Cross." Claire felt relief washing through her. "You're alive."

"Barely. They came for me three weeks ago. I got out with minutes to spare." His voice was tired but alert. "I've been watching from a distance. I saw what happened to Winters and that poor NSA analyst. I figured it was only a matter of time before you needed help."

"We need more than help. We need access to a facility called Relay Station Echo. Someone with credentials who can get us inside."

A pause. Then: "That's a big ask."

"I know, but it's the only way to get the evidence we need to bring down Harwood. He's now a contractor with plausible deniability spearheading SENTINEL's more lethal incarnation. They're calling it ORION."

"Harwood." Cross's voice hardened. "I've been dreaming about taking down that bastard for years. He was always the worst of them, even Rennick knew it." Another pause, "I might know someone. Someone who owes me, and who has reason to want ORION destroyed as much as we do."

"Can you set it up?"

"I can try. Give me twenty-four hours. I'll be in touch."

The line went dead. Claire lowered the phone and looked at Elise.

"We have twenty-four hours," she said."

Elise kept driving, heading north into the mountains, putting distance between them and anyone who might be following.

CHAPTER TWENTY-SEVEN

Relay Station Echo

The facility sat in a hollow between two ridges, invisible from the public road. Claire studied it through binoculars from an overlook half a mile away, memorizing the layout that Rennick had described. As expected, there was a cluster of low buildings surrounded by a chain-link fence that was topped with razor wire. There were guard stations at the main entrance and two secondary gates. The parking lot had just a dozen vehicles, probably a skeleton night shift. Beyond the fence, the dark mass of the Blue Ridge Mountains loomed on all sides.

It looked like what it pretended to be: a telecommunications research facility, the kind of anonymous government installation that dotted the rural landscape of western Virginia. Only the density of the security cameras and the alertness of the guards suggested something more.

"Time check," Cross said from beside her. He'd arrived at their rendezvous point six hours ago, looking like he'd aged ten years since she'd last seen him. Whatever he'd been through in the weeks since his disappearance, it had left marks that wouldn't fade easily.

"1:47 AM," Elise replied. She was crouched behind them, monitoring a laptop that showed feeds from traffic cameras they'd tapped along the access road. "Thirteen minutes until the maintenance window opens."

Claire lowered the binoculars and looked at the two people who had agreed to risk everything for this mission, again. The three of them were all that remained of the coalition that had brought down SENTINEL. The other living members were scattered and unreachable, too frightened to continue.

And now they were about to break into a classified government facility.

"You're sure about your contact?" she asked Cross.

"As sure as I can be." Cross checked his watch. "He's inside now and has been for three hours. He'll disable the corridor sensors at 2:00 AM exactly and meet us at the service entrance on the north side. He's putting it all on the line. He's seen what ORION does to people who ask questions. He doesn't want to be part of it anymore."

Another true believer turned apostate. Elise was thankful for this pattern, another person driven to betrayal by the gap between what they'd signed up for and what they'd been asked to do. The intelligence community had no shortage of them. The question was always whether they found the courage to act before the system found them.

"Movement at the main gate," Elise said. "There's a vehicle leaving. Looks like a shift change."

They watched the headlights wind down the access road until they disappeared around a curve. The facility settled back into its quiet routine, guards making their rounds, lights burning in a few windows, and the hum of equipment audible even at this distance.

"Eight minutes," Cross said. "We should move."

• • •

They approached through the forest, following a route Cross had mapped using satellite imagery and his contact's knowledge of the security patrol patterns.

The night was warm and moonless, the darkness almost complete beneath the thick canopy of leafy tree branches. Claire moved by feel and memory, trusting the others to maintain spacing, trusting the plan they'd developed over twenty-four hours of intense preparation.

The fence appeared through the trees. It looked formidable, twelve feet of chain-link topped with razor wire, sensors embedded in the posts that would trigger alarms if anyone tried to cut through. But there was a gap in the coverage, Rennick had said. A blind spot where the terrain created a dead zone in the camera angles, where someone who knew exactly where to step could approach the fence without being seen.

Cross found it first, signaling them with a low whistle. They gathered at the base of a large oak, its roots creating a depression in the earth that put them below the sight line of the nearest camera.

"Two minutes," Cross whispered. "When the maintenance window opens, the fence sensors go into diagnostic mode. We'll have forty-five seconds to get through before they cycle back online."

"And if your contact doesn't come through?"

"Then we run, fast, and in different directions." Cross's face was barely visible in the darkness. "But he'll come through. He's as committed to this as we are."

The worry of detection was hanging heavy over all three of them. They waited in silence, each lost in their own thoughts. Claire tried to keep her mind on anything but the fear that this wouldn't work. She found herself thinking about Thomas Winters and Meranda Caine, about all the people who had died because they'd dared to tell the truth. She thought about what would happen if they failed tonight. They couldn't fail everyone ORION was targeting. She thought of all the lives that would be quietly dismantled by algorithms and manipulation.

She thought about what success would look like. Harwood exposed and ORION destroyed. It had to be worth her recommitting herself despite everything she'd already sacrificed.

Cross's watch beeped once, softly. "Now." They moved.

• • •

The fence section had been pre-cut by Cross's contact while he worked earlier in the day. He created an opening that was invisible until you knew where to look.

They slipped through one at a time—Claire first, then Elise, then Cross bringing up the rear. The facility grounds stretched before them. There was large expanse of open lawn dotted with utilitarian buildings and pools of harsh white illumination cast by the security lights.

The service entrance was fifty yards ahead with its steel door set into the side of the main building. Cross's contact was supposed to be waiting there, ready to let them in.

They crossed the open ground in a crouch, moving from shadow to shadow, timing their movements to the rhythm of the security camera sweeps. Forty yards. Thirty. Twenty.

The door opened.

A figure stood in the dim light of the corridor beyond, a man in his forties, wearing the uniform of a facility security officer. His face was drawn with apprehension, but his movements were steady as he waved them inside.

"This way," he said, his voice barely audible. "The corridor sensors are down for another six minutes. After that, we're on camera whether we like it or not."

They followed him through the building's maze of hallways and security doors that matched the layout Rennick had described. Left, then right, then through a door that required the contact's badge and PIN. They raced down a flight of stairs to a basement level that wasn't supposed to exist.

"Server room's at the end of this hall," the contact said. "The ledger system is in the secure cage on the right side. You'll need this, " He handed Cross a keycard. "It'll get you through the cage door, but only during the maintenance window. Once the diagnostic's complete, it'll be worthless."

"How long do we have?"

"Eighteen minutes. Maybe less if someone notices the sensor gaps." The contact looked at each of them in turn. "I'll be at the north exit. When you have what you need, get out fast. Don't wait for me if something goes wrong."

"Thank you," Claire said. "For everything."

The man shook his head. "Don't thank me, just make it count. Make all of this count for something."

Then he was gone, disappearing back the way they'd come, leaving them alone in the basement corridor of one of the most secure facilities in the American intelligence apparatus.

• • •

The server room was cold at a temperature that would protect the equipment lining the walls.

Rows of black cabinets hummed with processing power, their LED lights blinking in a language only machines understood. At the far end, behind a mesh cage secured with a heavy-duty lock, sat a single terminal connected to an isolated server stack.

It had to be the ledger system containing everything Harwood had authorized, cryptographically signed, and biometrically verified. It was the proof they needed.

Cross swiped the keycard, and the cage door clicked open.

Elise moved to the terminal, her fingers flying over the keyboard as she navigated the system's interface. "It's partitioned," she said. "Multiple security layers, but the maintenance mode has disabled most of the authentication requirements."

"Can you access the ledger?"

"Working on it." Elise's face was lit by the screen's glow, her expression intense with concentration. "There, I'm in. I can see the authorization logs. Christ, there are hundreds of them with operations going back months."

"Can you copy them?"

"I will." She plugged a portable drive into the terminal's USB port. "The transfer rate is slow, this system was designed for security, not speed. It's going to take... eight minutes, maybe nine."

"We might not have nine minutes."

"Then we'd better hope we do."

Claire stationed herself at the cage door while Cross kept watch on the corridor. The minutes crawled by with each second feeling like an eternity. She could hear her own heartbeat and feel the sweat on her palms despite the cold air.

Five minutes. Six. Seven.

"Claire." Cross's voice was tight. "We've got movement. Someone's coming down the stairs."

"How soon?"

"Thirty seconds. Maybe less."

"Elise?"

"Ninety percent. I need another minute."

"We don't have a minute."

The footsteps in the corridor were getting closer. It sounded like multiple people moving fast. Someone had noticed something wrong, a sensor glitch, a missing guard, something that had triggered an investigation.

"Ninety-five percent," Elise said. "Almost there."

Cross drew his weapon, a pistol Claire hadn't known he was carrying. "Get ready to move."

"Done!" Elise yanked the drive from the terminal and shoved it into her pocket. "I've got it. Let's go."

They ran down the corridor and up the stairs they had used, leaving their pursuers behind on the lower level. Whoever was chasing them must have used a separate staircase to keep their approach stealthy.

The main corridor seemed longer than before. They weren't quite to the exit when they heard, "Stop! Federal agents!", followed by the crack of a gunshot that sent plaster raining from the ceiling.

Cross returned three quick shots that scattered their pursuers, buying precious seconds. They continued sprinting to the end of the corridor. The contact was there, at the north exit, holding the door open. "Go! Now!"

They charged across the open ground, not caring about cameras anymore, not caring about anything except reaching the fence. Alarms were sounding now, search lights were sweeping across the facility grounds, and guards began converging from multiple directions.

The cut section of the fence was still hanging loose. Claire dove through and felt the wire tear at her shirt. She scrambled to her feet and kept running. Elise made it through right after her, then Cross, all of them crashing through the forest, branches whipping at their faces.

Behind them were the sounds of pursuit—four-wheeler engines starting, dogs barking, and the crackle of radios coordinating tactics for a search.

The trees and darkness made efficient pursuit a bit more difficult. They had been fueled on pure adrenaline and were fortunate to have memorized the terrain. The car was half a mile ahead, hidden on an abandoned logging road.

They were gasping as they threw themselves inside the vehicle. Cross had the engine started before the doors closed, and then they were moving, lights off, navigating by memory down the rutted track until they reached the main road.

Only then did Claire allow herself to breathe.

"The drive," she said. "Tell me we have it."

Elise pulled the portable drive from her pocket and held it up as proof of their hard-earned efforts. "We have everything. Every authorization, every operation, every terminal action Harwood approved." Her voice was shaking with adrenaline and triumph. "We have him, Claire. We have the proof."

Claire stared at the small device in Elise's hand. It was the culmination of everything they'd fought for, everything they'd risked. This evidence would bring down ORION and expose James Harwood for what he was.

"Now we just have to survive long enough to use it," Cross said. He was pushing the car hard, putting miles between them and the facility. "They'll know what we took. They'll come after us with everything they have."

"Let them come," Claire said. "We have what we need. Now we finish this."

CHAPTER TWENTY-EIGHT

Endgame

They released the documents at dawn. Not through the Post or the Times, those channels were too compromised, too vulnerable to the legal pressure that Harwood's allies could bring to bear. Instead, they would use the architecture of the internet itself: distributed, decentralized, impossible to suppress.

Elise had spent the night preparing the release, breaking the ledger files into encrypted packages that were uploaded to dozens of servers across multiple continents. Reddit. The Tor network. Secure drop sites maintained by press freedom organizations. Academic repositories and journalist collectives who had built infrastructure specifically for moments like this.

At 6:00 AM Eastern, they pushed the button and held their breath.

The documents spread like wildfire through digital networks designed to resist exactly the kind of suppression ORION excelled at. Within an hour, journalists on three continents were poring over the files. Within hours, the first stories were appearing. They were not the carefully vetted, legally reviewed pieces that mainstream outlets would produce, but raw, urgent reports that captured the essence of what had been found.

SECRET U.S. PROGRAM TARGETED THOUSANDS OF AMERICANS read one headline. *FORMER SENATOR AUTHORIZED ASSASSINATIONS FROM PRIVATE CONTRACTOR ROLE* read another. *BIOMETRIC EVIDENCE PROVES HARWOOD PERSONALLY APPROVED 'TERMINAL ACTIONS'.*

They watched the coverage from a motel room in Pennsylvania, surrounded by the debris of their desperate night. Claire brushed aside the coffee cups and takeout containers to find a clean spot to sit and review multiple news feeds they appeared on the internet. Elise sat in a tall-backed easy chair with her head back and eyes closed letting the sound of the broadcast coverage wash over her. Cross stood guard at the window, watching for the pursuit that would inevitably come.

"It's happening," Elise said. Her voice was exhausted but triumphant. "They can't stop it. It's too distributed, too redundant. Even if they shut down ten sources, a hundred more have copies."

"They'll try anyway," Cross said. "They'll come for us."

"Let them." Claire stood and walked to the window to look out at the early gray morning. "The evidence is out. Whatever happens to us now, the evidence can't be undone."

Her phone buzzed with a number she didn't recognize, which was concerning.

Ms. Hensley. We should meet. I believe we have matters to discuss. JH

James Harwood. Reaching out directly, dropping all pretense.

"He wants to talk," Claire said, showing the message to the others.

"It's a trap," Cross said immediately.

"Probably, but he's in a corner. The documents are out. His operation is exposed. He's looking for a way to salvage something from the wreckage." Claire studied the message. "He might be willing to deal."

"Why would we meet him?" Elise said. "I get that he would want to make a deal for his freedom, but what's in it for us? What would we gain now that ORION's exposed?"

Claire didn't hesitate, "Information., names. We need the full scope of what ORION has done, things that might not be in the ledger files." Claire looked at Cross. "We have enough to destroy him, but we might not have enough to destroy the whole system. He could give us that."

"Or he could kill you," Cross added.

"He could try." Claire typed a response: *Where and when?*

The reply came thirty seconds later for an address in Alexandria, Virginia in four hours. The message offered a neutral location, where they could talk without interference.

"I'm going," Claire said.

"Not alone," Elise said.

"No. Not alone." Claire looked at her two remaining allies, the people who had risked everything to stand beside her.

• • •

The address led to an office building near the Potomac, a glass-and-steel tower that housed consulting firms, lobbying shops, and other parasites of the beltway bandit ecosystem.

Claire entered alone, as Harwood had specified. Cross and Elise waited nearby, ready to move if something went wrong. But, for this conversation, she would face the architect of ORION by herself.

The elevator carried her to the fourteenth floor and a vacant reception area. She followed a hallway leading to a corner office with a view of the river.

James Harwood was waiting inside.

He was smaller than she'd expected, a compact man in his sixties, with dull white hair and the bland, forgettable face of a career politician. He wore an expensive suit and an expression that mixed resignation with calculation. He may have had a setback, but it was clear he was still playing for position.

"Ms. Hensley." He gestured to a chair across from his desk. "Thank you for coming."

"I didn't do it for you."

"No, I suppose you didn't." He sat down, steepling his fingers. "You've caused me a great deal of trouble. You and Ms. Marston and Agent Cross. I underestimated you, and I assumed that once Rennick was gone, the threat was contained."

"You assumed wrong."

"Evidently." He turned to look out the window at the river below. "Do you know what ORION was designed to do, Ms. Hensley? Not the version in the documents, the real purpose, the underlying vision?"

"Surveillance. Control. The elimination of anyone who threatens your power."

"Stability." He said the word like a prayer. "We live in a world that's tearing itself apart with polarization and radicalization. The erosion of shared reality is dangerous for us all. Every institution that used to hold society together is crumbling. The power vacuum that creates is waiting to be filled by bad actors, foreign adversaries, domestic extremists, and ideologues of every stripe."

"So, you decided to fill the void first. Preemptively."

"I decided to protect it. In order to preempt those seeking to destabilize us, one must identify the forces of destabilization before they metastasize and neutralize them while they are still manageable." He turned back to face her. "Do you know how many attacks we've prevented? How many movements we defused before they could grow into something dangerous? ORION wasn't about power, Ms. Hensley. It was about preventing chaos."

"By killing Thomas Winters? By destroying careers and lives? By targeting journalists and researchers who were just doing their jobs?"

"By making hard choices. The kind of choices that leaders have always had to make." He sneered, "You think you're a hero. You think you've saved democracy by exposing ORION. But what you've done is create a bigger vacuum. Thanks to you, there will be a gap in our defenses that our enemies will exploit. The chaos you've unleashed will cost lives, far more lives than ORION ever took."

"That's not your decision to make," Claire said, ignoring the taunt of his sneer. She leaned forward. "You don't get to decide who lives and who dies in a democracy. You don't get to decide what ideas are acceptable and which ones need to be eliminated. The whole point of this system is that those choices belong to the people, not to you, not to any unaccountable group of bureaucrats and politicians who think they know better."

"The people." Harwood laughed bitterly. "The people can be manipulated, misled, and radicalized. They don't have access to the information I have. They don't understand the threats we face. Leaving decisions to 'the people' is how civilizations collapse."

"And yet ours is one of the longest lasting democracies the world has known. Our system of checks and balances isn't perfect, but we're determined not to let our system become the monster it was built to fight." Claire stood. "I didn't come here to debate philosophy with you, Senator. The documents are out, and your career is over. The question is whether you cooperate with the investigations that are coming, or whether you spend the rest of your life in prison."

"What are you saying. What can you offer me?"

"I can't officially offer you anything but I am suggesting you have a choice. Give us everything, every name, every operation, every piece of the infrastructure that made ORION possible, and we'll advocate with the authorities for leniency. Refuse, and we'll make every effort to ensure the full weight of what you did lands on your shoulders alone."

Harwood was silent for a long moment, his gaze moving from Claire to the window to some middle distance only he could see. The calculation happening behind his eyes was almost visible, weighing options, assessing probabilities, searching for any path to survival.

"There are people above me," he said finally. "People who authorized ORION, funded it, protected it from oversight. People whose names don't appear in any document you have."

"Give us those names."

"And if I do? What's in it for me?"

"Then maybe, just maybe, you get to spend your last years somewhere other than a federal prison cell." Claire moved toward the door. "You have until midnight. After that, we release everything that is remaining including the minor details, and you face the consequences alone."

She left him sitting in his corner office, staring out at the river, contemplating the ruins of everything he had built.

• • •

Harwood's statement arrived at 11:47 PM.

There were thirty pages of names, dates, and operations. Harwood detailed the full architecture of ORION and its predecessors, stretching back decades. He named names—intelligence officials who had approved domestic surveillance without authorization, politicians who protected illegal programs in exchange for information on their opponents, business leaders who provided funding in exchange for access to ORION's capabilities.

It was, Claire realized as she read through it, a roadmap to the rot at the heart of American power. It wasn't a conspiracy in the classic sense, no secret societies or shadowy cabals, but something more insidious—a network of mutual interests and shared assumptions. People who believed that the rules didn't apply to them. In the end, it wasn't even about protecting the nation. Greed and power were powerful temptations for the empty souls who had no other values.

"He's really doing it," Elise said, reading over her shoulder. "He's giving us everything."

"He's trying to save himself. He'll take down as many people as possible, so his own crimes look smaller by comparison." Claire set down the document. "This gives us a full picture, so we can expose it all."

Cross was already on the phone, coordinating with the network of journalists and activists they'd assembled over the past days. Their second wave of releases would begin within hours. They'd also spotlight Harwood's statement and distribute it through the same channels they'd used for the ledger files.

By morning, the full scope of what ORION had been, what it had done, and who enabled it, would be public knowledge. This time, Claire hoped the inevitable investigation would result in reforms that had teeth. The evidence they'd exposed was so damning that even the most compliant politicians couldn't ignore it.

James Harwood would face the consequences of his choices, just like Katherine Rennick before him.

"Is it over?" Elise asked.

Claire thought about the question. Once again, the immediate threat was neutralized. ORION was exposed, its architect broken, its infrastructure compromised beyond repair. The people who had built it and protected it would be held accountable, not all of them, never all of them, but enough to matter.

But she knew, in her bones, that it wasn't over. It would never be over. The impulse that had created SENTINEL and ORION originated with the belief that control was more important than freedom, and that security justified any violation. Somewhere, someone was already thinking about how to rebuild and profit from the excesses and secrecy. They, too, would learn from the mistakes made.

The fight would continue. It always continued. All you could do was keep fighting, keep watching, keep shining light into the shadows for as long as you could.

"For now," she said. "It's over for now."

And for now, that would have to be enough.

CHAPTER TWENTY-NINE

Epilogue

The congressional hearing room was packed, as it had been every day for the past two weeks.

Claire watched from the gallery as Senator Johnson, now the Chair of the newly formed Select Committee on Intelligence Accountability, questioned the Director of National Intelligence about the latest round of reforms. The questions were direct, informed by years of investigation and the hard-won knowledge that exposure alone wasn't enough. Systems had to be dismantled. Structures had to be rebuilt. The culture that had enabled ALTAR, SENTINEL, and ORION had to be confronted and changed.

It was slow, frustrating work. For every victory, there were setbacks, programs that survived under new names, officials who escaped accountability, reforms that were watered down by the very people they were meant to constrain. The intelligence community had learned from its failures. It was better at hiding and defending itself.

But so were they.

Claire had left the Post, taking her Pulitzer and her reputation to build something new. Newspapers were dying under the stress of a distracted and disinterested citizenry. With fewer eyeballs and shrinking ad budgets, most papers were either easily co-opted into survival mergers by powerful interests looking to shape the national narratives, or they were shuttered altogether. What was left were handfuls of impassioned journalists throughout the country who still believed that the Fourth Estate played an important role in a healthy democracy. Some struggled to survive by starting modest digital news efforts that returned to connecting communities to the issues that mattered to them. Some created issue-driven podcasts for longer conversations to explore important topics. While the low cost of entry was attractive for startups, misinformation and the atomization of credible sources competing for audience on YouTube made it nearly impossible to support a sustained, meaningful effort to counter the powerful.

Claire understood the odds; yet undaunted, she created a network of journalists, researchers, technologists, and activists, all connected through encrypted channels and shared purposes, to focus on the intersection of surveillance and power that had consumed her life.

They called it Lighthouse. It was a small operation with a growing reputation for exposing what others couldn't or wouldn't. They'd already broken stories about facial recognition abuse in three states, uncovered a private intelligence contractor's involvement in union-busting, and forced the resignation of a cabinet official who lied about his connections to surveillance technology firms.

They were small victories with incremental progress. They did what they could with the resources available to them.

• • •

Senator Johnson called for a short lunch break in the proceedings. Elise had arrived too late for a seat in the packed room. She was waiting outside the hearing room, two cups of coffee in hand.

"Anything interesting?" she asked, handing one cup to Claire.

"Johnson is pushing hard on the new disclosure requirements. The DNI is stonewalling, but she's got the votes. It will pass." Claire sipped her coffee as they walked toward the exit. "Another small win."

"They add up." Elise fell into step beside her, their movements synchronized by years of partnership. "Got a call from Daniel this morning. His foundation just received a grant to expand into Europe. They're going to set up offices in Berlin and Brussels."

"Good. The surveillance state isn't just an American problem."

"No, it's not." Elise was quiet for a moment. "Do you ever think about what comes next? After all this?"

"There is no after. This is the work. This is what we do." Claire pushed through the doors into the sunlight. "The fight doesn't end; it just changes shape."

They walked in silence for a while, past the Capitol dome, along with the ordinary citizens going about their lives. The city looked peaceful, almost innocent, a facade that hid the endless struggle for power happening behind closed doors and classified systems.

• • •

That evening, Claire sat alone in the Lighthouse office, reviewing files for their next investigation.

The Lighthouse office was modest. It occupied a converted warehouse in northeast D.C. In spite of, or maybe because of, the stripped-down space furnished with secondhand furniture and the bare necessities of their mission, it hummed with purpose. There were workstations where researchers tracked surveillance programs across a dozen countries. Secure servers stored documents too sensitive to trust to any cloud. They had a windowless conference room where they planned operations that would make powerful people very uncomfortable.

Claire heard a knock at her door. She wasn't expecting anyone at this hour, but she looked up to find Ryan Cross standing in the threshold.

He looked better than he had during the ORION crisis, healthier and more at peace with himself. After the exposure, he'd cooperated fully with investigators, testifying before three congressional committees, then quietly disappeared into an advisory role helping companies identify security threats. It was a quieter life, but one that seemed to suit his skills without compromising his principles.

"Got a minute?" he asked.

"For you? Always."

He sat down across from her, his expression serious. "I've been hearing things. Rumors from old contacts in the community. There's something new being developed, not government this time, or not primarily. Private sector. A consortium of tech companies and defense contractors working on next-generation behavioral prediction."

"We've been tracking similar developments. AI systems that look like what ORION was trying to build."

"This is beyond that." Cross leaned forward. "They're calling it CHIMERA. They're working on systems that can simulate human consciousness. The intent seems to model individual minds with enough fidelity to make decisions without the inefficiency of human interference. Essentially, they want to replace human reasoning."

Claire felt a chill run through her. "How is that even possible?"

"They've taken the emotional modeling capabilities of Copycat, the system you and Elise exposed during the ALTAR investigation, and they merged them with ORION's behavioral prediction algorithms." Cross's voice was grim. "Where Copycat learned to simulate how people feel, and ORION learned to anticipate what people do, CHIMERA is learning to model the way people think. The synthesis is more than the sum of its parts. It's not just watching or predicting anymore. It's control and extraction."

“It’s like the ultimate surveillance tool,” Cross continued. “One that wouldn't need to watch you because it would generatively know how you’re feeling, what you’re thinking, and with that, they’ll improve the probabilities of predicting your actions. High emotional resonance increases the intensity of an individual’s reaction; low resonance, probably more of a wait and see reaction.

"How far are they?"

"I don't know. Could be years away. Could be closer than anyone thinks." Cross stood. "I thought you should know in case Lighthouse wants to start tracking."

"We'll look." Claire rose to shake his hand. "Thank you, Ryan, for everything."

"Thank me when we've won." He paused at the door. "If that's even possible."

Then he was gone, leaving Claire alone with the knowledge of what was coming.

• • •

Later that night, Elise found her still at her desk, surrounded by printouts and half-empty coffee cups.

"You should go home," Elise said. "Sleep. Remember sleep?"

"Cross came by. He got wind of a new effort called CHIMERA." Claire pushed a printout across the desk. There are a couple of private sector consortium members racing to co-opt human decision making. Simulate individual minds. They've merged Copycat and ORION."

Elise picked up the document, scanning it quickly. Her expression shifted as she absorbed the implications. "This is..."

"Bigger than anything we've faced before. Yes."

Elise set down the document and was quiet for a long moment. When she spoke, her voice was different, softer, more reflective.

"We tried this before," she said. "After ALTAR. We said we were done. We said we needed to disappear, protect ourselves, find some way to live that didn't involve constantly looking over our shoulders."

"I remember." Claire thought about those months, the rural farmhouse, the analog existence, the desperate attempt to disconnect from a world that had become impossible to trust. They had intended to resist for a long time, but the pull of the fight had dragged them back. When SENTINEL emerged and old patterns started repeating, they couldn't stay silent and watch from the sidelines while everything they'd exposed regenerated under a new name.

"This time will be different," Elise said. "CHIMERA isn't like SENTINEL or ORION. At least keeping the government honest meant once we'd investigated, we had levers to pull, checks and balances that could serve as guardrails. The government had to respond even if the response didn't meet our expectations."

Elise went on, "Without new laws on the books, private sector actors in a distributed system will be insanely hard to hold accountable. Once the technology is built and powerful people realize how easy it is to take control, and how much money they can make from it, things get a lot more complicated than anything we've dealt with before. They'll have plenty of cover, too. The promise of new, innovative technology will get everyone excited, and once the buzz heats up, it's off to the races."

Claire got a funny look on her face as something disturbing took shape in her thoughts. It was the nagging realization that once you deploy these surveillance tools and behavioral models, optimized by a distributed base of power players with an unrelenting drive for king-of-the-hill profits, what would stand in the way of their usurping even more influence and control? What new vulnerabilities did that create for democracy? What happens if those systems are infiltrated by bad actors?

Elise saw the doubt and reached out and took Claire's hand. "We've been preparing for this our whole lives. Everything we've done, ALTAR, SENTINEL, and now ORION, it was all leading here. What is it we excel at, Claire?"

Claire shrugged. She was mentally exhausted.

"Patterns, Claire. We spot patterns. We detect the signal from the noise, as my nephew likes to say. We have our Lighthouse to help us through the fog."

Claire thought about the years ahead. The constant vigilance and the small betrayals. She thought about the technology being built to usurp human decision making. She thought about the rush to cash in and the compounding cybersecurity vulnerabilities that would result from sloppily deployed tools. She imagined millions of dollars lost and upended lives that would go unnoticed in the noise.

Someone had to fight for what was left. "Lighthouse stays regardless," Claire said slowly, working through the implications. "The network we've built, the people we've trained, must continue the visible work. You and I get to decide how, or even whether, to follow players in the attention economy and their increasing use of these tools into our democracy, our communities, and our lives. This is a particularly crucial inflection point for so much in our country—what does education become, who will have responsibility for medical decisions, how do these tools integrate with artificial intelligence and align with human interests?"

Elise nodded, "The stakes are incredibly high."

"Right now, I can't imagine how we'd make a difference," sighed Claire.

Elise turned to go. "Get a good night's sleep, Claire. Lots to do tomorrow."

THE END

Acknowledgements

Writing the first two books in this series has been both energizing and eye-opening. The line between reality and fiction is often thinner than we imagine.

We would like to thank Gwen Kinsey, Jason Rhodes, and Glenn Higgins for their additions, corrections, ongoing editing, and constant help and support as this novel was created.

We would also like to thank our Editor, Brieann Kinsey, for her many hours of editing and support.

www.ingramcontent.com/pod-product-compliance
Lightning Source LLC
LaVergne TN
LVHW020702110826
845149LV00012B/2074

* 9 7 9 8 9 9 4 2 7 3 6 0 9 *